THE ~~~~~~~~~~~ AN
PREACHER'S
MASSACRE

THE FIRST MOUNTAIN MAN
PREACHER'S MASSACRE

WILLIAM W. JOHNSTONE
with J. A. Johnstone

PINNACLE BOOKS
Kensington Publishing Corp.
www.kensingtonbooks.com

PINNACLE BOOKS are published by

Kensington Publishing Corp.
119 West 40th Street
New York, NY 10018

PUBLISHER'S NOTE
Following the death of William W. Johnstone, the Johnstone family is working with a carefully selected writer to organize and complete Mr. Johnstone's outlines and many unfinished manuscripts to create additional novels in all of his series like The Last Gunfighter, Mountain Man, and Eagles, among others. This novel was inspired by Mr. Johnstone's superb storytelling.

All Kensington titles, imprints, and distributed lines are available at special quantity discounts for bulk purchases for sales promotions, premiums, fund-raising, educational, or institutional use. Special book excerpts or customized printings can also be created to fit specific needs. For details, write or phone the office of the Kensington special sales manager: Kensington Publishing Corp., 119 West 40th Street, New York, NY 10018, attn: Special Sales Department; phone 1-800-221-2647.

ISBN-13: 978-0-7860-3106-1
ISBN-10: 0-7860-3106-9

First printing: January 2013

10 9 8 7 6 5 4 3 2 1

Printed in the United States of America

CHAPTER 1

Springtime in the Rocky Mountains was mighty pretty, thought Preacher, but not so much when some varmints were trying to kill you. It was hard to appreciate the beauty of nature stretched out behind a log with a handful of bloodthirsty savages closing in.

He sure wished he could get to his pistols. All four of them were double-shots and heavily charged, and would cut a wide, bloody swath through the warriors who had jumped him first thing, just as the sun was coming up.

He had gone down to the creek to get some water for the coffeepot. Normally he would have tucked a couple of the flintlock pistols behind the broad leather belt cinched around his waist, but he hadn't put the belt on yet.

It was a greenhorn mistake, and that bothered Preacher as much or more than the fact that he might die in the next few minutes. He'd always figured on dying, but he didn't like the idea of it happening because he'd done something foolish or careless. He had spent most of the past twenty-five years in these mountains, dealing with the frontier's dangers on a daily basis, and he should have known better.

"You're gettin' old, Preacher," he said aloud. "And you're gonna have to be mighty lucky to keep on gettin' any older."

He was fortunate the first arrow that came flying out of the trees hadn't killed him. If he hadn't twisted and bent down to fill the coffeepot at just the right time, the arrow would have buried itself between his shoulder blades instead of slicing a little gash in the side of his neck as it went past him. He'd reacted instantly by launching into a dive that carried him behind a fallen tree at the edge of the stream.

More arrows had whipped through the air above him. Others thudded into the log. He got a good enough look at them to tell that they were Blackfoot arrows.

That eliminated any chance of talking his way out of it. The Blackfeet hated him with a special passion stronger than any of the other tribes. He had killed many of their warriors over the years, often by slipping into the sleeping villages and cutting throats. Some of the Indians called him Ghost Killer because of his ability to get in and out of their camps without being seen and leaving death in his wake.

Once, many, many years earlier, when he was just beginning to get the reputation that still followed him, the Blackfeet had captured him. They had tied him to a stake, and come morning, they would have lit a fire at his feet and burned him to death. He was powerless to do anything except talk.

So talk he did. Recalling a street preacher he had seen back in St. Louis, he began exhorting his captors with a voluminous intensity that would have put many a hellfire-and-brimstone sin-shouter to shame.

Kept it up all night, he did, and by morning, when the Blackfeet had planned on killing him, they were curious to see how long he could keep going. Too curious to kill him, which was just what Preacher had intended.

He wasn't sure how many hours that ordeal had lasted, but in the end the Blackfeet let him go, impressed by his oratory. They'd had plenty of reasons to regret that decision since then, but Preacher surely didn't.

The story of how he'd escaped from certain death got around, as such stories will, and the young man who'd gone by the name Art got tagged with the moniker Preacher. He'd been called that for so long it seemed like his given name.

However, the warriors who had him pinned

down behind the log weren't interested in hearing any preaching. All they wanted was his hair, which was thick and dark, with a few flecks of silver, like his beard.

Preacher looked around, taking stock of his situation. He had his hunting knife in a sheath strapped to his right calf. He had the coffeepot, which was heavy enough to serve as a bludgeon. A couple of feet away lay a fairly thick broken branch. If it wasn't too rotten, it might make a decent club.

Those were close-quarters weapons, though. They wouldn't do him any good against bows and arrows.

He knew at least three enemies lurked in the trees and brush. He'd seen arrows flying from that many locations at the same time, which proved it wasn't an actual Blackfoot war party that had attacked him. But the warriors might be scouts from a larger group so there could be more. One of them might have even gone back to fetch the others already.

If he was going to fight his way out, he had to draw them closer, and that wasn't likely to happen unless they thought he was dead. He'd have to try something pretty risky.

But since he was likely to wind up dead anyway, what did it matter?

Moving fast, he pushed himself halfway to his feet as if he were about to make a run for it. Instantly, bowstrings twanged and arrows sliced through the air. Preacher twisted out of the way of a couple, but the third arrow raked along his side, ripping his buckskin shirt and drawing a fiery finger of pain across his flesh.

That was just what he wanted. He let out a yell and flopped gracelessly to the ground behind the log, landing on his back with the arrow between his arm and his body where he had clamped his arm down on it. The shaft stuck straight up in the air as if the arrow had gone all the way through him.

He shuddered and twitched like his body was going through its death throes, and the arrow jumped around accordingly.

Hidden in the trees, the warriors watched that arrow sticking up above the log jerk and dance.

After a moment Preacher grew still and lay absolutely motionless.

Time dragged by. Blackfoot warriors were no fools. They watched carefully, wary of a trick.

But they were also curious, and eager to take the scalp of the notorious mountain man who was responsible for the deaths of so many of their fellows.

Little animal noises that had fallen silent earlier started up again. Had the Blackfeet left? Impossible, Preacher decided. Even if they had decided not to scalp him, they wouldn't go off without making sure he was dead.

In the early morning quiet, he heard his stallion moving around a few yards away. Horse wasn't happy. He snorted and snuffled and danced around skittishly, smelling the bear grease on the warriors' hair. If he had caught that scent earlier, he would have given Preacher some warning, but the lurkers had skillfully avoided getting upwind of the camp.

Dog, the big, wolf-like cur who was Preacher's other long-time trail companion, was off hunting somewhere. He would be back, but maybe not in time to help.

Preacher couldn't hold that against him. Dog had saved his life more times than the mountain man could count.

It was up to him, he thought as the sun climbed above the trees and began to shine down in his face. He closed his eyes against the glare.

More time crawled by. Preacher breathed as shallowly as possible so the arrow wouldn't move around enough for the Blackfeet to notice. What were they going to do, let him lie there all day before they came to lift his hair?

He felt a shadow over his eyes, surprised something had moved between him and the light. He hadn't heard any footsteps. Just like him, the Blackfeet could move mighty quiet when they wanted to.

His eyes flew open just as one of the warriors stepped over the log, knife in hand to cut Preacher's scalp away from his head. Preacher snatched the arrow from between his arm and body and rammed the sharp flint head as hard as he could up into the warrior's groin.

The man screamed in agony and dropped his knife. Preacher snatched it out of midair and rolled to the side. His arm drew back and snapped forward. The knife flashed through the air and caught one of the warriors hanging back a few yards in the throat. The blade went deep, causing blood to spurt out around it. The man gurgled and staggered as he dropped his bow to paw futilely at the wound.

Preacher grabbed up the coffeepot and hurdled the log as the third warrior was trying to nock an arrow to his bow. The Blackfoot threw the bow and arrow aside, knowing Preacher was too close, and grabbed for the tomahawk at his waist.

The move came too late. Preacher swung the coffeepot and smashed it against the side of the warrior's head. Bone crunched under the brutal impact. The Indian fell and began to twitch and shudder much as Preacher had done earlier. The death spasms were real this time.

Preacher dropped the pot and grabbed the warrior's tomahawk just in case either of the other Blackfeet was still alive. He quickly saw that precaution wasn't necessary. Both men had bled to death from the wounds he'd inflicted on them.

Somehow he was still alive, with nothing to show

from the encounter except a couple of scratches that didn't amount to anything.

"Horse, I reckon you're lookin' at the luckiest son of a gun on the face of the earth," he told the restive stallion.

But a strong possibility still existed that a Blackfoot war party was in the area. Preacher needed to clear out, get up higher in the mountains, and find a place where he could fort up.

If the three dead men were indeed scouts for a larger group, one thing he could count on was that the men in the war party would come looking for him as soon as they discovered the corpses.

And he didn't want to be found.

CHAPTER 2

Preacher had gotten his gear packed up and was tightening the cinch on Horse's saddle when Dog came bounding into the clearing beside the creek. "Now you show up," he drawled as the big cur stiffened and approached the bloody bodies to sniff at them. "Could've used a hand a little while ago."

Dog just looked at him and cocked his head a little to the side.

"Naw, I ain't mad at you," Preacher went on. "We got to pull out, though, and can't waste any time doin' it."

Less than five minutes later, Preacher was riding away from the campsite. He sent Horse into the shallow stream and followed the rocky bed with Dog splashing along beside them. The water was cold, but it stayed that way year-round because of the snowmelt from the white-capped peaks around them.

Tall pines covered the steep slopes higher up. In the valleys where he was, aspen, juniper, and birch lined the creeks. Wildflowers bloomed in some of the meadows. Birds flitted from branch to branch in the trees. Preacher saw a moose raise its antlered head at the other end of a long, grassy park.

He liked nothing in the world better than being in these mountains, which was why he always returned to them when life took him to other places for a while. They were the only real home he had ever known. Even when he'd been a kid, living on his folks' farm back East, he hadn't felt like he'd belonged there. He had left as soon as he could, setting out to see the elephant, as the old-timers said.

He had seen the elephant, all right. Seen it and then some.

A smaller creek flowed into the stream he'd been following. He turned Horse and sent the stallion walking upstream. Within a few hundred yards, the creek bed began to rise and soon became too rocky and steep for Horse to keep going in the water. Preacher rode out onto the bank.

He dismounted and all three rested for a few minutes. Then, holding Horse's reins, he led the stallion up the slope with the waters of the creek dancing and bubbling down alongside them. Dog bounded ahead to lead the way through the brush.

An hour of walking lifted them a long way above the valley where Preacher had encountered the Blackfeet. The view was spectacular from the spot where Preacher paused to rest again. Mountains and valleys fell away all around them. He could see so far the distance became hazy even to his eagle-keen eyes.

He didn't spend a lot of time taking in the scenery. He searched the landscape below for any sign of pursuit.

At first it appeared there wasn't any, but then he spotted a flash of motion and color. Might have been a bird, might have been a face painted for war, he told himself. He concentrated on the area. A few moments later, sunlight winked on something metal.

A rifle barrel or a knife, Preacher thought. Definitely not a bird.

"Let's go," he said quietly to Horse and Dog. "They're down there lookin' for us."

He used the trees for cover as much as possible. They reached a spot where the creek had carved a narrow canyon into the rock, forming a pass of sorts on the side of the mountain. It looked wide enough for Preacher to get through with the stallion. He worried about being spotted while they crossed the short stretch of open, rocky ground to reach it, but the canyon was the best route he could see away from the war party.

A hundred yards in, it grew narrower. If it came to a dead end at a waterfall, he and his friends might be trapped in there, Preacher mused.

But if that turned out to be the case, within the cramped confines of the canyon the Blackfeet could only come at him one or two at a time. He would have his pistols and his rifle ready, and he would take them on until he ran out of powder and shot, and then he'd meet them with knife and tomahawk. They would kill him in the end, but they would pay a hell of a price to do so.

He pressed on. After a mile or so of the rock walls so close they scraped on Horse's flanks and the sky was just a thin ribbon of blue overhead, the canyon opened out again into several valleys branching off through the mountains. To Preacher's left was a small pool. Water trickled down an almost sheer cliff and gathered there before forming the creek he'd been following.

It was a good place to stop for a while. He hunkered on his haunches next to the pool and made a late lunch on jerky and pemmican he took from a pouch tied to his saddle.

High above his head, a couple of eagles rode the wind currents, swooping and gliding in apparent joy at being free and living in such a place. Preacher knew how they felt.

After he had eaten and rested, he found a game trail that curled around the shoulder of the mountain and followed it to a ledge where pronghorn antelope grazed. They bounded away at the sight of him. If he hadn't been trying to dodge those Blackfeet, he might have stalked and killed one of the antelope and had fresh meat, but under the circumstances he wasn't about to risk a shot.

At the base of a granite cliff, he found several giant slabs of rock that had sheered off and slid down the mountain sometime during the last centuries. They leaned against the cliff forming a cave-like area. It was big enough for him and his two companions. He led Horse into the shelter. Dog wasn't far behind. The sun was low by the time he unsaddled Horse. It had been a long day, starting early with that fight with the Blackfeet, and he had pushed himself and his friends pretty hard. They'd climbed high and it was quite cool at that altitude.

Once the sun went down the night got pretty chilly. He built a fire right up against the leaning rock so its face would reflect the heat. After it burned down, its embers ought to keep them fairly warm the whole night, he hoped.

After another skimpy meal, he spread his bedroll and crawled into his blankets. All four pistols and his rifle were loaded and close beside him. He hoped he wouldn't need them. He had put a lot of distance between himself and the three dead warriors, and had used every trick he knew to cover his tracks. All he could do was hope it had been enough.

He didn't fall asleep right away. It was very dark behind the rocks, but bits of starlight filtered in around them. Dog lay against him on the side away from the guns. He felt the big cur's steady breathing. If not for the worry about the Blackfeet, it would have been a mighty peaceful night.

His thoughts strayed back over the past few months. Preacher and three of his friends had spent the winter with a Dutch trader named Horst Grunewald, who was better known in the mountains as Blind Pete, even though he wasn't blind.

Pete's trading post had been burned down by some of Preacher's enemies—now deceased—so it only seemed fair that Preacher help him rebuild it. That was what he had done, with assistance from Audie, Nighthawk, and Lorenzo. The diminutive Audie and the taciturn Nighthawk were old friends who had shared many a camp with Preacher. The black man Lorenzo had come west from St. Louis with Preacher after helping him settle a score back there. They were all boon companions, as the storybooks might have phrased it.

But once the weather had turned nicer, Audie and Nighthawk had set out to do some trapping on their own, and Lorenzo had decided to remain at the trading post with Pete, who was glad to have the help.

"My rheumatism's gettin' worse, and I ain't gettin' any younger," Lorenzo had explained to Preacher. "I don't think I'm in any shape to go trampin' around all over these mountains with you, Preacher, much as I might like to."

"Well, that's fine, Lorenzo," he'd said. "I'll miss your company, but I understand."

"You can come by here any time you want to, whilst you're traipsin' around gatherin' up them beaver pelts."

"Yah," Pete had put in. "You are always most welcome here, Preacher."

Preacher had smiled and told them he would see them again, and then he'd set out, alone except for Dog and Horse, not sure exactly where he was going but knowing he had to shake the dust off his feet and rattle his hocks. He never stayed in any one place for too long. For Preacher, alone had never meant lonely.

Sometime while he was remembering the winter he had spent with his friends, he dozed off.

He slept soundly until Dog stiffened against him and a soft growl came from deep within the big cur's throat.

The gray light inside the shelter of the rocks meant that dawn was approaching. He listened and heard voices. The guttural sound told him they were Blackfeet.

He pushed the blankets aside, then rolled over

onto his belly and picked up the rifle. Crawling over to a tiny crack between the rocks a few feet away, he put his eye to the gap.

His field of vision was narrow, but he was able to see several warriors on horseback riding through the newly green grass about seventy yards away. Preacher spoke the Blackfoot language fluently, so he had no trouble understanding them as they talked to each other. At this distance he couldn't pick up all the words, but he garnered the gist of the conversation.

They were looking for him, of course, but they hadn't actually followed his trail. Their war chief— Red Knife, Preacher thought the name was—had his warriors scattered all to hell and gone searching for the man who had killed the three scouts beside the creek.

Preacher had heard of Red Knife, although he'd never run into the man before. He'd heard the stories. The Blackfoot war chief had a special hatred of white men and killed them anywhere, any time he could.

A couple of the passing riders glanced toward the rocks where Preacher, Horse, and Dog were hidden, but they looked away again without showing any interest. They couldn't tell the little pocket was behind the massive stone slabs.

They rode on to the far end of the ledge, turned around, and circled back. Preacher couldn't see them the whole way, but he tracked their movements by the sound of their voices. From time to time Dog growled, and Preacher put a hand on his thick fur and whispered, "Easy, old son, easy."

By the time the sun peeked over the horizon, the Indians were gone. Preacher figured they would join up with Red Knife and the rest of the war party and report that their quarry wasn't to be found in this direction. That was a good break for him, he thought. They would all move on and look elsewhere for him, and eventually they would give up the search.

"We're gonna squat right here for a day or two and give those heathens time to leave this part of the country," Preacher told his animal companions. "Then we'll work our way north and find some good trappin' country."

That sounded like a fine plan to him, and it probably would have been, if he hadn't seen the dust cloud a couple of days later as he was getting ready to leave the hideout among the boulders.

But there it was, too small and moving too steadily to be caused by a buffalo stampede but big enough to tell it came from a large group of horses or some other animals. He was curious, since that was his nature, but more than that, he knew if he could spot the dust cloud, so could somebody else, namely Red Knife . . . if the Blackfoot war party was still around.

So he saddled up and headed east out of the mountains, down onto the plains.

CHAPTER 3

After resting for a couple of days, Horse was more than happy to stretch his legs. Preacher let the big stallion run. He knew he was kicking up dust of his own that might draw attention, but if it was a party of white men up ahead, he wanted to warn them about Red Knife prowling around, looking for trouble.

The problem with being able to see a long way was that it always took longer than it seemed like it should to reach a destination. Preacher had covered several miles when he reined Horse back to a walk. The dust cloud looked like it was still as far away as it had been when he started.

The stallion tossed his head impatiently.

Preacher said, "Take it easy. I'll let you run again in a little while."

They kept going, angling northeast to intercept whatever was raising the dust cloud. With tireless energy, Dog bounded ahead and then came back, again and again.

Preacher heeled Horse into a faster gait, not a gallop but rather a ground-eating lope the stallion could keep up for hours if he had to. Gradually they drew closer to their goal.

Then the dust cloud stopped moving.

Preacher frowned and reined in. As the pounding of Horse's hoofbeats stopped and the echoes faded away, he heard a distant popping and cracking that could be only one thing.

Gunfire.

Whoever was up there had run smack-dab into trouble, and Preacher figured that trouble was named Red Knife. "I reckon we'd better see what this is all about. Come on."

Horse galloped again, swiftly carrying Preacher closer to the scene of battle. Instead of a single column of dust, it had diffused into a haze hanging over the plains. A lot of folks were moving around in a hurry up there.

Despite the way it looked from a distance, the prairie wasn't completely flat. Ridges and gullies crisscrossed it, and sometimes the land swelled upward into something that could almost be called a hill. Preacher spotted one of those grassy mounds and used it to cover his approach.

Reaching the slope, he swung down from the saddle and dropped the reins, letting them hang loose. Horse wouldn't go anywhere. With the flintlock rifle in his hands and Dog beside him, Preacher hurried up the rise.

Before he reached the top, he dropped to hands and knees and took off the wide-brimmed felt hat he wore. He crawled higher, bellied down, and stuck his head up just far enough to take a gander at the scene playing out before him.

Dog lay beside him and growled.

"I don't blame you," Preacher said quietly. "I don't like the looks of it, either."

About two hundred yards away, three canvas-covered wagons drawn by mule teams had come to a halt. What appeared to be a dozen or so men were using the wagons for cover as they fired at three times that many Blackfoot warriors on horse-back racing around the embattled vehicles.

On the far side of the wagons was an entire herd of horses, fifty or sixty of them, Preacher judged. Maybe more. They had been driven up into a little draw and were being held there by several riders who divided their attention between keeping the horses penned up and fighting back against the Blackfeet.

As Preacher watched, one of those men grabbed his shoulder and toppled off his mount. The man rolled over and came up on his feet. He broke into a shaky run as one of the Blackfeet charged after him.

Preacher brought his rifle to his shoulder, eared back the hammer, and sighted over the long barrel. The distance was pretty far, but certainly within his range. When he was sure of his aim, he pressed the trigger. The hammer fell, the charge under it detonated with a crack, and the heavier charge at the base of the barrel boomed.

A second later, the warrior who'd been giving chase to the fallen white man threw his arms up and pitched from the back of his pony as the back of his head flew apart. The ball from Preacher's rifle had shattered his skull, killing the warrior without him ever knowing what had happened.

Preacher reloaded.

With all the shooting already going on—the defenders at the wagons all had rifles, and so did some of the attacking Blackfeet—Preacher doubted anybody would notice right away that he was firing from the top of the rise. He drew another bead and shot another Blackfoot off his horse.

The Blackfeet weren't exactly skilled riders. Being more at home in the mountains, they hadn't adapted to the use of horses as well as some of the other tribes that spent most of their time on the plains.

But they could stay mounted when they wanted to, having learned that horses gave their raiding and hunting parties more range. They probably wanted that herd for their own use, Preacher thought, and they wanted to kill the white men who had driven the horses out here because, well, because they were white. The Blackfeet didn't need any more reason than that.

Preacher reloaded and fired several more times, and with each shot one of the attackers fell. He knew that sooner or later the other warriors would realize they were being cut down by somebody who wasn't forted up inside the wagons. Unlike a herd of buffalo, they wouldn't just go on about their business, unaware they were being slaughtered.

Sure enough, several of the Blackfeet spotted the spurts of powder smoke from Preacher's rifle muzzle and broke off from the others, galloping toward the rise. Preacher calmly finished reloading, then socketed the rifle butt against his shoulder, aimed at one of the onrushing warriors, and squeezed off another round.

The Blackfoot flew backward off his pony as the heavy lead ball slammed into his chest, leaving three others still intent on killing Preacher. They were covering the ground too fast for him to reload the rifle.

He set it aside and waited in the tall grass until the Indians were closer. Then he reared up, pulling the two loaded pistols from his belt, and cocked them as the barrels rose.

Both guns roared. Smoke and flame geysered from their muzzles. Blood fountained from a warrior's throat as a pistol ball ripped through it.

One of the horses screamed and went down, crushing its rider beneath it.

The fourth and final warrior in the charge yanked his horse to a stop and let fly with an arrow. Preacher dove forward and let the shaft whistle over his head.

The Blackfoot didn't get a chance to try again. A gray streak flew through the air and crashed into him, knocking him off his horse. By the time the warrior hit the ground, Dog had his massive jaws locked around the man's throat. More blood flew as the big cur came close to ripping the warrior's head right off his shoulders.

"Come on, Dog," Preacher called as he dropped to one knee at the top of the rise. He picked up the rifle and began reloading it again. He turned to the cur and smiled. "Good job."

Down below, the Blackfeet had broken off their attack. Between Preacher's efforts and those of the men in the wagons, they were taking too many casualties. White men had been coming regularly to the frontier for less than forty years, but the Indians had already figured out they were vastly outnumbered. No matter how many whites they killed, there were always more to take their place.

Resources, including warriors, had to be used carefully. The price paid for victory in battle couldn't be too high, or that victory would actually be a defeat. Any time a fight wasn't going as well as hoped, it made more sense to abandon it and fight again another day.

It wasn't a blind retreat, however. The Blackfeet intended to flee right over Preacher and kill him in the process. To their way of thinking, he had it coming because he'd interfered with their attack on the wagons.

Preacher lifted the rifle. Once again the flint-lock cracked and boomed. One of the warriors slewed around but managed to stay mounted as he clutched his shattered shoulder. He stood a good chance of never being able to fight again.

The men in the wagons weren't finished. Shots roared from down below as they continued firing. A Blackfoot pony went down.

The warrior leading the charge, close enough for Preacher to see the designs daubed in red paint on his face, waved an arm and veered his horse. The rest broke off their charge and turned sharply, angling into a swale between a couple of ridges. Preacher watched them go while he re-loaded the rifle yet again.

Setting the flintlock aside, he reloaded both pistols. He crossed his arms and shoved the guns behind his belt, butts forward. Then he picked up his hat and rifle. "Come on, Dog."

He mounted and rode around the rise, keeping an eye on the place where the Blackfeet had fled just in case they decided to double back and try again. He headed slowly for the wagons.

As he came closer he saw that several of the mules were down, skewered by arrows. Only a few Blackfoot warriors had been armed with rifles claimed from victims of previous raids. Most of them had been using bows and arrows.

Men moved around the wagons. Some unhitched the dead mules while others stood facing outward, vigilantly holding rifles. One of the guards waved an arm over his head as Preacher approached, making a circling motion to let him know it was all right to ride on in.

The man lowered his arm and strode forward, meeting Preacher about fifty yards from the wagons. "Hello! You showed up just in time, friend. I assume that was you taking those potshots from the top of the hill?"

"It was," Preacher replied as he brought Horse to a stop.

"Well, you turned the tide for us, I don't have any doubt of that. Come on. We've got coffee and food, and we're more than willing to share!"

CHAPTER 4

Preacher dismounted, and the man extended a hand. "My name's Wiley Courtland." He was a medium-size man, a couple of inches shorter than Preacher, but probably weighing just as much. Hatless and clean-shaven, he wore high-topped brown boots, whipcord trousers, a linsey-woolsey shirt, and a brown leather vest. He was fair-skinned and a little sunburned. His hair was so pale it was almost white, even though he was only around thirty years old.

The mountain man shook hands with him. "They call me Preacher."

"Is that because you're a minister?"

Preacher grinned. "Not hardly. Some would say I'm pretty much a heathen, but I like to think me and the good Lord are still on speakin' terms. It's just that the nearest church is more 'n five hundred miles away, and I never was much for bein' cooped inside, anyway."

Courtland spread his arms wide and smiled. "Where would you find a more spectacular tabernacle than this?"

"You're in pretty good spirits for a fella who was in danger of losin' his hair just a few minutes ago."

"Yes, but the danger is over now. The savages are gone. We lost some mules, but no men or horses. I'd say we were lucky."

"Mighty lucky," Preacher agreed. As they walked toward the wagons, he went on. "What are you and your pards doin' out here?"

"Driving that horse herd to Fort Gifford, of course."

The answer didn't seem that obvious to Preacher. For one thing, he hadn't heard of Fort Gifford. "Where's that?"

"It's a new trading post established by the American Fur Company, about fifty miles west of Fort Union on the Missouri River."

Preacher knew Fort Union, all right. He had been there several times in the past seven or eight years. Traders who worked for John Jacob Astor's fur company had built it at the spot where the Yellowstone and Missouri Rivers ran together.

He hadn't heard that Astor was trying to extend his enterprise's reach farther west, but the news didn't surprise him. As ambitious as Astor was, Preacher wouldn't be shocked if the fella wound up running the whole blasted country someday.

"And you're in charge of this bunch?" he asked Courtland.

"That's right. It was my idea to put the horse herd together and bring it out here. I financed the expedition, too. I don't mind telling you, it took just about everything I had. But I expect to reap some handsome profits once we get to Fort Gifford."

"How do you figure?"

"I'm going to trade some of the horses directly to the Indians for pelts. The others I plan to sell to fur trappers who are in need of mounts."

"You might come out ahead that way, all right." Preacher thought Courtland was being overly optimistic about the amount of profit the horses would bring in, but he didn't see any need to point it out. As a rule, he minded his own business and let other men tend to theirs.

As the two of them walked up to the lead wagon, one of the men approached them. "We got four men wounded, Wiley, but only one of 'em is pretty bad. I think he'll live once we get the arrow out of him."

"That's good," Courtland said with a nod. "Preacher, this is my second in command, Otis Freeman. Otis, meet the fellow who pitched in to help us. He says he's called Preacher." Courtland frowned slightly. "You didn't explain why they call you that if you're not a minister."

"It's a long story." Preacher gave Freeman

a crisp nod as he shook hands with the man. "Howdy, Freeman."

Courtland's lieutenant was a tall, heavy-shouldered man with a mournful face. Calling him plain would have been generous. His appearance bordered on ugly. "Preacher, eh? "I think I've heard of you. You're famous among the mountain men. Supposed to be as wild and dangerous as a ring-tailed Wampus Cat."

Preacher grinned. "The Wampus Cat might not take kindly to bein' compared to me. You say you've got a man with an arrow in him?"

"That's right. You know anything about tending to wounds like that?"

"I've patched up a few of them," Preacher replied, dryly understating the case. He had taken care of more arrow wounds than he could count, including quite a few in his own hide. "I'd be glad to take a look at the fella, if you'd like."

"That's mighty generous of you, Preacher." Courtland nodded to Freeman. "Otis, show him where the wounded man is."

"Right back here on this tailgate." Freeman waved at the second wagon in line.

Preacher looped Horse's reins around one of the spokes in a rear wheel on the lead wagon, then told Dog, "Stay." He walked with Freeman back to the spot where the injured man had been placed.

The man lay on his left side on the second

wagon's lowered tailgate. The right side of his shirt was red with blood. Not surprising, the color had drained from his face, which was covered with beads of sweat. He was conscious, but looked pretty groggy.

Several men stood at the back of the wagon. One said, "We gave him a few slugs of whiskey, Otis. Figured he'd need it when you go to pull that arrow out."

Freeman nodded. "That was good thinking. If some of you will hold him down now, I'll get a good grip on that shaft and see if I can pull it out of him."

"Hang on." Preacher grabbed Freeman's arm. "I thought you were gonna let me take a look at it first."

"Well, sure, if you want," Freeman said with a shrug. "But you can tell by looking at him he's in a lot of pain."

"He'll be in a lot more if you pull that arrow straight out of him. It'll rip a hole in him big enough to put a fist through. He'd likely bleed to death before you could stop it."

"What do you think we should do, then?" Freeman asked. The question didn't sound angry or resentful. He really wanted to know.

Preacher leaned closer to study the wound. The man's shirt had been ripped back to reveal the place where the arrow entered his body. It was low on his right side, a couple of inches above his waist.

Judging by the angle of the shaft, the arrow hadn't penetrated deeply. The head was probably no more than three inches under the man's skin.

Preacher laid a hand on the man's back and prodded with his fingertips, causing the man to gasp and stiffen. After a moment Preacher nodded. "What we need to do is push it on through."

It would have been obvious to any seasoned frontiersman, but he had a strong hunch it was the first time any of Courtland's men had been farther west than St. Louis. They appeared tough and competent, but lacked the experience that could keep a man alive out there. Preacher was surprised they had made it as far as they had before running into any serious trouble.

"If you push it on through, won't that just hurt him more?" Freeman asked.

"Oh, it'll hurt like blazes," Preacher admitted, "but it'll do a lot less damage, too. If you fellas will hang on to him, I'll be glad to show you."

Freeman thought about it for a moment and then nodded. "All right, go ahead. You heard the man, fellas. Let's get a good hold on poor Ben here."

As several of the men laid hands on him, the wounded man roused from his stupor enough to say, "Wha . . . what are you . . ."

Preacher patted him on the shoulder. "Don't you worry about a thing, son. We'll have you fixed up in no time."

"You . . . you swear?"

"Of course I swear," Preacher said. "Why, I've doctored fellas who were a heap worse off than you. One of them I got back in such good shape he spent the winter with some Injuns I know. He didn't have just one squaw to keep his buffalo robes warm. He had three."

"Th-three women . . . ?"

"You bet."

While Preacher was talking, he had taken hold of the arrow shaft and had a firm grip on it. When the wounded man's eyes widened at the thought of sharing his blankets with three women, Preacher suddenly gave the arrow a hard push. The flint head came straight out the man's back with a spurt of fresh blood.

The man screamed in agony and tried to buck up off the tailgate, and Preacher snapped, "Hold him!"

Freeman and the other men pushed hard to keep the man still.

Preacher pushed the arrow through far enough to get hold of the shaft with both hands, just behind the head, and snap it off. Then it was simple to pull the shaft back out through the hole it had made going in.

The wounded man's struggles subsided as the pain eased a little. Preacher told the others, "Don't let go of him yet. You'll need to hold him down again while somebody pours whiskey all the way through that hole. It'll need to be drenched good."

One of the men muttered, "Seems like a waste of perfectly good whiskey."

"It's the best way to keep the wound from festerin'," Preacher explained.

"Do what he says," Freeman ordered. "The man knows what he's talking about."

Preacher wiped off the blood on his hands on his buckskins and stepped back away from the wagon. "Once you've got the wound clean, you'll need to bandage it. Later I'll make a poultice and we'll put it on the holes to draw out any corruption."

From behind him, Wiley Courtland commented. "Frontier surgery at its finest."

Preacher looked around and shook his head. "I wouldn't call that surgery. Nothin' fancy about it."

"Medical attention doesn't have to be fancy, just effective. I was watching you, Preacher, and I'm more convinced than ever that my first impulse about you was right."

"What impulse might that be?" Preacher asked, suddenly wary.

"I want you to come to Fort Gifford with us."

CHAPTER 5

Preacher frowned. "Why would you want me to do that?"

"Well, just look at what you did for poor Ben there." Courtland waved his hand at the wounded man. "I didn't know the best way to treat such an injury. None of us did. We might have done more harm than good, and he might have died if you hadn't come along." Courtland paused. "For that matter, all of us might have died when those Indians attacked us if not for you, Preacher."

"You're givin' me too much credit."

"I don't think so. How many of the savages did you kill?"

Preacher shrugged. "Seven or eight, I reckon."

"That's more than all of us killed, even though we were shooting as fast as we could. The Indians probably wouldn't have broken off their attack when they did if you hadn't inflicted so much damage on them."

Courtland was probably right about that, Preacher thought. But that didn't mean he wanted to go all the way to Fort Gifford with these green-horns.

"I'm a fur trapper, not a horse herder."

"I wouldn't expect you to herd any horses. You'd be our guide and scout and surgeon, not to mention expert marksman. My plan was to engage the services of just such a person when we got out here, but so far we haven't run into anyone who fits the bill. Until you."

They could use his help, that was for sure, mused Preacher. But no matter how much he had appreciated the company of Pete, Lorenzo, Audie, and Nighthawk during the winter, he enjoyed being out on his own again. He was a solitary man and always had been.

"How long do you think it would take us to get to the fort?" Courtland went on.

"Well, since I don't know exactly where it is, that's a mite hard to say. But from what you told me earlier, I don't reckon it'd take much more than a week."

"So there you are." Courtland waved his arm about again. "A week's work on your part, and a healthy share in the profits I realize from the horses. You see, Preacher, I wasn't expecting you to accompany us out of the goodness of your heart. You'd be a partner in this enterprise."

That brought a healthy chuckle from Preacher. "I've never been what you'd call a businessman."

"But you've hired on with other expeditions, I'll wager."

That was true. Never just for the money, though. He'd always had other reasons. Usually, the folks he helped out really needed his help.

It was likely the same case. Courtland, Freeman, and the others had made it that far, but it had been mostly due to blind luck.

Preacher had a feeling their luck had run out when they encountered Red Knife's war party. Wherever Red Knife had gotten off to, he'd be smarting over the defeat handed to him.

Preacher looked across the rolling prairie in the direction the Indians had gone when they disappeared. Somewhere out there, he'd bet a couple of Blackfoot scouts were keeping an eye on the men and wagons at that exact moment. The war party would stalk them, and when the time was right, Red Knife would strike again, determined to avenge his warriors who had fallen in the battle.

Preacher decided there was a very good chance Courtland and the others would never make it to Fort Gifford alive without his help. Even with him along, it would be pretty doggoned risky.

He made up his mind. "All right. I reckon the

beaver can wait another week or two for me to trap 'em. I'll come with you."

A relieved grin spread across Courtland's sunburned face. "I'm about as glad to hear that as anything I've ever heard in my life!"

One man had been creased by a rifle ball during the fighting, while two more had scratches inflicted by arrows that had narrowly missed doing much worse. Once those minor injuries were tended to, the group was ready to move again. Ben was placed on a pile of blankets in one of the wagons since he was in no shape to ride.

Some of what Preacher had taken to be horses were actually extra mules. They were hitched to the wagons in place of the animals that had been killed. When the vehicles rolled out, heading north again, Preacher and Wiley Courtland rode at the head of the little procession.

Courtland wore a coonskin cap complete with the bushy tail and head. Preacher thought it looked a mite ridiculous and figured somebody back in St. Louis had sold it to Courtland, assuring him every frontiersman worth his salt sported headgear just like it.

In spite of the hat, Preacher had to give Courtland some credit. The backs of the wagons were loaded with plenty of supplies, guns, and ammunition.

Courtland had done a decent job of outfitting for the trip. It appeared the only thing he had failed to do was hire experienced men to come along with him.

Now he had Preacher for that. It remained to be seen whether it would be enough to get the party safely to Fort Gifford.

"Is this your first trip west of St. Louis?" Preacher asked as they rode along. He was just making conversation. He was pretty sure he knew the answer.

"That's right," Courtland replied. "I've always wanted to come west. I owned an interest in a freight line in Missouri, so I know horses and wagons. I finally decided to take the bit between my teeth, so to speak, and sold my part of the company so I could use the money to outfit for the trip out here."

"I know the feelin'. About wantin' to come west, anyway."

"Have you been out here a long time?"

"More than twenty years. I ran away from home when I was still a boy."

Courtland let out a low whistle of admiration. "That must have been pretty dangerous. And you've survived out here that long, under such hazardous conditions."

Preacher shrugged. "A fella learns how to get along and what to watch out for. If he doesn't . . ."

"Then nature takes care of it, eh?" Courtland finished up when Preacher's words trailed off. "It's true. The world is a harsh, unforgiving place." He put a smile back on his face. "But I try to keep my spirits up. It doesn't do any good to brood about things, does it?"

"I reckon not." After a few moments, Preacher went on. "Was there somethin' that decided you to make the move when you did?"

Courtland didn't answer right away. A grim expression came over his face, and he finally said, "It had something to do with a woman."

"A lot of times it does. Sorry if I stirred up bad memories."

"Oh, that's fine. I've put it behind me. That's all a man can do, really."

They fell silent for a while, which was fine with Preacher.

When Courtland spoke up again, it was to ask a question. "Do you think those Indians will come back?"

Preacher wasn't the sort to lie just to spare somebody's feelings. "I'd be mighty surprised if they didn't."

"Do you know what tribe they were?"

"Blackfoot."

"Those are supposed to be some of the worst Indians, right? The most hostile?"

"They ain't ever been overly friendly to me,"

Preacher said. "We've had our scrapes. Plenty of 'em."

"And that's why you think they'll attack us again?"

"Yeah. I've got a hunch the ones who jumped you are bein' led by a war chief called Red Knife. I know for a fact he's been on the prod in these parts, because I had a run-in with some of his scouts a few days ago. I don't know him, but I've been told he hates white men more than any of the other Blackfeet do. He won't like that we made him turn tail and run. He'll be lookin' to settle that score."

"We'd better double our guard at night, then, and be on the lookout for trouble," Courtland pointed out.

"Yeah," Preacher agreed dryly. "That'd be smart."

They didn't see any more signs of the war party, and Preacher was grateful. On the other hand, the longer Red Knife delayed attacking them, the longer the war chief would have to build up his forces. The Blackfeet already outnumbered Courtland's party. If Red Knife was able to round up more warriors, the odds might become overwhelming.

The horses were picketed when they made camp that evening. Some of the men got tents from the wagons and set them up. Preacher didn't have need of a tent; he would spread his bedroll under one of the wagons. and be just fine.

"Should we build a fire?" Courtland asked.

"Might as well. You won't be tellin' Red Knife anything he don't already know, if that's what you're worried about. I suspect he's had scouts trailin' us all day."

Courtland frowned, but he said, "Then you're right. We might as well have hot food and coffee."

Later, while they were sitting by the fire, Preacher asked the man, "Why didn't you just follow the Missouri River with your horses? You're well south of there."

"I studied all the maps available and decided we could save some time and distance by following this route."

"You know some of those maps likely was drawed by fellas who ain't never been out here, don't you?"

"But you know the territory. Aren't we headed in the right direction?"

Preacher shrugged. "If you're right about where this Fort Gifford is, then I reckon you're headed toward it. Anyway, if we keep goin' north, we'll hit the Big Muddy sooner or later, and the fort will have to be one direction or the other. Reckon we can backtrack if we have to."

"The Big Muddy . . . that's the Missouri?"

"Yep."

"Despite all the hardships you must have suffered, I envy you your adventurous life, Preacher."

"No need to," the mountain man said.

"Why's that?"

"Because by the time we make it to Fort Gifford, you're liable to get all the *adventure* you could ever want."

CHAPTER 6

Ben died from his wounds. He was buried quickly, without fanfare. As heartless as that may have seemed, Preacher knew it was better for the folks not to dwell too much on the loss.

Courtland had posted four guards instead of the usual two. Preacher would have preferred even more, but the men had to sleep sometime. He intended to do some prowling around during the night, which would help, and Dog and Horse would alert him if they sensed any danger lurking in the darkness.

"Stay close," he told Dog as he bedded down under the lead wagon. The campfire had burned itself down to embers giving off a soft red glow.

As was his habit, even when danger didn't threaten, Preacher slept lightly, waking after a couple of hours. He crawled out of his blankets and stood up. The night was dark, lit only by the stars and a sliver of moon. To his keen eyes, it was enough light to let him move around freely.

He put on his hat and took his rifle with him as he made the rounds of the camp. The guards were posted about twenty yards out at each of the compass points. Preacher called softly to them as he approached each in turn. He didn't want to spook any of them into getting trigger-happy.

The men reported that everything was quiet, with no sign of trouble. Preacher could see and hear that for himself.

His instincts nagged at him, though. He had learned that when his gut told him something was wrong, it usually was. The feeling grew stronger as he approached the fourth and final guard, the one on the east side of the camp.

The man was sitting cross-legged on the ground. Preacher spoke quietly to him, identifying himself. "Any problems over here?"

The sentry didn't reply.

Preacher's forehead creased in a frown. It could be the fella was asleep, which wouldn't be good.

There were worse things, though. Preacher dropped to one knee next to the man, put a hand on his shoulder, and shook him gently.

The man's head tipped far back at a grotesque, unnatural angle. Preacher leaned forward and saw the dark stain on the front of the man's shirt where blood had flooded down. The man's throat was cut down to the bone, giving him the appearance of having a wide, gaping second mouth.

Preacher's hand moved to the man's back. A stake had been pushed into the ground behind the guard and through his shirt so it held him up in a sitting position. Whoever had killed him—Preacher had no doubt it was one of the Blackfeet—hadn't wanted the man's death to be discovered right away.

Something else was going on, Preacher thought as his head jerked around and he peered toward the wagons. More than likely the killer had crawled on into camp . . .

A startled yell and a gunshot suddenly split the night. Preacher surged to his feet and broke into a run, leaving the corpse where it was.

It took only a few seconds for his long legs to carry him back into the camp. Men fought clear of their tents, waving pistols around and shouting curses and questions, but nobody really seemed to know what was going on. Confusion reigned, which was a bad thing.

Preacher spotted Otis Freeman and grabbed his arm. "Tell everybody to settle down!" he snapped. "Get your rifles and take cover by the wagons! The Blackfeet could be attackin' again!"

That would be a good tactic, sending one man in to throw the camp into an uproar, then attacking while everybody was running around like chickens with their heads cut off.

"Where's Courtland?" Preacher went on.

"I don't know! His tent's over there!" Freeman leveled an arm and pointed.

Even in the dim light Preacher could tell somebody was thrashing around inside it. He ran over to the tent, thrust his rifle barrel through the opening, and ripped the canvas aside, revealing Wiley Courtland rolling around on the ground, locked in deadly struggle with someone.

The Blackfeet had borrowed a trick from him, Preacher realized. One warrior had used stealth to creep up on the guard, cut his throat, and then slipped into the camp to murder as many men as he could before he was discovered.

Preacher didn't know if Courtland was the warrior's first target, or if more men lay dead in their tents. He could check on that later. At the moment, he had a more pressing problem, and so did Courtland. The Blackfoot had a knife gripped in his raised fist, and Courtland's desperate grip on the warrior's wrist was all that kept the blade from falling.

Locked as closely together as the men were, Preacher couldn't risk a shot. But when Courtland rolled over his attacker was on top momentarily, and Preacher struck. He stepped in and drove the butt of his rifle against the back of the Blackfoot's head in a swift, deadly stroke. He felt bone shatter under the force of the blow.

The warrior died without a sound.

Courtland jerked his head aside to avoid the falling blade as the knife slipped from the Blackfoot's fingers. The dead man collapsed on top of him.

With a curse, Courtland shoved the warrior's corpse aside and scrambled away from it. By then, the other men had gathered around, and a couple hurried forward to help Courtland to his feet.

"Spread out, blast it," Preacher barked. "Bunched up, you're a better target."

"Do what he says," Freeman ordered. "Wiley, are you all right?"

Courtland nodded. "I think so. Thanks to Preacher . . . again."

The men scattered, resuming defensive positions around the wagons. The surviving guards had rushed in to see what all the commotion was about. Preacher did a quick head count and came up with eleven, not counting himself.

The guard whose throat had been cut was the only fatality.

Preacher called Dog over and knelt beside him, putting an arm around the big cur's shaggy neck. "Hunt, Dog."

When Preacher let go, Dog bounded off into the night, vanishing rapidly in the darkness. Preacher knew he would range all around the camp, searching for enemies.

If Dog came across any more Blackfoot warriors

out there, Preacher would be able to tell by the snarling and snapping and yelling.

Instead, silence lay over the prairie for a good twenty minutes before Dog came trotting back. He snuffled Preacher's hand, and the mountain man ruffled the fur on the animal's head. "Good boy."

He turned to Courtland and Freeman. "There ain't any more Injuns out there. Not anywhere close to the camp, anyway."

"You're sure?" Courtland asked.

"If they were there, Dog would've found 'em. That varmint who snuck in was by himself."

"What did he think he was going to accomplish, one man like that?"

"You'd be surprised." Preacher smiled. "If he'd been slick enough to crawl in here, cut three or four throats, and get back out without anybody knowin' until morning he'd been here, that would've played hell with everybody's spirit."

Preacher didn't mention he had done the same thing to his enemies himself, many times.

He went on, "It's bad enough he managed to kill the guard out yonder on the east side of camp."

"Jenkins?" Courtland exclaimed. "Jenkins is dead?"

"Yeah. Throat was cut ear to ear. Maybe he dozed off when he should've been watchin', or maybe the fella was just that good. It don't really matter, does it?"

"No, it doesn't," Courtland agreed with a weary sigh. "Poor Jenkins is just as dead either way. Otis, have a couple men bring in his body. Go with them to guard them."

Freeman nodded. "Sure." He moved off to pick some men for the grim chore.

"What happened in the tent?" Preacher asked Courtland.

"Luckily, I'm a fairly light sleeper. I woke up and sensed something was wrong. Smelled something, maybe."

"Could be. That bear grease they use is pretty rank."

"When I opened my eyes, I could see just well enough to make out a shape above me. I reacted without even thinking about it and threw myself aside. He was already trying to stab me. The knife went in the ground, I guess. I felt his arm come down right beside my ear. So I grabbed his wrist and hung on for dear life."

"That was the right thing to do," Preacher told him. "You could've hollered for help, though."

"I know. I should have. But I was concentrating so hard on keeping him from killing me . . ." Courtland shrugged. "I just didn't think of it at the time."

A few minutes later, Freeman and the two men he had taken with him came back with the dead sentry's body. They wrapped it in a blanket and placed it next to one of the wagon wheels.

"We'll bury him in the morning," Courtland said, "before we get moving again."

"Speakin' of that," Preacher said. "If I'm not back by mornin', you fellas head north and I'll catch up to you as soon as I can. You can just leave Horse here. He won't wander off before I get back."

"Catch up?" Courtland repeated with a puzzled frown. "What do you mean? Aren't you coming with us?"

"Yeah, but there's somethin' else I got to do first."

"What's that?"

"Figured I'd give ol' Red Knife and his boys a taste of their own medicine."

CHAPTER 7

"I don't much like this, Preacher," Courtland said a few minutes later as the mountain man was getting ready to leave. "Won't you just make this fellow Red Knife even more angry if you're able to kill some of his men?"

"I don't figure it's possible Red Knife could get much more out of sorts with us than he already is," Preacher replied. "Besides, it ain't really Red Knife I'm tryin' to spook. It's the warriors who are with him. He's their war chief and they'll mostly do what he tells 'em to, but if enough of 'em decide it ain't worth it to keep comin' after us, they can make him change his mind. That's been known to happen, anyway."

"But what if you get killed instead?"

"That's a risk I'm runnin', all right."

"And the rest of us as well. I was counting on your help to get us to Fort Gifford."

"If we can shake those Blackfeet off our trail, it'll be a lot easier," Preacher pointed out.

Courtland shook his head. "I suppose I can't argue with that. Anyway, you're not the sort of man to be talked out of something once your mind is made up, are you?"

Preacher chuckled. "If that's your way of sayin' I'm stubborn as a mule, I reckon you're right about that!"

He called Dog over and gave the big cur a good whiff of a piece of buckskin shirt he'd taken from the dead warrior. Once Dog had the scent, Preacher ordered simply, "Trail!", and Dog bounded off into the night. He would be able to backtrack the Blackfoot without much difficulty, Preacher knew.

Preacher said so long to Courtland and Freeman and trotted out of the camp, taking the same direction Dog had. He carried the long-barreled flintlock rifle and had all four pistols tucked behind his belt. His powder horn bumped lightly against his hip as his long legs carried him over the prairie. He planned to do his killing with the big knife on his calf, but if it came down to a gunfight, he was going to be prepared.

From time to time, Dog circled back to make sure Preacher was still following him. With tireless ease, the mountain man's leathery muscles bore him onward, across plains, up and down rises, and through buffalo wallows. The trail led in a generally eastward direction.

The miles fell away under Preacher's high-topped moccasins. The stars wheeled through the ebony sky overhead, and the sliver of moon dipped toward the horizon. Preacher didn't slow down until the faint tang of smoke drifted to his nose. He stopped, went to a knee, and let out a low whistle easily mistaken for the call of a night bird.

After a moment, Dog answered the summons, padding out of the shadows. Preacher whispered, "Good job. You brung me right to 'em."

The fire was a small one fueled by buffalo droppings and gave off little smoke, but Preacher could smell it anyway. He was within a few hundred yards of the Blackfoot camp. On hands and knees, he crawled toward it, following the smell of the smoke. Dog crept along beside him.

Eventually both bellied down on the ground. Preacher took off his broad-brimmed hat and left it lying there with his rifle. He would come back to reclaim them when his mission was finished, if he was able to.

If he wasn't, it wouldn't really matter what happened to the hat and the gun.

He moved in utter silence as he crawled toward the camp. The Blackfeet had stopped for the night in the lee of a grass-covered knoll. Somewhere nearby trickled a little creek; Preacher could hear it. He also heard the Indian ponies shifting around and pawing at the ground. There was no wind.

Red Knife would have posted guards, just like Wiley Courtland had. The difference was the Blackfoot sentries would be more alert, as well as more dangerous if they discovered him before he was ready to make his move.

Preacher stopped and lay absolutely still, with his head lifted just enough for him to see the camp and the tiny red glow of the fire's embers. Slowly, he turned his head from side to side, searching for the guards. He spotted a dark shape off to his left that might be a man.

"Stay," he breathed to Dog, then started crawling toward the shape. The big cur wouldn't budge from that spot unless Preacher told him to, or unless a fight broke out. Then he would be right in the middle of it as fast as his legs would carry him.

Slowly, so the new grass barely stirred around him, Preacher crawled toward the guard. He couldn't afford to get in any hurry. It was still hours until dawn, and he would put all the darkness to use.

Eventually he was close enough to see the patch of darkness he'd been closing in on was definitely man-shaped. He smelled the bear grease on the guard's hair.

Preacher circled so he could take the sentry

from behind. When he rose from the grass, he was like the head of a coiled snake, coming up to strike.

His left arm went around the guard's neck and clamped down like an iron bar, shutting off any sound as he jerked the man backward. At the same time, he drove the knife in his right hand forward. The long, razor-sharp blade sliced through the buckskin shirt and into the Blackfoot's body with hardly any resistance.

The man's muscles spasmed, but they were no match for Preacher's strength. A deep shudder went through the warrior as the knife's tip penetrated his heart. His back arched for a second, and then he went limp in Preacher's grip.

Preacher lowered the body to the ground and withdrew his knife. He wiped the blade on the dead man's shirt to clean it off. The thrust had stilled the guard's heart so quickly there wasn't much blood.

No sounds disturbed the night. Preacher knew he could crawl back to where he had left Dog, along with his hat and rifle. The dead guard evened the score for Jenkins' death back at Courtland's camp, and that lone, mysterious death might be enough to demoralize the rest of the Blackfeet.

But Preacher figured he could do more damage. He stretched out on his belly again and crawled toward the men sleeping on the ground near the remains of the fire.

They were scattered out some, which made his job easier. During the next hour, three more men died, the ones farthest on the outskirts of the camp. Their desire for a bit of privacy, if that was what had motivated them to separate themselves from their fellows, cost them dearly.

In each case, Preacher clamped his hand over the mouth of his quarry and slashed the man's throat with a swift, silent move. Blood fountained from the wounds, bringing death in a matter of seconds.

It was grim work, the sort of thing that ate at the souls of some men, but Preacher would never lose a minute of sleep over it. Blackfoot warriors lived to kill, and would have done the same thing to him without hesitation if they'd had the chance.

He didn't want to push his luck, so after the fourth kill, counting the guard, he backed away. Darkness and silence still hung over the camp. Hardly daring to breathe, Preacher worked his way back to where he'd left Dog. His instincts guided him unerringly to the spot.

Dog didn't make any noise, but he licked Preacher's face in welcome. Preacher grinned in the darkness, happy to be reunited with his old friend and relieved his foray into the Blackfoot camp had been successful.

In the morning, the Indians would have a new,

terrifying story to tell about the man they called Ghost Killer, he thought.

A line of gray appeared in the sky along the eastern horizon by the time Preacher came trotting up to Wiley Courtland's camp with Dog at his heels. When he got close enough, he knelt down and called, "Hello, the camp! Hold your fire. It's me, Preacher."

One of the guards leveled a rifle in his general direction, and for a second Preacher thought the man was so spooked he was going to pull the trigger anyway. But the guard held off. "Preacher? Preacher's back!"

His call roused the whole camp. As he stood up, several men came hurrying out to meet him. Courtland gripped his arm and slapped his shoulder excitedly. "I didn't know if we'd ever see you again!"

"Didn't have much faith in me, did you?" Preacher drawled with a grin on his bearded face.

"All the faith in the world! But you have to admit, the odds of you coming back alive from a mission like that were pretty small." Courtland paused. "You did find the Blackfoot camp, didn't you?"

"I did," Preacher said, "and there are four of them who won't be comin' after you, or anybody else, ever again."

Freeman let out an impressed whistle. "You

killed four Blackfeet and still were able to fight your way out?"

"Wasn't any fightin' to it," Preacher explained. "Nobody knew I was there. They're probably just wakin' up and findin' the bodies right about now."

"That's remarkable," Courtland turned to give orders. "Build the fire up and get the coffee on. I want to get an early start and put as many miles behind us as we can today."

"That's a good idea," Preacher told him. "I'm hopin' that losin' four more men will convince Red Knife to leave us alone, but I sure wouldn't count on it."

"What do you think the chances are that he will?" Courtland asked.

"I don't know," Preacher answered honestly. "But whatever they are, there's an even better chance he'll come after us with blood in his eye!"

CHAPTER 8

It had been a long, harrowing night, and Preacher hadn't slept much. He was used to being tired, though, and was ready to move out with the rest of the men. A hot breakfast and some coffee had done wonders to restore his vitality. After a somber ceremony in which Jenkins, the dead guard, was laid to rest in the prairie sod, the wagons rolled out again, heading north.

Preacher rode at the head of the group with Courtland. The horse herd brought up the rear, raising its customary cloud of dust. That dust was going to make them mighty easy to track if Red Knife decided to come after them, Preacher thought, but nothing could be done about it, short of figuring out a way for the critters to sprout wings and fly.

That idea put a faint smile on his face. He wasn't given to fanciful notions, but every now and then one occurred to him.

Courtland was a talkative gent. "Tell me about some of your adventures. Otis said he's heard people talking about you in St. Louis. They claim you've killed thousands of Indians, wrestled with bears and mountain lions, and explored more of the frontier than any white man west of the Mississippi."

"Yeah, well, people like to talk," Preacher said. "And whenever the facts ain't interestin' enough, they'll just make up a story or three."

"But you *have* fought a lot of Indians, right?"

"I suppose. But I've been good friends with even more of 'em. It don't pay to make an enemy when you can make a friend instead."

"You don't run away from trouble, though. I can tell that about you."

"I'll allow that the good Lord didn't put in any backup when He was stirrin' the pot to make me," Preacher said. "It's just a matter of common sense. You can't run away from trouble without turnin' your back on it, and the second you do, that's when it'll jump right on top of you."

"That's actually quite profound," Courtland said with a smile.

"Like I said, common sense."

After a few more minutes, Courtland asked, "Have you ever been married?"

"Depends on whether you reckon there's got to be a church and a minister involved for that. I've known a heap of women I was mighty fond of, and I reckon they felt the same way about me."

"You're talking about squaws?"

"I'm talkin' about women." Preacher spoke with a slight edge in his voice. "Out here on the frontier, folks is folks, and it don't take you long to get to where you don't care what color their skin is. I just spent the winter with a Dutchman, a dwarf, a Crow Indian, and a fella as black as the ace of spades. I got the same name for all of 'em. *Friend.*"

Courtland nodded. "That's a very admirable attitude. I meant no offense."

"None taken. As for the gals I've knowed . . . some were Indian, some weren't." He thought back to his first love, the beautiful, tragically doomed girl called Jenny. "And before you ask, I don't know if I've got any kids. Could be, but I just don't know."

"Doesn't that uncertainty ever bother you?" Courtland asked with a slight frown.

"Not really. Everybody has to make his own way in the world." Preacher scratched at his beard. "Might have me a real son one of these days. That wouldn't be bad, I suppose. Not until I'm ready to settle down, though, and Lord knows when that'll be."

Courtland smiled. "Not any time soon, I expect. And I can say that having known you less than a day!"

* * *

The group didn't encounter any trouble that day or the next. They didn't see any Indians, either, only wildlife. The antelope and moose they came upon impressed the men, but they watched from a rise in absolute awe as a herd of several thousand buffalo rumbled past.

"And that's just a little herd," Preacher told them. "It don't amount to much. Sometimes the buffs stretch as far as the eye can see, and they move past all day without ever stoppin'. Might still be at it the next mornin', too."

"There must be millions and millions of them out here," Courtland said.

"More than you can ever imagine," Preacher agreed.

Late in the afternoon, they entered a range of low, rolling hills. After traveling for miles on the treeless plains, the sight of trees was a welcome one for Preacher, but he knew the terrain would be slightly more rugged from there.

They were looking for a good place to make camp when Preacher spotted three riders coming toward them. Courtland saw the men at the same time and exclaimed, "Indians!" He started to lift the rifle he carried across the cantle of his saddle.

"Hold on," Preacher said as he raised a hand and motioned for his companion to stop. "Those are Crow. They're friendly . . . at least they were the last I heard."

"How can you tell that from this distance? They just look like Indians to me."

"You learn how to tell the difference pretty quick out here. You'd better, or else you're likely to make a mistake that could turn out to be fatal. Stay here, and hold the wagons and the horses where they are. I'll go talk to those fellas."

Preacher heeled Horse into motion again and trotted toward the three men, who had brought their own mounts to a halt. As he came closer, his first impression was confirmed. The men were Crow, members of the same tribe as his friend Nighthawk.

It wouldn't have surprised Preacher if he knew them, but all three men were strangers to him. As he reined in, he lifted his right hand, palm out in the universal sign of peace and greeted them in their own language. "Hello to my friends of the Crow people."

The three men were warriors, no longer young but still vital, and obviously seasoned fighting men.

"You are the one called Preacher," one of them said.

"You know me. Then you know I am a friend to the Crow. I have eaten meat with you and slept in your lodges. I have fought at your side against your enemies."

"As the Crow have fought with you against *your* enemies," the spokesman for the trio responded.

Preacher inclined his head in acknowledgment of that point.

The warrior lifted a hand toward the wagons and the horse herd in the distance. "Why have these white men come here?"

"They take those horses to Fort Gifford. You have heard of the place?"

"It is there, beside the muddy river," the Crow said with a grave nod. "Some of our people go there to trade."

The slight note of scorn in the man's voice prompted Preacher to say, "But not you and your brothers."

"We are not traders. We are hunters."

"And that's why you're out here today. You're looking for game."

"Our families would eat. We must hunt."

Slowly but surely, many tribes were coming to doubt the wisdom of that idea, thought Preacher. In a way he found it sad, because every time one decided to trade for his and his family's sustenance instead of hunting for it, their way of life died a little more. Someday, if the trend continued, that change in attitude might do more to defeat the Indians' resistance than all the guns brought into this country by white men.

Preacher cleared his head. That wasn't his concern at the moment. "A Blackfoot war party roams somewhere behind us. They are led by Red Knife. Do you know of him?"

All three warriors grimaced in anger. They'd heard of Red Knife, all right, Preacher told himself. The Blackfeet and the Crow had hated each other and warred against each other almost unceasingly for as far back as anybody could remember. They were constantly raiding, stealing horses, and taking captives from the other tribe.

"Red Knife is worse than the other Blackfeet," said the Crow who had done all the talking so far. "He is like a bear driven mad by hate, especially toward white men."

"Do you know why?" Preacher asked.

"Because a worm of madness crawled into his ear while he slept, perhaps."

That was the Crow's way of saying he didn't know why Red Knife was so loco. And it was as good an explanation as any, Preacher supposed. "You might want to go see how the hunting is elsewhere."

All three Crow drew their shoulders back haughtily and glared at him.

"We do not fear the Blackfeet!"

"Never said you did," Preacher replied. "But Red Knife has more men than the fingers on all of your hands. You would not come up to a bear and slap it on the snout. Only a fool would do that."

"We ride where we please," the Crow insisted, but Preacher had a feeling that as soon as they were out of sight, the three warriors would hotfoot it out of those parts. They were proud, but they weren't fools.

"How far is it to Fort Gifford?"

"Four days' ride from here. With those wagons . . . five, perhaps six."

Preacher nodded. "Thank you. May the Spirits smile upon you."

"And on you, white man." The Crow paused, then added in a bit of dry humor. "You may need all the assistance you can get from the Spirits."

Preacher turned and rode back to the wagons and the horse herd. A glance over his shoulder told him the three warriors were angling off to the west.

"What did they say?" Courtland wanted to know when Preacher rode up and reined in. "Have they seen those Blackfeet?"

"No, but they've heard of Red Knife, and their opinion of him matches what I've heard. He's got a powerful hate for white men, and he ain't likely to give up once he starts after somebody."

"Did they say anything else?" Freeman asked.

"Yeah," Preacher replied with a smile. "They said we're liable to need all the luck we can get before we make it to Fort Gifford."

CHAPTER 9

The guard shifts were doubled again, which was no problem. The men were so nervous, nobody wanted to sleep very much anyway. They were too busy looking over their shoulders, worried a Blackfoot bent on bloody murder might be sneaking up on them.

And after what had happened to Jenkins, there was no chance of anybody dozing off on duty.

Two more days of steady progress passed. Preacher began to hope they would reach Fort Gifford without being attacked again, but nagging doubt still lurked in the back of his mind.

As they came to an area of rugged badlands the doubt grew stronger. The rocky, pine-dotted buttes thrusting upward with narrow gaps between them looked like perfect places for an ambush.

He thought about suggesting they take the

horse herd around the buttes rather than through them, but he knew from previous visits the badlands stretched for a number of miles east and west. Detouring around them would add several days to the trip, giving Red Knife more time to marshal his forces against them, if he wasn't doing it already.

"Everybody best keep his eyes open," Preacher advised Courtland as they rode into the badlands. "There are plenty of places in here for Red Knife to hide."

"We'll be riding with our hands on our guns, you can be sure of that."

Courtland turned in the saddle and waved Freeman forward from beside the third wagon.

"Spread the word for everyone to be especially alert."

"You think those Blackfeet might've got ahead of us?" Freeman asked.

Preacher nodded. "Yeah, they could be lurkin' up there in those buttes."

Freeman looked like he wished he could turn around and ride the other direction, rather than continuing on into the badlands, but he said, "I'll tell the fellas."

"Dog, go take a look around," Preacher told the big cur. Dog soon disappeared around a rocky knob with a single pine jutting from its blunt top.

"It's like that dog understands everything you say to him," Courtland commented.

"Dog and me been together a long time. Reckon we know how each other think. Same's true for ol' Horse here. We're all gettin' a mite long in the tooth, but we ain't ready to be put out to pasture just yet."

Courtland laughed. "Having been around you for a few days now, Preacher, I think the day you're ready to be put out to pasture is still a long, long time in the future."

"Maybe . . . assumin' I don't get shot or stabbed or skewered with an arrow or have my head stove in with a tomahawk." The mountain man grinned in dry humor. "Other than that I might be all right."

It didn't take long for the group to fully penetrate the badlands. The open terrain fell behind them. The passages between the buttes were wide enough for the herd to travel through without going single file, but the steep, pine-dotted slopes were close enough on both sides to seem looming and dark.

Preacher watched for Dog to return, but the minutes dragged past and eventually turned into an hour with no sign of the big cur. No gunshots had disturbed the warm silence, but the whistle of an arrow through the air wouldn't travel very far.

Dog had fought grizzly bears and mountain lions and all manner of bad men, so Preacher wasn't overly concerned about him being able to take care of himself. Still, he would have been relieved to see Dog bounding back into sight.

It didn't happen.

The skin on the back of Preacher's neck began to crawl under the long, thick dark hair. Every instinct in his body told him something had happened.

And it wasn't over. The threat still loomed, just as surely as those piney slopes on either side of them.

He wasn't sure what warned him. A flicker of movement, perhaps. Maybe even the flutter of the arrow's fletching as it flew through the air. Whatever it was, he suddenly leaned forward over Horse's neck.

The arrow that would have transfixed his throat and killed him brushed across the back of his neck and buried its flint head harmlessly in the ground. Preacher had a pretty good idea of the spot in the trees where the arrow had been launched, so he straightened, flung his rifle to his shoulder, and touched off a shot.

The heavy .52 caliber ball ripped through the lower branches, clipping several of them, and smashed into the chest of a Blackfoot warrior who tumbled into the open with blood gushing from the wound.

As if the shot were a signal, more reports roared

out from the trees to the left, followed by flights of
arrows from both sides.

Preacher kicked his foot loose from the stirrups
and dived out of the saddle. He landed running
and shouted to the others, "Use the wagons for
cover!"

"What about the horses?" Courtland yelled.

"We'll have to round 'em up later! We're
hemmed in!"

Horse ran clear of the wagons, and Preacher
was glad to see the stallion go. He'd stay out of the
line of fire, but close by so Preacher could find
him when the fighting was over.

If Preacher was still alive then. As the mountain
man scrambled for cover, he wasn't sure that
would be the case.

"Pull the wagons up side by side!" he called,
waving an arm over his head to indicate where
they should go.

The drivers, pale-faced with fear as arrows flew
around them, thudding into the vehicles' side-
boards, stayed cool-headed enough to line up the
wagons all three abreast. The men crowded in between them for cover.

The wagons served another purpose. They
blocked the gap for the most part, so the horse
herd couldn't stampede past them. Spooked by the
gunfire, the horses were milling around, but they
hadn't turned to bolt back the other direction.

Judging by the number of arrows flying out of

the trees, Red Knife had indeed increased the ranks of his war party, Preacher thought as he reloaded his rifle. Shots blasted from the men behind the wagons as they aimed over tailgates and drivers' boxes.

"Shoot almost anywhere in those trees and you got a chance of hittin' one of the varmints!" Preacher shouted. "Keep firin'!"

Ragged volleys continued to ring out for the next several minutes. As always in the heat of battle, time seemed to slow down. It already seemed like they had been pinned down for an hour, when really only a fraction of that time had passed.

Preacher's keen eyes searched the slopes. Whenever he saw a flash of movement or a bit of cover, he was ready to press the rifle's trigger. As a result, his fire was very effective. He saw several of the attackers fall, some of them toppling from behind the trees to land in the open.

The other men scored some hits, too. Courtland let out a whoop and called, "I got one! I saw the ball hit him in the head!"

"Good job," Preacher said. "Now see if you can get another one."

One of the men in between the wagons suddenly grunted in pain and staggered back with an arrow embedded deeply in his chest. He dropped his rifle and pawed futilely at the shaft for a second before his eyes rolled up and he collapsed. Preacher knew by the limp way the man fell that he was a goner.

Well, he hadn't expected the party to come through this unscathed, he told himself. That would have been a miracle beyond any they could have hoped for. At that moment, he was happy to settle for *some* of them making it out alive.

He began to watch for puffs of powder smoke marking the location of warriors armed with rifles. Every time he spotted one, he sent a round whistling back toward it. Three times those rifles fell silent after his shot, so he knew he had at least winged the gunners.

Arrows continued to rain down. Several of the mules in the wagon teams were hit and screamed in agony, but the others stood stolidly, preventing the wounded animals from bolting. The horse herd was still milling around. Preacher grimaced as he heard the cries of horses that had been hit.

"We have to do something!" Courtland exclaimed with a note of desperation in his voice. "Those horses represent my life's savings! If I lose the herd I'll be ruined!"

If it was him, Preacher would have been a mite more concerned with his hide and his hair than he was with business reverses, but he supposed every man had his own priorities.

Courtland had a point. They couldn't stay where they were. Those arrows would begin to take a heavier toll. They needed a way to break out of the trap.

Fewer arrows and none of the gunshots were coming from the right. Red Knife had put all his men armed with rifles on the left, which was a mistake. And, the Indians hadn't been using firearms for all that long. Fighting with them still didn't come natural to many of the warriors.

"We're gonna pull the wagon on the right all the way up to the front to make an opening," Preacher told Courtland. "Then I'll drive the herd through as fast as I can."

"They'll stampede!" Courtland objected. "There's no telling how far they'll run!"

"If they stay here, they'll wind up stuck full of arrows, and so will we," Preacher snapped. "As soon as the horses are through, the wagons will light a shuck after them. They'll kick up quite a bit of dust, which ought to help. Red Knife's men won't be able to draw quite as good a bead on us."

"It seems awfully risky."

"So's gettin' up in the mornin'. Let's go! Move that wagon!"

CHAPTER 10

Otis Freeman leaped to the wagon seat, jerked the reins free from the brake lever, and grabbed the whip from its socket. He sent the lash biting at the backs of the mules and yelled, "Hyaaahhh! Move, you jug heads, move!"

One of the mules was wounded, but the arrow hadn't penetrated far enough to be fatal so the team was able to pull. As the mules surged forward and the wagon lurched into motion, an arrow whisked Freeman's hat right off his head. He ignored the loss.

Preacher gave a shrill whistle, and Horse answered the summons, pounding up through a storm of arrows. Preacher swung up onto the stallion's back and ducked low in the saddle. He galloped around the herd, circling to get behind the horses, which brought him pretty close to the trees. Arrows whizzed around his head as the Blackfeet concentrated their fire on him. Only

Horse's speed and sheer providence kept Preacher from being hit.

He guided Horse with his knees, using his hands to yank the brace of pistols from behind his belt. Thrusting the weapons toward the slope, he pulled the triggers. The double-shot charges raked through the trees as Preacher hoped they did some damage.

Thrusting the empty guns behind his belt, he swung into position behind the herd. He drove his mount toward the nearest of the horses and snatched his hat off his head to swat it at the animal's rump.

The stallion got into the act, too, reaching over and using his teeth to nip another of the horses.

Preacher continued to yell and swing his hat, prodding several horses to run, and the others naturally followed suit. It took only seconds for a full-fledged stampede to develop. The horses raced through the gap created by Freeman pulling the wagon on the right ahead of the others.

Preacher raced after the herd, waving the wagons on. Freeman whipped up the lead wagon's team and got it moving again. The other vehicles fell in behind him full of men who'd let their mounts run free and taken cover among the supplies, firing out the backs and from the sides where they had raised the canvas coverings.

Preacher jerked his other two pistols out of holsters he had fashioned and strapped to his saddle.

He emptied them at the slopes up ahead, firing in both directions at once.

Somebody needed to come up with a good repeating pistol, he thought. If that ever happened, he'd be the first in line to buy one.

The arrows were thick around him, almost like flint-tipped horizontal rain. Dust from the hooves of the stampeding horses clogged the air and stung his eyes. The thunder of hoofbeats was deafening, but even over the awful racket he heard someone scream.

The driver of the second wagon tumbled off the seat with two arrows lodged in his body. One of the men riding in the back of the vehicle scrambled up onto the seat and grabbed the reins. The mule team never slowed down.

With the frantic horse herd leading the way, the party of white men fled through the gap. As they neared the end of it, where the landscape opened up into a wider, roughly circular flat surrounded by buttes, some of the Blackfeet rushed out of the trees, trying to intercept the fleeing men. Too close to the horses, a warrior was trampled under their flashing hooves, flinging his arms up and screaming before he went down to gory death.

Another warrior lunged at Preacher and reached up to drag him off the stallion. Preacher lifted his right foot and launched a kick. His heel caught the Blackfoot on the jaw and drove his head back so far his neck snapped. The warrior dropped like every bone in his body had turned to jelly.

From the corner of his eye Preacher saw a tomahawk spinning through the air at him. He ducked his head. Only superb reflexes and instantaneous reactions allowed him to snatch it from its flight—along with a generous helping of luck.

The Blackfoot who had thrown the tomahawk was so amazed by Preacher's feat he stopped and stood there staring for a second, and that proved to be a fatal mistake. Preacher whipped the tomahawk right back at him. It struck the warrior in the center of his forehead and cleaved into his skull.

Preacher spotted another Blackfoot lining up a shot at him with bow and arrow. The mountain man's guns were all empty.

Just as the warrior loosed the arrow, more than a hundred pounds of gray fur struck him from behind. The arrow flew well over Preacher's head as the man who had fired it was driven to the ground by Dog's weight. Dog savaged his throat. The Blackfoot didn't have time to do anything but shudder once before he died.

"At least you got here before all the fightin' was over this time!" Preacher yelled at Dog.

The big cur ignored him and twisted away to launch himself at another Blackfoot.

The horses stampeded out of the gap and ran loose on the flats. All three wagons careened after them, rolling swiftly across the level ground.

Preacher didn't know how many men the party had lost, but some had survived, obviously. He fell back and galloped alongside the lead wagon. Otis Freeman was still at the reins, apparently unharmed. Wiley Courtland raced up on the other side of the team. He hadn't even lost his coonskin cap in the melee.

"Head for that butte over there!" Preacher called to Freeman and waved a hand to indicate which one of the rocky knobs he meant. "There are some boulders at the base of it where we can fort up!"

Freeman nodded to show he understood. He hauled on the reins to make the team veer in the right direction.

Preacher fell back some more to let the wagons pass him, and so did Courtland. Once the wagons had gone by, the two men rode side by side.

"You hurt?" Preacher lifted his voice to ask.

"A couple scratches where arrows nicked me!" Courtland replied. "But that's all. How about you?"

"I'm all right."

"We lost a couple men!"

Preacher nodded grimly. "Could've been worse. Might be yet."

"Are they going to come after us?"

Preacher looked back. "I reckon you can bet that furry hat you're wearin' on that!"

Mounted warriors charged out of the trees. The

Indian ponies stirred up more dust as they galloped after the white men.

They weren't going to be able to catch up before the wagons reached the boulders at the base of the butte, though, Preacher figured. That would give him and the other men a fighting chance.

A man really couldn't ask for much more than that in this life, he mused.

Courtland hadn't forgotten the reason they were there. "It's going to take a long time to round up all those horses, if we're ever able to!"

"As long as you're alive to give it a try, I reckon you've come out ahead," Preacher told him.

"Yes, I suppose you could look at it that way." Courtland's tone made it clear he was having a hard time doing that.

Preacher wasn't going to worry about it. He was a lot more concerned about saving their scalps.

Freeman and the other drivers arranged the wagons in a half circle behind the rocks and were unhitching the teams when Preacher and Courtland rode up. The spaces among the boulders were large enough for mules and the saddle horses, but it would be crowded.

Preacher swung down from the saddle and reloaded his guns as soon as his feet hit the ground, pausing only to reach down and ruffle the fur on Dog's head when the big cur came up to him.

"Load every gun you've got," he told the men. "They're likely so mad right now they'll charge us flat out. We need to mow down as many of 'em as we can, so they'll decide it makes more sense to give up than to keep losin' men."

"Do what Preacher says," Courtland added.

Until that moment, Preacher hadn't even realized he had taken command. It was a natural, instinctive thing for him to do, especially in a situation where he was the only seasoned frontiersmen and his allies were all greenhorns.

Courtland didn't seem to mind. He was smart enough to know their best chance for survival lay with Preacher's experience and wisdom.

The men worked quickly to get ready in the few moments they had. Preacher counted them again and came up with nine. They had lost two men in the battle.

Inside the boulders was a good defensive position, but it wasn't perfect. The wagons and boulders provided good cover only against a frontal assault. If the Blackfeet were able to get on the butte behind the wagons, they could fire down into the party of white men.

Preacher stood beside the drivers' box on the middle wagon and watched the mounted warriors slow and finally stop. He figured they were letting the rest of the war party catch up to them. As the dust began to settle, he saw that was the case. More and more men rode out of the gap to join the ones already facing the butte where the white men had taken cover.

"Good Lord!" Courtland exclaimed as he looked at the riders gathering in the distance. "How many of them are there?"

"Looks like fifty or sixty," Preacher said calmly. He placed all four loaded pistols on the floorboard within easy reach. Then he rested the long rifle in the crook of his arm and waited.

"And only nine of us plus you, Preacher," Courtland went on. "Those are five to one odds, at least!"

"Reckon we'll just have to work a mite harder than they do to stay alive."

Courtland took off his coonskin cap and raked his fingers through his fair hair. "You're taking this awfully well."

"No reason to get worked up. That won't do any good. Man who stays calm and steady shoots straighter."

Courtland put his cap on again. "I suppose you're right. And I suppose I really shouldn't be worrying about those horses right now, should I?"

Preacher shifted the rifle in his grip. "Nope. It's time to worry about stayin' alive, because here come those varmints now!"

CHAPTER 11

With a ferocious, bloodthirsty howling intended to jangle the nerves of any man facing them, the members of the war party surged forward. Not very good shots under the best of circumstances, let alone from the backs of galloping ponies, they didn't bother with the few rifles they had. They stayed with what they did best, launching a flight of arrows from horseback.

"Keep your heads down!" Preacher called to his fellow defenders. "Hold your fire and let the varmints get closer!"

The arrows rained down, thudding into the wagons, ripping the canvas covers, and smashing into the rocks.

"Now!" Preacher ordered when he judged the time was right. "Let 'em have it!" He put his rifle to his shoulder and fired.

The men behind the wagons followed his lead.

They might not be experienced frontiersmen, but they were able to reload quickly and aim straight as long as they kept their nerves under control.

Preacher snatched a pair of his short guns from the wagon's floorboard, leaving the other two loaded pistols there in case he needed them quickly, and fired into the mass of warriors. Shoving the empty guns behind his belt, he grabbed up his rifle, reloaded it, aimed at a warrior, and shot again.

There was nothing ragged about the volley of gunfire. Pistols and rifles rang out strong and pure, and the heavy lead balls sliced through the ranks of Blackfeet like a scythe mowing down wheat. Horses tumbled, and men flew screaming through the air.

The charge fell apart, dissolving into dusty, roiling confusion.

In a matter of moments, a considerable amount of damage was inflicted on the war party, so Preacher wasn't too surprised when the Blackfeet suddenly wheeled their ponies and galloped away from the butte.

Otis Freeman let out a triumphant yell. "Look at 'em run! We beat 'em!"

Preacher lowered his rifle, which still had smoke curling from its muzzle, and shook his head. "I wouldn't count on that. They've just realized they're payin' too high a price to kill us. They'll get over bein' so mad and start tryin' to figure out a better way to go about doin' it."

"You mean they'll attack us again." Courtland's words weren't a question. They had a note of grim finality about them.

"There's a better than even chance," Preacher agreed. "No point in worryin' about it now, though. We need to load all the guns again. Anybody hurt?"

One of the men kneeling beside a wagon wheel called, "Johnny is! You better come quick, Preacher."

The mountain man hurried over, dropped to a knee, and peered under the wagon. One of the men was lying with his legs pulled up, his body curled around the arrow embedded in his belly.

In the heat of battle, Preacher hadn't seen the man fall. Pain must have driven the poor fella to crawl under the wagon in a futile search for relief, he thought. He could hear the man's harsh, ragged breathing.

"A couple of you get hold of him and ease him out from under there so I can take a look," Preacher instructed. "I want two men on guard. Keep your eyes wide open, and don't just watch the spot where the Injuns rode off. Look all around, 'cause they could come at us from any direction."

Carefully, two men rolled the wounded man onto his back and moved him from under the wagon. Both hands were clenched around the arrow's shaft where it entered his body.

Preacher tried to be gentle as he pried the grip loose. He could tell the arrowhead had penetrated deeply into the man's vitals. "What's his name?"

"Johnny McKittrick." The man who answered swallowed hard. "We've been friends for a couple of years."

Preacher nodded. "Get him some water." He leaned forward and went on. "Johnny? You hear me, Johnny?"

McKittrick's eyelids fluttered open. He groaned. "I . . . I hurt awful bad," he managed to say. "I think . . . I think they got me."

"Yeah, they did," Preacher said. "They got you pretty bad, Johnny. I'm afraid you're done for."

Angrily, Wiley Courtland asked, "Was there really any need to tell him that?"

Preacher glanced up and snapped, "Sometimes a man needs to know the truth. Might be things he wants to say." He turned his attention back to McKittrick. "Is there anybody you need word sent to about this, Johnny?"

"I . . . I don't know . . . My ma . . . might still be alive. Her name . . . is Neva McKittrick. She lives in . . . Ohio . . . little town called . . . Glendora."

"Neva McKittrick in Glendora, Ohio," Preacher repeated with a nod. "We'll all remember that, all of us who are here with you, Johnny."

McKittrick's friend knelt beside them with a canteen in his hand. He held it out. "I got the water."

Preacher took it and asked, "You thirsty, Johnny?"

"Yeah, I . . . I am. Can I have . . . a drink?"

"Sure, but it's liable to make you hurt worse."

"Don't care . . . I'm mighty . . . thirsty."

Preacher held the canteen to McKittrick's lips and trickled a little water into his mouth. McKittrick swallowed and sighed, and then winced as the pain hit him. The reaction lasted only a second. He sighed and whispered, "Thank . . ."

His eyes closed and his head fell to the side.

"Damn, damn, damn!" his friend exclaimed. "He . . . he's gone?"

"Yeah, and it's a blessin' he went that fast. I've seen men with arrows in their guts who lasted seven or eight hours. And it was seven or eight hours of hell for 'em, too, let me tell you." Preacher put the cork back in the canteen and handed it to the man. "Sorry for your loss."

"We knew it would be dangerous out here, I reckon," the man said in a dull voice. He began to breathe harder. "I'm gonna kill all those redskin ba—"

"That's enough," Courtland snapped. "We're not going to lose our heads about this. We're going to stay calm. That's our best chance of fighting back and surviving." He looked at the mountain man. "Isn't it, Preacher?"

"That's right." Preacher nodded, but Courtland's level-headed response surprised him a little. Maybe the fella was learning something, he thought.

Preacher looked at the men gathered around him "We're still outnumbered, but we've got more guns and ammunition than the Blackfeet have, and we're better shots, too."

"But there are only nine of us left. Ten, counting Preacher." Freeman said. "They keep whittling us down. Without Preacher, it's likely we'd all be dead by now."

"We've killed a dozen of them for every man we've lost. Sooner or later they're bound to get tired of that."

Courtland rubbed a hand over his face wearily. "Preacher's right. Somebody wrap McKittrick's body in a blanket. We'll go ahead and lay him to rest properly while we've got the chance." He detailed a couple of men to dig a grave at the foot of the butte.

While they were doing that, Preacher made sure all the guns were loaded and that the guards were keeping a good watch.

Satisfied for the moment with the precautions, he went over to the spot inside the cluster of boulders where Dog lay on the ground next to Horse.

The big cur's head rested on his paws, his ears pricking up as Preacher approached.

Preacher knelt beside Dog and ran a hand over the animal's shaggy flanks. Not finding any wounds, he explored Dog's head next and paused as he felt a sticky welt between the ears. He parted the fur and saw that the injury didn't appear too serious. "One of those varmints loosed an arrow at you that bounced off that thick skull of yours, didn't he? Knocked you out for a little while. That's why you didn't come back right away. But when the fightin' started, you heard it and came a-runnin'."

Dog's tongue lolled out by way of answer.

"You've always been a hard-headed critter," Preacher told him. "Reckon that came in handy this time."

While he was at it, he checked the stallion for injuries as well but didn't find any. Somehow Horse had avoided all the arrows and rifle balls. His knack for doing that had saved Preacher's life more than once.

Spotting Preacher, Courtland walked over and asked, "Is there any reason the men shouldn't boil some coffee and have something to eat?"

"No reason at all," Preacher replied. "It's a good idea. We're liable not to be sleepin' much tonight."

Courtland frowned. "I thought Indians didn't usually attack at night."

Preacher managed not to snort in disgust. "An

Injun attacks when it best suits him, any hour of the day or night. You ain't forgot about the one who killed Jenkins, have you?"

Courtland shrugged. "Actually, I guess I had. Before we started out here, I was told so many things about the Indians. It seemed like everyone I met in St. Louis had an opinion."

"And most of 'em was wrong, I'll bet," Preacher said. "Here's what I want to do. We're gonna split up, six of your men down here with the wagons where most of the Blackfeet will attack. I'll take three up that butte behind us."

"Are you sure it's a good idea, splitting a force that's already so small?"

"We can't let the Blackfeet take the high ground behind us. If they do, they'll hit us from two directions at once, and we won't stand a chance. Not only that, but from up there we'll have a better shot at the ones out on the flat. That's why I want your three best shots to go up there with me."

"I suppose that makes sense," Courtland admitted. "Otis is an excellent shot. Better than me, that's for sure. I'll find out who's the best among the others."

Preacher nodded and glanced at the sky. "Couple hours of daylight left. They may come at us again at dusk, when the light's mighty tricky for shootin'. If they don't, it'll be tonight, once it's good an' dark."

The Blackfeet hadn't reappeared by the time night began to settle over the badlands. Johnny McKittrick and Ben had been laid to rest, and the men had had a grim, mostly silent meal. They stood watchfully, waiting to see what was going to happen.

Nothing did. Quiet descended over the landscape along with darkness.

The two men who would be climbing the butte along with Preacher and Otis Freeman were Clyde Woodbury and Lew Elkins. They were all taking plenty of powder and shot with them.

"How do you reckon they'll come at us, if they do?" Freeman asked as the men got ready to climb to the top.

"There's no tellin'," Preacher replied. "Might be sneaky about it, or they might just charge up the other side of the butte yellin' and shootin' arrows. We got to be ready for whatever comes, and we got to hold the high ground. Otherwise they'll overrun us all, and that'll be the end of it."

"Don't worry about us," Elkins said. "We'll fight."

"I know that." Preacher had seen the men in battle and knew they had plenty of grit, but they needed somebody to take charge. They needed someone familiar with the dangers of the West and who knew how to command them.

For better or worse, Preacher was that commander.

"Stay alert," he told Courtland, and then the four men started up the slope. It wasn't sheer, but it was steep. They had to lean forward and use their hands to help climb most of the way.

Dog went along and made it without much of a struggle, as did Preacher. Freeman and the others were winded by the time they reached the top.

The butte was fairly level and formed a rough square about forty feet on each side. Stunted pines grew around the edges. In the center was a dark heap of stone rearing about a dozen feet high. It hadn't been visible from below. Freeman stared at it and asked, "Is that a natural formation?"

"Hard to say. It might be, or Injuns might've built it sometime in the past."

"Why would they do that?"

"Could be this is a holy place for them," Preacher said. "Not for the Blackfeet, though. That ain't why they're tryin' so hard to kill us. This ain't really their stompin' ground. They roam pretty far afield when they're out lookin' for war, and it's our bad luck they come across us."

Freeman grunted. "Yeah. Our bad luck, all right." He regarded the stone pile in the starlight and went on. "It looks almost like . . . an altar of some sort. You think whatever tribe built it ever had, well, human sacrifices here?"

"Don't know," Preacher replied honestly.

But even if blood had never been spilled there in bygone days, chances were good it would spill before the night was over.

CHAPTER 12

Using the trees for cover, the men spread out on the far side of the butte to wait. Preacher stretched out on the ground with Dog close beside him. He had the veteran frontiersman's ability to fall asleep almost instantly, under any conditions, and seized the opportunity to get a nap.

He dozed, knowing Dog would awaken him if anything threatened, assuming his own instincts didn't rouse him. They both slept lightly, like wild animals.

Time passed. Preacher woke up and checked on the other men, all of whom were still wide awake and tensely alert. "Anything movin' around out there?" he asked Freeman in a whisper.

"Nothing that I can see or hear," Freeman replied. "Of course, that don't really mean much, does it?

Those savages can move around without being seen or heard, can't they?"

"They're pretty sneaky," Preacher agreed. "By the time you know they're there, it's liable to be too late to do anything about it. But keep watchin' and listenin' anyway. It's really the only thing we can do."

Preacher moved back to his spot and settled down to wait again. The night was so quiet he could hear the horses and mules moving around, down at the base of the butte. A bird called somewhere nearby.

Except it wasn't a bird, no matter what it sounded like, Preacher thought as he stiffened. It was a signal. He let out a soft whistle to warn the others and picked up both pistols. Dog growled quietly beside him.

"Take it easy," Preacher whispered. "They'll be here in a minute."

It didn't take quite that long. A dark figure suddenly flitted from behind one of the trees on the slope, a short distance down from the crest, and started toward the top.

Preacher lifted his right-hand pistol and shot the man in the chest.

The gun's dull boom was shockingly loud in the night, almost like a cannon had gone off. The warrior bounding toward the top of the butte was thrown backward by the impact. He cried out in pain as he tumbled down the slope, a cry that cut off abruptly as he slammed into the trunk of a pine.

With no longer any reason for stealth, a dozen Blackfoot warriors let out blood curdling whoops as they leaped up from where they had crawled and lunged for the top, They were met by a wave of fire from Preacher, Freeman, Woodbury, and Elkins.

Each man was armed with a rifle and two pistols. They emptied the weapons as fast as they could and cut down more than half of the attackers.

But five warriors were still alive to reach the crest.

Preacher surged to his feet and leaped forward to meet the charge of the closest one.

The warrior swung a tomahawk at Preacher's head. The mountain man used the barrel of his empty rifle to parry the blow, then stepped closer and smashed the rifle butt into the Blackfoot's throat. The man stumbled and gasped as he tried to drag air through his crushed windpipe. Preacher struck again, using the rifle butt to shatter the warrior's jaw and put him down and out. The Blackfoot would likely suffocate without ever regaining consciousness.

A few yards away, a flurry of snapping and growling marked the spot where Dog had another of the warriors down on the ground. Preacher knew the big cur could handle that, so he turned and hurried toward Freeman, who was locked in a desperate struggle with one of the Blackfeet.

Before Preacher could get there, Freeman wrenched a tomahawk out of the man's hand and slashed it across his face. The warrior staggered back, and Freeman went after him, hacking and clubbing. Preacher hurried on to see if one of the other men needed a hand.

He was too late to help Clyde Woodbury. One of the Blackfeet was rising to his feet, blood-dripping knife in hand, after cutting Woodbury's throat. He let out a shrill shout and threw the knife at Preacher. The mountain man avoided it, and a second later, his tomahawk crashed into the warrior's forehead and all the way through the bone into the brain.

Lew Elkins had his hands locked around his opponent's throat as they rolled on the ground. It was hard to see them in the shadows, but when Preacher heard a sharp crack, he knew someone's neck was broken. He was ready with his tomahawk if the Blackfoot was the one who got up.

It was Elkins who stumbled to his feet. "Preacher? Is that you?"

"Yeah. Looks like this batch is done for." Shots roared down in the rocks. "But it sounds like the other fellas got their hands full."

The men grabbed their guns and hurried to the other side of the butte. As they reloaded, Freeman asked, "Where's Clyde?"

"He didn't make it," Preacher said. "One of the Blackfeet cut his throat."

Freeman cursed bitterly as he rammed a ball down the barrel of his rifle. "Clyde was a good man. We'll never even the score for the fellas we've lost."

"I expect the Blackfeet feel the same way." Preacher brought his rifle to his shoulder and looked over the edge of the butte. In the light from the stars and the quarter moon he could see bodies scattered on the flat below.

The other members of the war party had launched their attack when the fight started on top of the butte. Courtland and the other four men had inflicted quite a few casualties.

Preacher could see shadows moving on the flat. Figuring anybody still moving out on the flat was an enemy, he took aim and told his companions to do the same.

They each fired three rounds before the leading edge of the attack broke past the wagons. Suddenly the fighting was hand to hand.

Preacher called, "Come on!" and slid down the slope to join in the battle.

With Dog at his side, he plunged into the melee among the boulders. Using his rifle as a club, he struck right and left until one of the Blackfeet tackled him from behind and knocked the weapon out of his hands. Preacher went down with the man on top of him. He drove an elbow

backward and dislodged his attacker before the
man could jerk his head back and cut his throat.
As Preacher rolled over he snatched his knife
from its sheath and buried the long blade in the
warrior's body.

He was on his feet again an instant later. He
caught another warrior from behind and drove
the knife into the man's back, then ripped it
free and cast the dying warrior aside. The knife
turned aside a tomahawk strike from another
man. Preacher kicked him in the belly and then
slashed his throat open.

It was grim, bloody, chaotic work. Preacher
received several minor wounds but barely noticed
them as he continued killing at close range. Blood
soaked the arm of his knife hand up to the elbow.

Gunshots, shouted curses, and screams of pain
filled the air. The terrible racket was so loud
Preacher almost didn't hear a powerful voice bel-
lowing commands for the attackers to retreat. It
took a second for him to realize those orders were
being given in Blackfoot.

With pistol shots and arrows still being traded,
the surviving warriors withdrew, taking many of
their dead and wounded comrades with them.

As the Blackfeet fled, Preacher leaned against a
boulder. His chest heaved and his pulse thundered in his head. Caught up in the frenzy of
battle, his hot blood wanted to go after the war
party and keep on killing, but part of his brain

remained cool enough for him to control the violent impulse.

"Let 'em go," he called to the survivors. He knew the Blackfeet hoped a retreat would draw them out of their cover.

Wiley Courtland stumbled over to him. Courtland's face was grimy with powder smoke and he had lost his coonskin cap, at least for the time being.

"My God, Preacher, are you all right? You're covered with blood!"

"Most of it ain't mine," Preacher replied with a weary grin. "At least, I think it ain't. Haven't really had time to check. How about you?"

Courtland nodded. "I'll be all right. Some more cuts and bruises, that's all. What do we do now?"

"Reload and maintain your positions," Preacher snapped. "Red Knife could come back. Unless he was killed in the fightin', which is what I'm hopin'. If he was, the rest of that bunch will be more likely to figure it ain't worth it to keep comin' after us."

A hollow laugh came from Courtland. "They might as well try to finish us off. There aren't that many of us left, and we don't have much to live for. Those horses are long gone."

So he was still worried about the horses, thought Preacher. Some men just couldn't forget about trying to make money, no matter what the situation.

Courtland and the others followed Preacher's orders loading their guns and taking up positions behind the wagons. The canvas covers were so shredded they were almost useless, but the thick boards would still stop an arrow or a rifle ball.

Preacher walked around the camp talking to the men. In addition to Clyde Woodbury on top of the butte, the party had lost two more men, which left their numbers at six, plus Preacher.

That was actually a pretty good showing, considering how many Blackfeet they had killed, the mountain man mused. The close quarters among the wagons and the rocks had helped. Unable to overrun them, the warriors had been forced to attack in small groups.

"I'm goin' back up on top of the butte where I can keep an eye out for 'em if they come back," Preacher told Courtland. "You should send a couple men to fetch down Woodbury's body."

"You're not going to slip off and leave us here, are you?"

Preacher's eyes narrowed in anger at the question. "A frontiersman wouldn't do that," he said in a hard, level voice.

"I know." Courtland sighed. "I meant no offense. I just . . . I've never had to deal with anything like this before."

"You're doin' fine. It won't go on for much longer."

"What do you mean by that?" Courtland asked with a puzzled frown.

"I mean those varmints are bound to give up pretty soon. Either that . . . or they'll wipe us out."

Preacher left Courtland to ponder that while he and Dog climbed back to the top of the butte. They sat down behind a tree to wait for morning or the next attack, whichever came first.

CHAPTER 13

As it turned out, morning came first. There had been no sign of the Blackfeet returning by the time the sky grew light in the east with the approach of dawn.

Once the sun had risen, Preacher stood up and surveyed the surrounding countryside. From the top of the butte, he could see a long way in every direction. He noted two things of considerable interest.

Several miles to the south, a haze of dust hung in the air, as if a number of riders were on the move. It was moving away from the badlands.

To the north, he spotted a number of dark shapes drifting through one of the grassy gaps between buttes about half a mile away. Courtland's horses, Preacher decided. The herd had run itself out after the stampede and stopped to graze well away from the fighting.

Preacher and Dog made their way down to the

camp. Courtland, Freeman, and the other men were obviously exhausted, but they were awake and relatively alert. Three blanket-shrouded shapes lying on the ground were grim reminders of the price they had paid.

A few dead Blackfeet were sprawled around the camp as well.

Preacher said, "We'd best drag those bodies out of the rocks. Some of the others will come back for them later, so they can be took care of Blackfoot fashion."

"Why should we be that considerate of their feelings?" Courtland wanted to know.

"Because if they *have* decided not to come after us again, we don't want to rile them back up," Preacher said bluntly. "You can fight somebody—hell, you can even hate 'em—without disrespectin' 'em."

"You really think they might let us go this time?" Freeman asked.

"Maybe. We've killed a whole heap of 'em. Red Knife wouldn't want to go back to his people with the entire war party wiped out and nothin' to show for it."

"All right," Courtland agreed. "However much time we have, we'll take advantage of it. As soon as we've buried our men, we'll move out and start looking for those horses, even though they're probably scattered clear to hell and gone."

"You're wrong about that," Preacher told him.

"I spotted them from the top of the butte. They're grazin' in a little pocket about half a mile north of here."

Courtland stared at him in disbelief. For a moment he seemed unable to speak. Then he asked, "All of them?"

"Well, I couldn't say about that. I saw a good-sized bunch, though. Should be most of them. This is new territory to them. They'll stick together for the most part. Makes 'em feel safer that way."

"Then there's still a chance to salvage something from this," Courtland said with growing excitement. "Let's get busy. I don't want something to spook those animals and make them bolt again before we can round them up."

Courtland didn't want to take the time for breakfast. He was impatient enough when it came to burying Woodbury and the other two men who had been killed, Preacher thought.

But when the moment came to say words over the graves, Courtland was eloquent in his prayer. Preacher had to give him credit for that much.

Several saddle horses and mules had been killed in the latest battle. There were enough mules left to pull the wagons, but that was all. Every man had a mount, but again, there were no extras.

Horse had come through fine. Preacher saddled the stallion and swung up to take the lead along with Courtland. Freeman drove one of the wagons, Elkins another, and a man named Dalton was at the reins of the third vehicle. A couple of men named Prince and Boylan served as outriders along with Preacher and Courtland.

All the guns were loaded, but the party's numbers had been carved down so far having superior firepower didn't mean much anymore. Despite that, the only thing to do was to keep going forward and hope for the best.

Courtland's spirits rose visibly when, ahead of the others, he and Preacher reached the pasture where the horses were grazing. They reined in a distance away so as not to spook them.

Courtland tried to count them but was too excited and gave up after a moment. "We may have lost a few, but nearly all of them are here. Now if we can just get them to Fort Gifford. It won't be easy . . . but nothing about this trip has been easy so far, has it?"

"I reckon you fellas were actually pretty lucky to make it as far as you did before things went to hell," Preacher stated.

Courtland sighed and nodded. "I know. I should have hired more men. Men like you, Preacher, who knew what they were doing. Instead I hired men who had experience working with horses."

"Those boys are good fighters. I can't fault 'em for that. If you'd run into a smaller war party, or one that wasn't led by somebody as loco as Red Knife, chances are you would've been all right."

"Well, your share of the profits will be bigger now. There's something to be said for that."

Preacher just grunted. Courtland's comment struck him as pretty callous. He was a business-man, first and foremost.

The drivers brought the wagons to a halt before they reached the horse herd. Preacher, Court-land, Prince, and Boylan rode ahead to round up the animals, taking it slow and easy.

By mid-morning they had the herd headed north again, with the wagons following along behind.

Since the others seemed able to keep the herd moving, Preacher split off from the group in the afternoon, telling Courtland he was going to do some scouting. He, Horse, and Dog fell back a couple of miles to search for any sign of pursuit.

Not seeing any, they ranged in a big circle to make sure the Blackfeet weren't trying to slip past and set up an ambush somewhere ahead of Court-land's party.

Other than some bear, elk, antelope, and moose, along with eagles soaring through the sky and beavers building dams in the streams, Preacher and his animal companions seemed to be alone in the vast, beautiful frontier. The rocky, pine-dotted buttes fell behind them at last, and they entered an area of grassy prairies and rolling hills. Preacher could see snowcapped mountains in almost every direction he looked, but none of the peaks were close. He and Courtland's men would reach the valley of the Missouri before they had to cross any of those ranges.

Wiley Courtland had an anxious expression on his face when Preacher rode up to rejoin the party. "You were gone a long time. I was afraid something had happened to you, even though I know how unlikely that is."

"We took a good long look around," Preacher told him. "Didn't see hide nor hair of those Blackfeet, nor any other hostiles."

"You're serious?"

"I wouldn't josh about a thing like that.

Courtland took off his coonskin cap, which was starting to look a little ratty, closed his eyes, and wearily passed a hand over his face. Relief made his shoulders sag. When he looked at Preacher again, he asked, "So we're out of danger?"

"I didn't say that," the mountain man replied. "It's still gonna take us three or four days to make it to the fort. Plenty of things can happen in that much time. Red Knife could catch up to us. You never can tell what we'll run into betwixt here and there, either."

"But right now . . . ?"

"Right now it appears nobody's fixin' to try to kill you." Preacher grinned. "Count your blessin's, eh?"

"Oh, yes. Most definitely."

After getting very little sleep the night before, the men were exhausted, but they pushed on until early evening, finally making camp beside a small creek.

"Three men will stand guard all the time, in two-hour shifts," Preacher said as they sat around the campfire finally having a hot meal.

"But you said the Indians weren't chasing us," Elkins said.

"I said they ain't close. That don't mean they couldn't catch up to us durin' the night."

"You've gotten us this far, Preacher," Courtland said. "We'll do whatever you think is best."

"Yeah, I didn't mean anything by what I said," Elkins added. "Hell, I'll bet you've forgotten more about staying alive out here than all the rest of us will ever know, put together!"

The night passed quietly, and the party was on the move again early the next morning. The terrain was rugged in places, but for the most part they made good time. Preacher stayed with the group part of the time, but he and Dog also scouted ahead and behind quite a bit.

When the day passed with no sign of the Blackfeet, Preacher began to hope Red Knife—or whoever was in charge—had been killed or had given up. Not wiping out the party of white men would be a bitter pill to swallow, but losing more warriors would likely be worse.

Two more days passed, with the men once more falling into a routine—easier to do when nobody was trying to kill them. Preacher made sure they didn't relax too much, though. As he had told Courtland, just because there was no immediate threat didn't mean they were out of the woods. The frontier always held dangers, often unseen and unexpected.

The middle of the fifth day, they reached a broad valley with mountains to the north. A line of trees in the middle of the valley marked the course of a stream. Preacher saw sunlight winking off the flat, slow-moving surface of the water. "That'll be the Big Muddy," he told Courtland. "The Missouri River."

"At last." Courtland frowned. "But I don't see the fort."

"It really would've been a stroke of luck if you'd hit the river right at the spot where they built the fort. We should be in the right area, though. You said it was about fifty miles west of Fort Union. I've been through here before, a few years ago, and I calculate we're in the general vicinity." Preacher lifted a buckskin-clad arm and pointed. "The Missouri and the Yellowstone flow together 'bout fifty miles over yonder, so we can't be far from Fort Gifford. You fellas hold the herd here and let 'em graze. I'll find the fort and come back to get you."

"I can come with you," Courtland offered.

Preacher shook his head. "No, I want all of you to stay here. Keep your eyes open. Wouldn't want to get this close and then have somethin' bad happen again."

"Certainly not," Courtland agreed. "All right, we'll make camp and wait for you to get back." He paused. "I hope it doesn't take too long. I'm eager to see civilization again."

Calling an isolated fur company outpost "civilization" was stretching things a mite, thought Preacher, but he supposed Courtland was right. Fort Gifford was the closest thing to civilization they were liable to find out there.

CHAPTER 14

Preacher headed west along the river, figuring it was the most likely direction for the fort to lie. He followed the southern bank, since he was already on that side and didn't know on which side of the river the fort had been built.

The spot where he had left the wagons and the horse herd fell out of sight behind him. He estimated he had ridden about two miles when he suddenly spotted movement on the riverbank ahead of him. Three men on horseback had ridden out of the trees.

Preacher reined in sharply. He lifted his rifle from where it lay across the saddle in front of him and rested it in the crook of his left arm. The thumb of his right hand went around the hammer as he gripped the stock. He used his knees to nudge Horse into motion again and said quietly to the big cur, "Stay close, Dog."

The three men had seen him and reined in for

a moment, too. Then they rode forward cautiously, just like Preacher. As the distance between them lessened, Preacher could see the men were bearded, which meant the strangers were all white.

But just because they weren't Indians didn't mean they were friendly. Preacher had plenty of enemies out there who were white.

Suddenly, though, the man on the right, who sported a bristling red beard, let out an excited whoop. "Preacher!" he yelled. "Preacher, is that you, you mangy ol' coyote?"

Preacher relaxed and a grin spread over his rugged face. He lifted his rifle with one hand and held it over his head in greeting. "Quint Harrigan!" he shouted back. He urged the stallion into a trot.

The redbearded man hurried toward him, too. Harrigan's two companions followed at a more deliberate pace. Preacher didn't recognize either of them, but Quint Harrigan was an old friend. If the other two men were riding with him, Preacher figured they must be all right.

The mountain men brought their horses alongside each other and reached out to clasp hands.

"Dang it, how long's it been, Preacher?" Harrigan asked. "Four years?"

"More like five," Preacher said. "At that rendezvous where three different Arapaho gals realized poor ol' Audie had been romancin' 'em at the same time."

Harrigan whooped with laughter and slapped his thigh in its buckskin leggings. "Yeah, Nighthawk told me later he coulda warned Audie, but he didn't say nothin' 'cause he wanted to see Audie's reaction when he got found out. That Crow's one hell of a jokester!"

That comment would have surprised anyone who didn't know Nighthawk well. The Crow never smiled and seldom said anything except "Umm." But Preacher grinned and nodded knowingly.

"You seen those two lately?" Harrigan went on. "I ain't heard how they're doin'."

"Just wintered with 'em, in fact," Preacher replied. "They're fine. They never really change."

"No more than you or the mountains do, you ol' stone face." Harrigan waved the other two men forward. "You know Rollin Brown and Bob Mahaffey?"

Preacher shook his head. "Don't think I've had the pleasure."

"They've only been out here a few years. They ain't old-timers like you and me. Boys, say howdy to Preacher."

Brown, who had a curling blond beard, shook hands. "I've heard a lot about you, Preacher. Didn't know I'd ever have the honor to cross trails with you."

"It's my pleasure, Rollin," Preacher told him.

Mahaffey was dark and lean, his beard cropped so closely it wasn't much more than stubble. He shook hands as well and gave Preacher a friendly nod. "Hear tell you're the big skookum he-wolf in these parts, Preacher."

"Folks like to talk," Preacher replied with a grin and a shrug. "That don't make it all true."

"In this case, though, it is," Quint Harrigan put in. "Ain't nobody from Canada to the Rio Grande who's been as many places and done as many things as Preacher here. Or fought as many fights, for that matter."

"What brings you to this neck of the woods?" Brown asked.

"I'm lookin' for an outpost called Fort Gifford."

The three men exchanged glances, and Harrigan pointed over his shoulder with a thumb.

"It's back that way about a mile. We just come from there. We was about to do a little huntin'. The Booshwa hired us to bring in some fresh meat for ever'body."

Preacher was relieved to hear the fort was so close. That meant the likelihood of hostile Indians venturing into this area was small. He was curious about something else, though. "You're workin' for the American Fur Company now, Quint?" Ever since he'd known him, Harrigan had been an independent trapper, like Preacher himself.

Harrigan shook his head. "Naw, not so's you'd notice. We just took on this huntin' job to help out and earn some extra supplies. Soon as we're done outfittin', we'll be headin' for the mountains to get us some pelts. Ain't that right, boys?"

Brown and Mahaffey nodded.

"You're plannin' on spendin' the season trappin', ain't you, Preacher?" Harrigan went on.

"Yeah, but I got another chore to finish takin' care of first. Been helpin' out some pilgrims who are bound for Fort Gifford with a herd of horses." Preacher inclined his head back the way he'd come. "They're camped a couple miles downriver. I need to go back and get 'em."

"Horses, you say?" Harrigan scratched his beard. "They brought a whole herd of horses out here?"

"Yep. Good saddle mounts. They figure on tradin' some of 'em to the Injuns and sellin' the rest to fellas like you."

"We've got good horses," Mahaffey said. He added with a shrug, "But not everybody does. Those fellas might make out all right."

"It ain't really my business one way or the other. I'm just tryin' to get 'em there alive. We've had some run-ins with the Blackfeet. A war party led by Red Knife dogged our trail for a while."

Harrigan let out a low whistle. "Red Knife," he repeated. "I've heard plenty of stories about him. All bad ones, too."

"He lives up to that reputation," Preacher said

without hesitation. "He wiped out half the bunch I've been travelin' with. He finally gave up, but not before I began to have my doubts about makin' it through."

Harrigan snorted. "I ain't seen the redskin yet that can keep Preacher from goin' where he wants to go." He turned to his companions and went on, "Fellas, I think I'll help Preacher herd them pilgrims on to the fort, if you don't mind makin' this huntin' trip without me."

"You mean we'll split the money the Booshwa promised us two ways instead of three?" Brown asked with a smile. "I reckon I can live with that."

"Me, too," Mahaffey nodded. He lifted his reins. "See you later, Quint."

The two men waved their farewells and turned their horses to ride back into the trees. They quickly disappeared from view.

"I appreciate the company, Quint," Preacher told Harrigan, "but I didn't really need the help."

"Nah, I didn't figure you did. But we got old times to catch up on. Like you said, it's been five years." As they rode east along the river, Harrigan added, "I see you still got that mangy ol' mutt."

"Yeah, Dog and Horse and me are still trail partners."

They traded reminiscences and talked about old friends for a mile or so, then Preacher asked,

"Tell me about this fort. I thought Fort Union was as far west as the outposts had come."

"Gifford's been there less than a year. John Jacob Astor sent some fellas out to build it last spring. Took 'em all summer because they kept havin' to stop to fight the Injuns."

"Blackfeet?"

"Yeah. The Arapaho, the Crow, even the Arikara seem to be settled down a mite right now, if you can believe that. They didn't give no trouble."

"The Arikara have tried to lift my hair more times than I can remember. Seems hard to believe they've turned peaceful."

"Well, I said they ain't givin' no trouble *right now*," Harrigan reminded him. "Might be different tomorrow. Anyway, once the fort was established, even the Blackfeet left it alone. Don't know how long things'll stay that way, though. You know how those varmints are. Just knowin' the fort's there probably sticks in their craw."

Preacher nodded. He could well imagine the Blackfeet would attack the fort sooner or later, especially with firebrands like Red Knife always stirring up trouble. Fort Gifford, like the other outposts belonging to the American Fur Company, was probably pretty sturdy and well defended. John Jacob Astor wasn't in business to lose money.

"How about the booshwa?" Preacher asked. "What sort of fella is he?"

"Mr. Langley? Mighty fine fella, if you ask me. He's fair in his dealin's. Sharp enough, mind you. Nobody's likely to snooker him, and anybody who tries likely won't try twice. But I like him."

That was important, thought Preacher. The booshwa—a frontier corruption of the word *bourgeois*, brought to these parts by French trappers who came down from Canada—ran the fur company's outposts. He had to be part businessman, part military leader, and all fighter, otherwise the rough-edged mountain men with whom he dealt would never respect him. A good booshwa made the difference in whether an outpost thrived or failed and was abandoned, left to rot and disappear back into the wild.

"Mr. Langley's got somethin' else goin' for him," Harrigan continued. "But I'll let you find out about that for yourself."

Preacher frowned. "Dang it, Quint, you know I never did like it when folks go to actin' mysterious-like."

"Maybe not, but I don't want to ruin the surprise for you." Harrigan changed the subject by standing up in his stirrups and peering along the riverbank. "Doggoned if you weren't tellin' the truth! That's a whole herd of horses."

"Of course it is," Preacher said with a snort. "I ain't in the habit of lyin'."

"Didn't mean to make it sound like you were. That's just the most horses I've seen in one place for a long time. It's pretty impressive."

Spread out on the grassy bank like they were, the horses were a pretty sight.

As Preacher and Harrigan trotted toward the wagons, Wiley Courtland and Otis Freeman rode out to meet them.

"Preacher, did you find the fort?" Courtland asked excitedly. He looked at Harrigan. "Who's this?"

Preacher answered the second question first. "This here's an old friend of mine, Quint Harrigan. I haven't yet laid eyes on the fort myself, but Quint knows right where it is. He's been stayin' there while him and some friends get outfitted." He nodded toward the two men. "Quint, meet Wiley Courtland and Otis Freeman."

Harrigan shook hands with them.

Courtland said, "We're very pleased to meet you, Mr. Harrigan. I don't know if Preacher told you or not, but we've gone through quite an ordeal to get here."

"Yeah, he said you'd had a little scrape or two with the Blackfeet," Harrigan replied dryly. "You shouldn't have any more trouble, though. Things are tamed down a mite in these parts."

"How far is it to the fort?"

"About three miles," Preacher said.

"Then we can get the horses there before dark!"

"That's right."

Courtland turned to Freeman. "Otis, tell the rest of the men to get ready. We're moving out as soon as possible."

That didn't take long, since the teams were still hitched to the wagons. Freeman was already mounted, so he told Boylan to handle the lead wagon.

"I ain't really a horse herder," Harrigan said, "but I don't mind pitchin' in and helpin' drive these animals to the fort."

"I appreciate that, Mr. Harrigan," Courtland said. "I have to say, everyone we've encountered out here has been uncommonly helpful."

"Except for the ones who were tryin' to kill you and scalp you."

"Well, yes, there was that," Courtland agreed with a smile.

The horses wouldn't be rushed, but it really didn't take that long to push the herd along the river to the fort. When they topped a hill and came in sight of it, Preacher saw that the place resembled Fort Union and the other outposts he had visited, which were largely self-sufficient. A high stockade fence made of logs, with a blockhouse at each corner, surrounded a compound full of sturdy-looking log buildings. Fort Gifford had a trench dug into it from the river to supply water. There was a smokehouse for meat, what looked like a blacksmith shop, numerous storage buildings, a barracks, and the centerpiece, the big trading post where the booshwa lived and did business.

Preacher noted the outpost even had a small vegetable garden behind the trading post. That was a touch he hadn't expected.

Smaller blockhouses flanking the gates were built on the parapet behind the stockade wall. The gates themselves were extra thick. It would take a cannon to blow them open, and luckily the Indians hadn't mastered the concept of artillery . . . yet.

"I better ride ahead," Harrigan offered as they approached the gates. "All the fellas know me. I reckon it's this red brush o' mine. Come on with me, Preacher."

Not seeing any harm in that, Preacher urged Horse into a trot and fell in alongside Harrigan. Dog bounded ahead of them.

Several men stood on the parapet holding rifles, and more rifle barrels protruded from the windows of the blockhouses on either side of the gates.

"You boys don't take any chances, do you?" Preacher said.

"You know as well as I do that peace don't usually last out here," Harrigan said. "And nobody wants to be took by surprise when trouble comes callin'."

"That's sure the truth."

Harrigan took off his hat and waved it over his head. His long red hair blew in the wind. "Open up, fellas," he called. "It's me."

A man leaned over the parapet and shouted back, "I thought you left to go huntin', Harrigan!"

"I did, but I found me a whole passel of horses instead!" Harrigan grinned and swept his hat toward the herd.

The heavy gates began to swing open slowly as men inside the stockade heaved on them. When the gap was wide enough, Preacher and Harrigan rode through.

"There's plenty of room for the wagons," Harrigan said, "but I ain't sure what your friend Courtland is gonna do with those horses. The corral ain't big enough for all of them."

"He can put the best ones inside and build a pen outside for the others," Preacher suggested. "Plenty of cottonwoods along the river to use for peeled poles."

Harrigan nodded. "Yeah, I reckon that'd work." He smiled again. "Remember I said Mr. Langley, the booshwa, had somethin' else interestin' about him?"

"Yeah."

"Well, there she is now." The red-bearded trapper nodded toward the big trading post.

Preacher turned his head and his eyes widened in surprise, just as Harrigan had predicted. A beautiful woman stood on the building's gallery with her hands clasped on the railing.

CHAPTER 15

The trading post was too far away across the compound for Preacher to make out many details, but he could tell the woman had long, thick, honey-colored hair that was pulled back from her face and braided at the back of her head. The appealing curves of her body were clearly visible in a high-necked gray woolen dress.

It had been months since he had seen a white woman, and he sure hadn't expected to encounter one at the isolated frontier outpost. There might not be another within several hundred miles.

He looked over at Harrigan and raised a quizzical eyebrow.

That drew a chuckle from the red-bearded trapper. He kneed his horse to move toward the trading post. "What'd I tell you?"

Preacher rode alongside Harrigan. "Who is she?"

"Mrs. Langley. The booshwa's wife."

"He brought a woman out here?"

"That's her standin' right there on the porch. Unless every man jack in this whole fort is seein' things that just ain't there."

Preacher shook his head ruefully. "That probably wasn't a very smart thing for him to do."

"Maybe, maybe not. One reason Mr. Astor had these forts built out here was to spread civilization into the wilderness, wasn't it? Ain't nothin' spreads civilization faster than womenfolks."

Preacher grunted. As far as he'd ever been able to tell, the only reason John Jacob Astor had built the frontier forts was so his American Fur Company could make more money.

"Havin' a beautiful woman in a fort full of men is just askin' for trouble," Preacher said.

"She is mighty comely, ain't she? And sweet as she can be, too. But the boys all mind their step around her, let me tell you. Nobody wants to get crosswise with Mr. Langley, since he's the one who decides how much he'll pay for the pelts. Anyway, he's pretty tough. He's been in a few tussles since he came out here, and not many fellas want to tangle with him."

That didn't surprise Preacher. It took a strong, stubborn man to run a wilderness outpost and do a good job of it.

Before they reached the trading post, a tall man stepped out of the building and moved up behind the woman. He rested a hand on her shoulder in an unmistakable gesture of possession.

Preacher wondered if his presence had prompted that gesture. The man had to be Langley, the booshwa. Certainly he knew everyone else there was aware of the woman's status as his wife. But Preacher was a stranger, and he figured Langley wanted to make the situation clear to him right away, so he wouldn't get any troublesome ideas in his head.

As Preacher and Harrigan reined their horses to a stop in front of the trading post, Langley said, "I thought you were going out to hunt with Mahaffey and Brown, Quint."

"Yes, sir, I was, Mr. Langley," Harrigan said, confirming Preacher's hunch about the man's identity. "But I ran into an old friend and decided to come back to the fort with him instead. This here is Preacher."

Langley cocked a bushy black eyebrow. "Preacher, eh? I've heard a lot about you, mister. You're Lewis and Clark, John Colter, and Jim Bridger all rolled into one."

"Not hardly," Preacher said, "but I've been honored to know John Colter and Jim Bridger. Those Lewis and Clark fellas were a mite before my time."

As Preacher and Harrigan dismounted, one of the men from the gate walked up to the trading post and addressed the booshwa. "We've got some wagons and a herd of horses comin' in, Mr. Langley. What do you want us to do?"

Langley was a tall, broad-shouldered man, obviously powerful, and handsome in a rugged way. He wore high-topped boots, whipcord trousers, a white shirt, and a brown leather vest. He was clean-shaven and had a shock of dark hair.

He squeezed his wife's shoulder and moved past her to go down the steps from the porch. "Let the wagons in. Hold the horses outside until I find out what's going on here."

"Reckon I can tell you that," Preacher said. "The fella those horses belong to brought 'em out here to sell and trade 'em."

Standing next to Preacher it was easy to see Langley was close to the same height. The booshwa probably weighed more, since Preacher's musculature was lean and wolf-like, but the two men were pretty evenly matched.

Langley frowned at Preacher. "The American Fur Company handles all the business in these parts. And I represent the American Fur Company."

"You handle the business in pelts. These are horses."

Anger flashed in Langley's eyes. He didn't like being challenged that way.

Langley and Wiley Courtland were liable to have some trouble, Preacher thought.

Luckily, that was none of his affair. He had

agreed to help Courtland get there, and had kept his word.

The woman on the porch spoke up, momentarily dissolving the feeling of tension in the air. "Ethan, where are your manners? You haven't properly introduced yourself or me."

"That's true," Langley admitted. "I'm Ethan Langley. This is my wife Judith."

Preacher shook hands with the booshwa, then took off his hat and nodded to the woman. "It's an honor and a pleasure to meet you, ma'am."

It was no lie about the pleasure. Judith Langley was even more attractive close up. Her face was lightly tanned, and her eyes were an intriguing shade of blue. Preacher thought she was probably in her mid-twenties, six or seven years younger than her husband.

"Thank you, Mister . . . Preacher, was it?"

He shook his head. "No mister. Just Preacher. And before you can ask, I ain't no sin-shouter or sky pilot, just an ol' trapper."

"Don't believe him, dear," Langley said. "As I indicated before, Preacher is something of a legendary character. He's one of the best-known trappers, explorers, and adventurers west of the Mississippi."

"Then it's an honor to have you visit us," Judith said. "You'll join us for supper tonight, I hope?"

Preacher saw the expression of disapproval flicker over Ethan Langley's face, even though the man concealed the reaction quickly. Langley didn't think much of his wife's idea.

As much to be contrary as for any other reason, Preacher smiled and said, "Why, I'd be plumb dee-lighted, ma'am."

"Good. I'd better go start preparing the meal." She smiled and turned to go back into the trading post.

As the wagons rolled into the compound Preacher noticed the guards along the parapet seemed more alert while the gates were open. That was a good sign, he thought. The air of crisp efficiency about the outpost impressed him, despite that he didn't feel any instinctive liking for Langley. A fella didn't have to be likable to be good at his job.

The wagons were directed toward a large open area. Courtland and Freeman rode beside the vehicles.

"I suppose I'd better go welcome our guests. We'll have to talk about what we're going to do with those horses, too." Langley looked at Preacher. "Who's in charge of the group?"

"That fella right there in the coonskin cap," Preacher replied, pointing at Wiley Courtland.

Langley gave him a curt nod of thanks and strode toward the wagons.

"Buy you a drink, Preacher?" Quint Harrigan suggested.

"Mighty generous of you, and I'll take you up

on it later," Preacher said. "Right now, I better go introduce those fellas so they can work out their business." Leading Horse, with Dog padding along behind them, he walked toward the wagons behind Langley.

Harrigan shrugged and went along, too. "You know"—he nudged an elbow into Preacher's side— "I never got asked to dinner by the booshwa's missus."

Preacher grinned. "That's 'cause you ain't legendary."

Courtland had brought his mount to a stop next to one of the wagons. As he swung down from the saddle, his back was to the approaching men. He turned to face them, and Langley came to an abrupt halt.

"You!" he exclaimed. "You bastard!"

CHAPTER 16

Courtland stiffened as his face twisted in anger and recognition.

"Langley! What are you doing here?"

"I'm in charge of this outpost." Langley's voice trembled slightly. Obviously he was furious, and was having trouble controlling that emotion. "Those are your horses out there?"

"They are," Courtland answered in clipped tones.

"Then you might as well turn around and drive them back to St. Louis, or wherever you came from, because there's nothing for you here."

Courtland took a step closer. His chin jutted out defiantly. "We'll just see about that."

"The hell we will," Langley snapped. "This fort belongs to the American Fur Company, and as the company's representative, my word is law!"

"Maybe when it comes to setting prices for furs, but not in any other way!"

Freeman had dismounted and moved up carefully beside Courtland. "You two fellas know each other, Wiley?"

That seemed like an unnecessary question to Preacher. Courtland and Langley knew each other, all right . . . and they didn't like each other. Not one bit.

"We're acquainted," Courtland said without taking his eyes off Langley. Both men were tense, and the feeling of impending violence hanging in the air dwarfed the minor friction between Preacher and Langley a few minutes earlier.

"Well, what do you know about that?" Harrigan said quietly to Preacher as the two of them stood off to the side, watching the confrontation.

"You knew I was here, didn't you?" Langley accused.

"I had no idea," Courtland responded. "I wouldn't have come if I did. If I'd never seen you again, Langley, it would have been just fine with me."

"You knew," Langley insisted, his voice growing more harsh as he went on. "And you knew *she* was here, too!"

Well, now, thought Preacher, that made things more interesting.

Courtland's eyes widened, shocked by what he

had just heard. His voice dropped to a whisper. "You mean Judith?"

Realizing the truth, he cried, "You brought *Judith* into this godforsaken wilderness filled with bloodthirsty savages and wild animals? My God, man, are you completely mad?"

Langley's hands balled into fists at his side as he took a quick step forward. "Keep your filthy tongue off her name," he warned in a low, menacing voice.

Courtland moved closer and his fists were clenched as well.

Preacher knew that within seconds, one or both would start throwing punches. "Hold on, hold on." It was none of his business, but he had fought for his life alongside Courtland and that created a certain bond. "There's no need for you fellas to go to beatin' on each other."

"Stay out of this," Langley snapped. "You don't know anything about it."

"I'd almost rather die than agree with this lowlife," Courtland ground out, "but he's right, Preacher. This is between him and me."

Preacher shrugged and stepped back. He had done what he could to prevent trouble. What happened next was up to the two men glaring at each other.

"Wiley!" The surprised cry came from the other side of the compound. "Wiley, is that you?"

Everyone turned to look. Judith Langley had come back out onto the trading post's porch.

Courtland snatched the coonskin cap from his head, smiled at her, and called, "Hello, Judith."

Langley held up a hand toward her and began, "Judith, wait—"

She ignored him. Going down the steps quickly, she picked up the skirt of her long dress a little, and hurried across the compound toward the men. Langley took a step like he intended to get in her way and stop her from reaching Courtland, but then his mouth twisted bitterly and he moved back.

Langley was going to let this play out, Preacher thought, and see what happened.

Judith went straight to Courtland and threw her arms around his neck.

"Wiley, I didn't think I'd ever see you again."

"And I didn't think I'd ever see you," Courtland told her.

Off to the side, Harrigan nudged Preacher again and asked quietly, "You reckon they're brother and sister?"

"Not from the way Langley's lookin' at 'em," Preacher replied.

The booshwa's face was creased in a scowl. His expression darkened when Judith turned her head to look at him and asked, "Ethan, why didn't you come and tell me Wiley was here?" She still had her arms around Courtland's neck.

"He just got here," Langley said. "Besides, I wasn't sure you'd want to see him again."

"Of course I want to see him! Someone from back home—"

"You weren't on such good terms the last time you saw him. As I recall, you'd just told him you were going to marry me instead of him."

Preacher glanced over at Harrigan. "Nope, not brother and sister."

Courtland said, "All that's in the past, Langley. Judith and I are just old friends now. I'm glad to see her, just as she's glad to see me."

"You knew she was here," Langley accused again. "That's why you brought those horses out here. They're just an excuse to come and butt into our lives where you're not wanted."

Judith finally stopped hugging Courtland and stepped back. She turned to face her husband. "Ethan, don't be ridiculous."

"That's a pretty far-fetched idea," Courtland added. "I invested my life's savings in those horses. I risked my life and the lives of the men who came with me to bring them out here." His voice caught a little as he went on, "And some of those men didn't make it. Do you really think I'd go through all that just to try to come between you and your wife, Langley?"

"Are you saying it's just an accident you showed

up at the fort where we're living?" Langley demanded.

"That's exactly what I was trying to tell you," Courtland replied with a note of exasperation in his voice. "The fact that Judith is here is a happy accident as far as I'm concerned, but an accident nonetheless." He looked at her. "But you really shouldn't be here. He shouldn't have brought you with him. It's too dangerous out here on the frontier. I know that from firsthand experience now."

"Nonsense," Judith answered without hesitation. "Ethan has always taken good care of me. I'm sure he'll continue to do so." She laid a hand on Courtland's arm. "Now, I've already invited Preacher to join us for supper tonight. You're going to do so as well, of course."

"Judith!" Langley cried.

She gave him a look that silenced him before he could go on. "This is my home now, Ethan. I believe I can invite whoever I want to join us for a meal."

Preacher could tell from the look on Langley's face that the booshwa knew when he was licked. The expression of resignation sort of made Preacher glad he had never taken a wife.

"All right," Langley said with a rough growl in his tone. "Courtland can come to supper. We need to talk business anyway, I suppose."

"That'll have to wait until after we've eaten. Wiley and I have a lot of catching up to do." Judith linked her arm with his. "In fact, if you want to come over to the trading post with me now, we can get started."

"I'd love to," Courtland said as he smiled and gently disengaged his arm from hers. "But I have to make arrangements for my horses and men. I have certain responsibilities. . . ."

"Of course. Later, then."

"You have my word," he assured her.

As Judith started back toward the trading post, Langley and Courtland faced off again.

"You can't bring those nags in here," Langley barked.

"They're not nags. They're fine specimens of horseflesh. And it looks like you have room in your corral for some of them, anyway."

"That corral belongs to the American Fur Company."

"So the trappers who come here to the post aren't allowed to put their horses in it?" Courtland demanded.

"That's different. They're doing business with the company." Langley grimaced and rubbed his chin. "I reckon if you wanted to pay rent on the corral space . . ."

"At a rate you set that's highway robbery?" Courtland shook his head. "No, thanks. We're going to have to build a corral of our own for some of the horses. We might as well build one big enough to hold all of them." He paused, then added scathingly, "Or are you going to claim the trees belong to the American Fur Company, too?"

"Do whatever you want outside the fort," Langley grated. "Just don't come crying to me for help if you get into trouble."

"I wouldn't even think of it. But just remember . . . we're the ones who successfully fought off Red Knife and his war party. If the Blackfeet show up again, *you're* liable to need *our* help."

Langley snorted. "That'll be a cold day in hell."

Harrigan leaned over to Preacher and whispered, "I'm sorta glad I ain't goin' to supper with those folks after all."

Preacher felt the same, but didn't see any way to gracefully decline Judith Langley's invitation without hurting her feelings, especially after he'd already accepted.

So after unsaddling Horse, leading the big stallion into the corral next to the blacksmith shop, and giving him a good rubdown, Preacher headed for the trading post. Dog trailed along behind him and lay down on the porch when Preacher told him to.

The gates were still open, and from the porch Preacher could see Courtland's men holding the horses. He heard axes ringing and knew some of the men were felling saplings along the river to fashion them into poles for a new corral. It would take several days to build, and in the meantime

Courtland would have to have men guarding the herd all the time.

Under most circumstances, Preacher would have volunteered to help, but as Courtland and Langley had pointed out, the disagreement over the horses was between them. Preacher was determined to stay out of it.

The disagreement over Langley's wife was between the other two men, as well, and Preacher danged sure intended to stay out of that one. He might have to witness more of it at supper, but he was determined to remain strictly a bystander.

He went into the trading post and found it to be large and reasonably well stocked, although some of the shelves were bare. Ethan Langley stood behind the counter at the rear, where he sold goods and traded for pelts, which was his main job. By the end of summer, the big log warehouse on one side of the post ought to be full of beaver pelts.

Langley gave Preacher a nod that was civil, if not overly friendly. "I owe you a bit of an apology."

"How do you figure that?" Preacher asked.

"When I found out Courtland was the leader of the group you came in with, I was angry with you as well. But Harrigan told me you hadn't really been traveling with Courtland for very long, that you just joined forces with them because a Blackfoot war party was on the prowl."

"Courtland keeps talkin' about makin' me a

partner in his horse-tradin' business because I gave him a hand, but I don't want any part of it. I was tryin' to help those fellas get here without losin' their hair."

"You're right not to make any sort of deal with Courtland. He's not to be trusted."

Preacher shook his head. "Wouldn't know about that."

"I would. I saw how miserable he made my wife back in Missouri."

"But she wasn't your wife then." Silently, Preacher chided himself for ignoring his vow not to get curious about those folks and their personal problems, but it was too late.

Langley said, "That's right. We were both courting her. Judith was a young widow, and one of the most beautiful women I've ever known. You've seen her."

"She's a handsome woman," Preacher said carefully.

Langley laughed, but he didn't sound particularly amused. "She's more than that. She had men swarming around her like flies. But she narrowed her choices down to me and Courtland . . . and he lost."

"He didn't take it kindly?" Preacher guessed.

"You could say that. He was very angry with her. Told her she was making a huge mistake and that I would never amount to anything. I told him to stay away from her and not bother her anymore."

Langley hesitated. "I'm afraid the argument came to blows."

"Who won?"

"I handed him quite a thrashing," Langley said with a note of pride in his voice.

From behind him, Judith said, "You don't have to boast about it." She frowned at her husband.

Preacher looked past Langley and saw that she had come through a door behind the counter that undoubtedly led to their living quarters.

"I wasn't trying to boast," Langley pointed out. "It's true, though. I gave Courtland exactly what he deserved."

"The way I saw it, you both deserved the lumps you got," Judith chided. "Brawling like a couple of schoolboys. You should have been ashamed."

"For standing up for the woman I love? Never!"

"You weren't standing up for me. You took offense at the things Wiley said about *you*."

"Well, who wouldn't?" Langley wanted to know.

Judith sniffed and turned away from him. "I think we've aired quite enough of our dirty laundry in front of Preacher." She smiled at the mountain man. "I'm sorry you had to hear all that."

"Shucks, ma'am, I don't pay it no never mind," he told her.

"Supper will be ready in a little while. Until then, why don't you break out the cider, Ethan?"

Langley chuckled. "That sounds like a good idea. Could I interest you in a cup of cider, Preacher?"

"You sure could."

Judith went back to the couple's quarters while Langley got a jug and a couple of cups from under the counter. He filled them about half full of amber liquid from the jug and handed one of them to Preacher.

"It's pretty strong," Langley warned.

"Most of the whiskey you find out here will scald the rattles right off a rattlesnake." Preacher grinned. "This can't be any stronger than that."

He clinked his cup against Langley's and took a drink of the cider. It had a kick, all right, but a mild one. It was smooth and tasted good.

He was about to say as much when the door of the trading post opened and Courtland came in. Langley stiffened at the sight of his old rival for Judith's affections.

Courtland wasn't wearing the coonskin cap or his rough work clothes anymore. He had put on a pair of tight trousers and a waistcoat with a frilly white shirt under it. He had even donned a cravat. He was probably the fanciest-dressed fella who had ever set foot in Fort Gifford, Preacher thought.

Catching sight of the cups Preacher and Langley were holding, Courtland quipped, "Well, are you going to offer me a drink, too?"

Judith heard his voice, and before her husband could answer, she emerged from the living quarters again and exclaimed, "Oh, my word! Wiley, I think you're the most handsome man I've seen in a long,

long time. Certainly since we came out here to this wilderness."

"Why, thank you. I dressed so you'd know I'm honored by your invitation."

She came out from behind the counter and hurried along the aisle toward him. Linking her arm with his as she had done earlier, she led him toward the rear of the big, high-ceilinged room. "Come on back to our parlor. It's nothing like what you're used to in St. Louis, but I've tried to make the surroundings as comfortable and homey as possible."

Courland didn't pull away. "I'm sure it'll be lovely." As he walked past Langley with Judith, he smiled.

Langley returned the smug look with a murderous glare.

Preacher wondered if Judith truly didn't know what she was doing.

Innocent or not, she had just lit the fuse under a powder keg.

CHAPTER 17

Langley motioned for Preacher to follow him. The two of them went into the rear section of the building behind Judith and Courtland.

She must have packed several wagons full of furnishings to bring with her, Preacher thought as he looked around. The main room of the booshwa's living quarters had a good-sized dining table on one side, with six chairs around it. The table was covered with a white linen cloth. A china cabinet and sideboard sat against the wall nearby.

On the other side of the room, near the fireplace, were two comfortable-looking rocking chairs, one with a smaller table beside it. A loom stood within easy reach. Tucked into one corner of the room was a desk, and in another corner was a pianoforte and a bench.

Preacher could picture the two of them on a normal evening, Langley sitting at the desk going over the outpost's accounts while Judith played the pianoforte or worked on the loom. It was a nice domestic image, the sort that would appeal to most men.

Not to Preacher, though. All those things were nice, but to a man like him, they would be almost the same as shackles. He would chafe against their confinement just as much.

It was all right to visit this world, though, he thought as he walked across the thick rug laid in the center of the room.

An open door led into a small kitchen with a wood-burning stove, something else hauled out by wagon. Clearly, Langley wanted his wife to have some of the comforts of a home back East, even though she was living in a largely untamed wilderness.

The food was already on the table—a platter piled high with antelope steaks, another filled with biscuits, and a bowl of greens from the garden.

"I'm sorry we don't have any more vegetables than this," Judith apologized. "It's too early in the season. But the next time you're here, I'll have potatoes and carrots and onions."

"I'm sure this will be delicious," Courtland said. "It'll certainly be much better than what we've been eating on the trail."

"Yes, ma'am," Preacher added. "Them steaks smell plumb mouth-waterin'."

Judith waved a hand at the table. "Please, have a seat. I'll fetch the coffee."

The men moved toward the table. Standing fairly close to the chair at one end, Courtland reached out and started to pull it back so he could sit down.

"That's my seat," Langley said, his voice sharp.

"Oh, really?" Courtland replied coolly. "I thought since I'm a guest, you might want me to have it."

"Not hardly," Langley said through gritted teeth.

Preacher managed not to growl in exasperation at their posturing, but it wasn't easy. He pointed to one of the chairs on Langley's left. "Wiley, why don't you sit there?"

Putting his hand on the back of the closer chair on that side of the table, Preacher claimed it so he would be sitting between Courtland and Langley. It was like riding herd on a couple of squabbling kids, he thought. And he didn't like it.

Cooperating, Courtland sat down where Preacher indicated. Langley took the seat at the head of the table. The awkward silence that followed lasted only a moment, until Judith spoke as she returned from the kitchen carrying a tray with four china cups on it. "Here we are."

After that, the atmosphere didn't get all that much less awkward. She handed each of the men a cup, starting with her husband.

"We'll say grace," Langley said once Judith sat down at his right hand.

Preacher bowed his head while Langley asked the Lord's blessing on the meal. He wasn't looking, but he would have been willing to bet that Langley and Courtland were still shooting venomous glances at each other, even during the prayer.

"All right, everyone, help yourselves," Judith said when they all looked up again.

Preacher dug in, delighted when he found everything tasted even better than it smelled. He wouldn't want to make a habit of it, but having a home-cooked meal was a real treat. He washed the food down with sips of black coffee almost strong enough to get up and walk around by itself, just the way he liked it.

"So, you've become a horse trader, Wiley," Judith said as they ate. "I must say, I'm not surprised. Working in the freight business, you were around horses all the time."

"That's right," Courtland said. "I think I've become a pretty good judge of horseflesh over the years. It's easy to pick out the real thoroughbreds just by looking at the clean, smooth lines of them."

Langley frowned. They were talking about horses, but clearly he thought Courtland actually meant something else.

And it was possible that was true, Preacher mused.

He had seen for himself how Courtland liked to pick at Langley.

The booshwa had one huge advantage, though. He had wound up with the woman both of them wanted.

Judith had an inkling of what was going on, and changed the subject. "Why don't you tell Preacher how the two of us met, Ethan?"

Preacher didn't have a lick of interest in hearing that story, but he gave a half-hearted smile around a mouthful of antelope steak and nodded to Langley. That would be better than listening to the other two men snipe at each other.

Langley took a sip of his coffee. "I was working at a store in St. Louis."

"You ran the place," Judith put in.

Langley shrugged. "I did, but someone else owned it. That doesn't mean I avoided the hard work. One day I was unloading some bags of flour from a wagon, tossing them from the wagon bed into a wheelbarrow so they could be taken inside."

"Those were big, heavy bags, too," Judith explained, "but Ethan didn't have any trouble handling them."

Again he shrugged, downplaying his strength. "I wouldn't go quite that far, because I did have some trouble. I tossed one of the bags too hard, and it went over the wheelbarrow and fell on the loading dock. It busted open, and flour dust flew up into a cloud. Unfortunately, the bag had landed right next to—"

"Me!" Judith interrupted with a smile. "I was covered with dust almost head to foot! I'm sure I was quite a sight."

Langley smiled at the memory, too. "You were," he agreed. "You looked like a ghost, all covered with that white dust like that." He paused. "A beautiful ghost."

"I agree," Courtland said. "I thought you looked beautiful, too. It would take more than a little flour dust to change that."

"You were there, too?" Preacher asked, then gave himself a mental kick for encouraging them.

"Yes, what Ethan neglected to tell you is that it was a wagon from my freight line delivering the flour to the store," Courtland said. "I wasn't driving, but I had come along to supervise the delivery. And *that's* why Judith was there in the first place, because I'd told her I'd be there. She was coming to see me."

"It's true, I knew Wiley first. He was a dear friend." Judith paused. "I hope he still is."

"Of course." Courtland smiled. "But I was more than that back then. I was a serious suitor for your hand."

"That didn't last long after she met me," Langley snapped.

"Please, Ethan." Judith looked like she wished she hadn't brought up that bit of personal history.

"We should leave all the hard feelings in the past. There's no need for them now. Everything is settled."

Courtland said, "That's right. Judith is your wife, Langley. I just want to be friends with both of you."

Langley's expression made it clear he didn't believe that for a second.

Neither did Preacher, for that matter, but it was none of his business.

He was going to keep telling himself that until he left Fort Gifford . . . which might be pretty soon after all, the way things were going.

The tension didn't lessen throughout the meal. Courtland and Langley couldn't go more than a few minutes without one insulting the other or commenting on their rivalry for Judith.

She was increasingly aware of it, and it embarrassed her.

When the meal was finally over, she cleared the table. Preacher could see the relief in her expression as she left the room with plates and silverware.

"I brought some brandy with me," Langley said. "Could I offer each of you *gentlemen* a glass?"

Preacher heard the scorn in the booshwa's voice, and it irritated him. Even though Langley had apologized for getting angry at him because he'd come to the fort with Courtland, it appeared the man still wasn't very fond of him.

That was fine with Preacher. He didn't care one way or the other and didn't intend to be there long enough for it to make any difference whether Langley liked him or not. Once he put together a good load of pelts, he would trade them at Fort Union not Fort Gifford.

"Brandy, eh?" Courtland drawled. "I didn't know you had an appreciation for the finer things in life, Langley."

"You should have known," Langley shot right back. "I married Judith, didn't I? A man couldn't find anything much finer in this world than her."

Courtland's jaw tightened. "I can't argue with that. I could point out, however, that sometimes a man winds up with something much finer than he really deserves."

"Oh, I think things generally work out pretty much like they're supposed to."

Courtland's eyes narrowed, and he placed his hands flat on the edge of the table as if he were about to push himself to his feet. Langley tensed.

Preacher was between them and intended to stay there. As a courtesy to Judith, he figured he ought to keep the two fellas from fighting. She wouldn't want a brawl breaking out in her home.

Langley made a visible effort to relax, forcing a smile onto his face again. "I'll get that brandy."

He walked over to the nearby cabinet and took three heavy crystal tumblers from it. From a matching decanter, he splashed a couple of inches of amber liquid into each glass and carried them back to the table. He brought one of the tumblers to Preacher and went back to get the other two.

Preacher and Courtland got to their feet, and Courtland lifted his glass. "I'd like to propose a toast."

Langley's eyes were suspicious, but he said, "I suppose you've got a right to do that. Go ahead."

"To Judith. I wish her only the best . . . even though she deserves better than what she got."

"Dadgum it—" Preacher began as Langley's face flushed a deep red and twisted with anger.

With a flick of his wrist, the booshwa flung the brandy in his glass right into Courtland's smirk.

CHAPTER 18

Courtland was so shocked he seemed frozen into immobility for a second, brandy dripping from his face. But only for a second. Then he let out an enraged roar and lunged at Langley, swinging the glass in his hand as if he intended to smash it against the booshwa's head.

Preacher moved quicker, blocking Courtland's charge with his body and grabbing the man's wrist. He stopped Courtland from attacking Langley.

Not that Langley deserved protecting after pulling a stunt like that. If Courtland had bashed him in the head, Langley would have had it coming.

Preacher hung on to Courtland's wrist with his left hand, wrapped his right arm around Courtland's body, and wrestled the horse trader toward the door.

"What's going on out here?" Judith cried from

behind them. "What was that shout? Ethan, what did you *do*?"

"What any man would who found a predator in his house. I'm getting rid of it."

Courtland yelled at Preacher, "Let go of me, damn you! He's been asking for this for a long time!"

"Not here, blast it!" Preacher told him. "It ain't decent."

"Just let me at him!" Courtland raved. "I'll show Judith she picked the wrong man. She ought to be with me, not him!"

With her hands pressed together in front of her, almost like she was praying, she came toward them. "Oh, Wiley, please, don't act like this. I never wanted to hurt you—"

"Well, you did!" Courtland shot back at her. "Worse than that, you hurt yourself. You should have a fine home back East, not this . . . this squalid little hovel in the middle of the wilderness!"

"Wiley!"

"And you," Courtland shouted at Langley. "Bringing her out here where she's liable to lose her hair to bloodthirsty savages! You want her scalp hanging in some Blackfoot chief's lodge? Do you, Langley?"

"Judith is perfectly safe here—"

"You haven't had to bury your friends who were killed by those Indians!"

Despite the fact that Courtland had been pretty obnoxious, the man had a point, Preacher thought. As the westernmost outpost built by the American Fur Company, Fort Gifford was in a particularly precarious position. It had to be a tempting target not just for the Blackfeet but for every hostile tribe in the area. There had probably been plenty of medicine talk in the lodges already about attacking the fort. Whether or not such an attack would take place was uncertain, but it was definitely a possibility.

"Don't worry about my wife," Langley said. "I can protect her."

"You can't protect her!" Courtland insisted. "You're nothing but a damned coward!"

Almost to the door between the living quarters and the main room of the trading post, Preacher glanced over his shoulder, saw the way Langley blanched, and knew it wasn't over, even if he got Courtland out of there.

"Let him go!" Langley roared. "I thrashed him once, and I can do it again!"

"Ethan, no!" Judith said. "I won't have the two of you fighting over—"

"Don't worry, Judith," Courtland broke in. "He can't hurt me. I'm not afraid of him. He's the one who's afraid."

Langley started toward them with fists clenched.

Preacher had Courtland close enough to the

door that a hard shove sent him staggering through it. Preacher hurried after him and slammed the door behind them, hoping Langley would seize that excuse to let the sordid confrontation end.

"Preacher, stop protecting him." Courtland's normally fair-skinned face was bright red with rage, brighter than any sunburn.

"I ain't protectin' him," Preacher said. "I'm tryin' to keep you from makin' a fool of yourself. You won't do any good brawlin' over a married woman."

"Maybe once she sees what sort of man her husband really is, she won't want to be married to him anymore."

Preacher didn't believe that for a second, but Courtland obviously did. He thought he stood a chance of taking Judith away from Langley.

And maybe he did. Preacher couldn't say. He'd never been able to fathom why women did what they did most of the time, and he had just about given up trying.

But he was convinced it wasn't the time or place for a showdown and said as much as he grabbed Courtland again and hustled the man toward the front door of the trading post.

Preacher's hopes for at least a temporary end to the trouble were dashed as the door to the living quarters burst open behind him. Langley strode

into the trading post's main room. Judith came
with him, plucking at his sleeve.

He shook her off and stomped after Preacher
and Courtland. "Take him outside, Preacher.
We're going to settle this once and for all!"

Preacher doubted anything would be settled
as long as both men were still alive, but as long
as it was a fair fight and they weren't busting
up Judith's home, he didn't really care what
they did.

Courtland would have charged Langley again,
there in the trading post, but Preacher wouldn't
let him past. He gave Courtland another shove
toward the entrance.

Behind them, Judith said desperately, "You
don't have to do this, Ethan. You don't have to
prove anything to me."

"It's not you I'm trying to prove anything to,"
Langley replied. "I'm tired of Courtland trying to
come between us, and after tonight he never will
again!"

That sounded pretty final, thought Preacher.
Maybe Langley planned on a fight to the death—
probably not a good idea. If he died, Fort Gifford would be left without anybody in charge.
Preacher didn't want Langley to kill Courtland,
since he still felt a bond of comradeship with
the man.

Chances were it wouldn't come to that, no matter what Langley's intention. It was mighty hard for one man to beat another man to death, especially if they were as evenly matched as these two seemed to be.

Preacher jerked the door open and wrestled Courtland through it onto the porch. The compound was fairly quiet, but there were a few men moving around. Candlelight glowed through the open door of the barracks. Not everyone had settled down for the night.

When they reached the ground at the bottom of the steps, Courtland jerked loose from Preacher's grip. Actually, Preacher let him go. He wouldn't have been able to get free otherwise.

Courtland shook his arms and moved his shoulders. "All right, out here is fine. Just gives me more room to move around."

Langley stalked through the door onto the porch in time to hear Courtland's words. "More room for me to kick you all around the fort, that's what you mean," he boasted.

"Come on and try!" Courtland said as he lifted his fists and poised himself to do battle.

Preacher stepped out of the way. Now that they were outside, he wasn't going to interfere anymore. Those two stubborn varmints could do whatever they wanted to each other.

Judging by Courtland's stance, he expected

Langley to come down from the porch and start throwing punches.

Instead, Langley threw himself from the porch, taking Courtland by surprise with a diving tackle. He wrapped his arms around Courtland and both men crashed to the ground.

Judith ran down the steps and clutched Preacher's arm. "Can't you stop them?" she pleaded.

"I probably could, but it wouldn't do any good. They're bound and determined to have it out, and if I stopped 'em now, they'd just go after each other again some other time. Best let 'em go ahead and scrap. Maybe they'll get all that hate out of their guts." Preacher didn't think that was very likely, but he supposed it was possible.

He stood there watching with a very worried Judith at his side as Langley and Courtland rolled around on the ground, wrestling and slugging at each other.

Across the compound, a man yelled, "Fight! The booshwa's in a fight with that fella who brung in the horses!"

More cries of "Fight! Fight!" went up and echoed through the fort. Men hurried from the barracks and some of the other buildings.

Langley wound up on the ground, and Courtland tried to seize that momentary advantage by grabbing the other man's throat. Before Courtland could lock down the grip, Langley shot a fist straight up and caught him under the chin. The blow rocked Courtland back.

Bucking upward, Langley threw Courtland off. As he sprawled in the dirt, Langley lunged after him. Courtland lifted his right leg and sunk his boot heel in Langley's belly, doubling him over. Courtland straightened his leg, making Langley fly through the air above him.

Langley landed facedown and didn't move. He seemed to be stunned. Courtland rolled over and scrambled after him. He dug a knee into the small of Langley's back and looped an arm around his throat from behind. Bearing down with his knee to keep the booshwa pinned to the ground, Courtland hauled back on Langley's throat.

Preacher had been trapped in grips like that. He knew from experience how a man's backbone groaned and bent painfully in that position. A fella couldn't stand it for very long.

Judith's fingernails clawed at the mountain man's buckskin sleeve as she pleaded despairingly, "Preacher . . ."

He was ready to step in before Courtland broke Langley's neck, but didn't have to. Langley managed to drive an elbow backward into Courtland's midsection with enough force to break the grip himself. The blow made Courtland gasp for breath.

Langley rolled over and threw another elbow. It

landed alongside Courtland's jaw and stretched the horse trader out on the ground.

From the way Langley fought, Preacher could tell that the man had been in plenty of bareknuckles brawls.

Langley crawled away, putting himself a little distance from Courtland. Both men climbed to their feet, their chests heaving. Blood dripped from a scratch on Langley's face, and Courtland's jaw was already starting to puff up and turn purple.

"Please stop!" Judith cried. "There's no need to do this!"

Neither man seemed to hear her. They paid no attention to the shouts of the men gathered around to watch the fight, either. Some of the bystanders yelled encouragement to the booshwa, while others urged Courtland on.

Otis Freeman's leather-lunged bellow filled the night air as he shouted, "Go get him, Wiley!"

Langley and Courtland approached each other cautiously. They had taken each other's measure. They had each dealt out and absorbed some punishment, and were trying to figure out how to end the fight.

Neither man would give up, Preacher knew. He could tell from the determined expressions on their faces. They would slug away at each other until they were too tired to lift their arms.

That might be the best outcome, he thought.

Let them battle to a draw, with no clear winner, and they might decide the rivalry was over.

But if one man vanquished the other, the loser would nurse his hatred and resentment over that defeat, and sooner or later the whole mess would come bubbling back to the surface. Probably sooner. No telling how long Courtland would be around the fort. The loser would have to strike back quickly.

Preacher was rooting for a draw.

The two men circled each other slowly, their fists lifted and poised to strike. Courtland suddenly feinted, and when Langley went for it, Courtland stepped in and snapped a jab that landed on Langley's nose. Blood spurted.

"Oh!" Judith cried in horror.

Langley fought back, throwing a right that didn't get through and a left that did. It landed on the same spot where the bruise was already forming on Courtland's jaw from the earlier blow. Courtland staggered a step to the side, a little off balance.

Langley thrust a foot between Courtland's calves and jerked his right leg out from under him. Courtland went down hard. Langley bulled in, evidently intending to stomp his opponent to death. He lifted a foot high and drove it down.

Courtland flung his hands up and grabbed

Langley's boot, holding it off from his face. Grunting with effort, he heaved on Langley's leg and upended the booshwa. Langley crashed down on his back.

Courtland went after him and tried to ram his knee into Langley's groin. Langley twisted aside and took the blow on his thigh. He tangled both hands in Courtland's shirt front and threw him aside.

They rolled away from each other. The men surrounding them moved back quickly as the two combatants bumped their legs. Panting and cursing, Courtland reached his feet ahead of Langley. He rushed in as Langley was struggling to his feet.

Unexpectedly, Langley turned that to his advantage. He stayed low and ducked under the roundhouse punch Courtland swung at him. Courtland's momentum carried him forward. Langley flung both arms around his opponent's waist, letting out a roar as Courtland's own momentum helped Langley lift him off the ground.

"Oh, my God," Judith breathed as Langley hoisted Courtland over his head. "Ethan, no!"

Langley continued to ignore her. Still roaring from rage and the Herculean effort he was making, he lifted Courtland higher and then slammed him to the ground. Courtland actually bounced once from the impact and then lay there motionless in a huddled heap.

The fight was over. Courtland looked like he was out cold.

Langley stepped closer to his fallen opponent, and for a second, Preacher thought he was going to kick Courtland. Langley settled for spitting on him. He turned and walked away, but he was unsteady from exhaustion and his steps weaved a little.

He was bloody and bruised and his clothes were dirty and ripped, but he seemed well satisfied with himself as he came to a stop in front of Judith and Preacher.

"Well, that ought . . . that ought to do it," Langley struggled to say. "That . . . blackguard . . . will never bother us . . . again."

"Oh, Ethan," Judith wailed.

Langley gave a little shake of his head, as if his brain was filled with cobwebs and he didn't quite understand what was going on. "Judith, what . . . what's wrong? I . . . I beat him . . ."

With a choked sob, Judith turned and ran back into the trading post. Langley stared after her, blinking in confusion.

Some of the men gathered around Langley to slap him on the back and congratulate him on his victory. Otis Freeman, along with Elkins and Boylan, picked up Courtland to carry him back to their camp just outside the walls of the fort.

Langley didn't pay any attention to those things. He looked at Preacher. "What happened?"

"I reckon you won the battle, hoss," Preacher said, "but I ain't so sure about the war."

CHAPTER 19

Still looking befuddled and crestfallen, Langley went on into the trading post.

Preacher didn't follow him. Dinner was over, and whatever went on between Langley and Judith, Preacher figured it would be better to keep his distance. Clearly, Judith was angry with her husband for brawling . . . but she probably would have been hurt if he *hadn't* fought for her, too.

There were times when no matter which way a fellow jumped, he was going to land in a mess of trouble. And a woman was nearly always involved at those times.

The fort's gates stood open. Preacher strolled through them and walked toward Courtland's camp. In the moonlight he could see the men had worked hard and put together about half the corral. They would be able to finish it the next day. Until then, the horses were picketed, and a couple of Courtland's men were watching them.

Courtland sat on the lowered tailgate of one of the wagons. Otis Freeman was with him, using a rag to wipe away the blood from the scratches on Courtland's face. Elkins stood nearby holding a candle so Freeman would have some light to work by.

After a moment, Freeman set the rag aside and took hold of Courtland's chin. He carefully moved Courtland's jaw back and forth. Courtland winced but didn't make any sound.

"Well, it ain't broke, anyway," Freeman announced. "You'll still be able to eat, but it's liable to hurt a mite for a few days. You're gonna be pretty stiff and sore all over, I reckon."

"So is Langley," Courtland muttered. "I gave as good as I got."

That wasn't exactly true, thought Preacher, considering Langley had still been on his feet at the end of the fight and Courtland hadn't, but the booshwa sure hadn't come through it unmarked.

Elkins took a flask from his pocket, uncorked it, and held it out to Courtland. "Take a swig of this, boss. It's prime corn liquor. It'll dull the pain some."

Courtland shook his head. "I appreciate that, Elkins, but I want to feel the pain. I want to experience every ache and throb so I'll remember what Ethan Langley did. I won't forget any of it until . . ."

His voice trailed off, but Preacher knew what he meant. Courtland wouldn't forget until he had evened the score.

It was exactly what Preacher had worried about and why he had hoped the two men would battle to a stalemate. Being defeated by Langley—again—was going to rankle Courtland until he did something about it.

More and more it looked like it was time for Preacher to move on. If he stayed, he ran the risk of finding himself stuck in the middle of the mess, caught between the two men and the hate they felt for each other.

Elkins put away his flask and suggested, "Maybe that fella didn't exactly fight fair."

"He fought fair," Courtland snapped. "Ask Preacher if you don't believe me."

Freeman and Elkins looked at the mountain man. He shrugged. "I didn't see no dirty tricks on either side. There ain't no rules in a bare-knuckles brawl, but nobody tried anything underhanded. It was a good clean fight."

"The next time it'll be different," Courtland vowed. "Langley won't ever beat me again."

Freeman asked, "Are we still gonna stay here and try to trade and sell those horses?"

Courtland looked up at him and frowned, then

winced because even that much movement hurt him. "Of course we are. Why wouldn't we?"

"Well, I just thought, what with the trouble between you and that fella—"

"That's personal," Langley cut in. "The horses are business. I've got a lot riding on this, Otis. Everything, in fact."

Freeman nodded. "Yeah, I know. I just wasn't sure you'd want to stay here, that's all."

"I'm staying here," Courtland declared, "until I do what I came to do."

Preacher wasn't sure what that was anymore. He suspected Langley was right about Courtland being aware the booshwa and Judith were living at Fort Gifford.

Courtland went on, "What about you, Preacher? Are you going to stay?"

"Nope," Preacher answered without hesitation. "I never planned to hang around once I helped you fellas get here. Fact is, I'll probably be pullin' out early tomorrow mornin'. There are plenty of beaver out yonder just a-waitin' for me to trap 'em."

"Plenty of redskins waitin' to kill you, too," Freeman pointed out.

"That won't be any different than it's always been," Preacher said with a faint smile.

"We'll miss you when you go," Courtland said. "Are you sure you wouldn't like to stay and take a share in this operation for all the help you gave us?"

"No offense, but not hardly. I'm ready to head for the tall and uncut."

Courtland held out a hand. "We wish you well, then. And I hope our paths will cross again sometime."

Preacher gripped Courtland's hand.

The horse trader winced again and grinned. "Think I bruised a knuckle or two on Langley's ugly face."

He was pretty chipper again for a man who'd just been knocked out. But anger and hatred still lurked in his eyes.

Preacher had heard the old saying about good intentions and the road to hell many times in his life. That night he got proof of it when he returned to the fort from Courtland's camp. Quint Harrigan, who was sitting on a stump in front of the fur warehouse, hailed him and raised a jug.

"Quite a ruckus earlier," Harrigan said when Preacher ambled over to join him. "I didn't know who was gonna win."

"I ain't so sure but what they both lost," Preacher commented dryly.

That brought a chuckle from the red-bearded trapper. "Yeah, when two fellas go to fightin' over a woman, she's usually the only one who wins."

Preacher didn't think Judith Langley had won anything except more grief. He changed the subject by saying, "Are you just gonna wave that jug around, or is there anything in it worth samplin'?"

"Oh, it's worth it! Here you go. Have a swig."

Preacher took the jug and swallowed a healthy slug of the whiskey inside it. It had a nice kick and burned all the way down his gullet. "Not bad," he allowed. "For panther piss and rattlesnake pizen, that is." He wiped the back of his other hand across his mouth and returned the jug to Harrigan

Harrigan hooted with laughter, then downed a slug himself. "How about comin' out with me and Rollin and Bob tomorrow?"

"I thought those other two already brought in some fresh meat."

"Not enough," Harrigan said. "There's a supply boat on its way upriver that's supposed to get here in a week or two, and there'll be a lot more men on it. Langley wants to smoke enough meat and lay it aside so there'll be plenty of provisions on hand when those other fellas get here. So we're goin' huntin' again tomorrow. Langley pays pretty good for meat, and he's even more generous when he's tradin' for it."

Preacher frowned. "That smacks of workin' for wages."

"How's gettin' paid for bringin' in meat any different than gettin' paid for bringin' in pelts?"

Preacher supposed there wasn't really any difference, but it still didn't feel right to him.

When he hesitated and didn't answer, Harrigan went on, "You know, I turned back to the fort today because I wanted to give you a hand, Preacher. You could help us scare up some game tomorrow. Ain't nobody better at it than you."

His better judgment was probably getting tired of him not listening to it, Preacher thought. But Harrigan had a good point . . . or a point, anyway, and Preacher supposed one more day wouldn't hurt. "All right. I guess I ought to spend a little more time around folks before I head out into the big lonesome again."

The four men left before sunup. Preacher figured if they could bring down a few elk or antelope while it was early, he still might be able to pull out from Fort Gifford today. If that didn't work out, he would leave the next day.

Brown and Mahaffey were friendly enough, even though Preacher didn't warm up to them immediately. Harrigan was surly. He had polished off most of that jug of whiskey the night before, and he was paying the price for it. Preacher didn't mind; he figured Harrigan would perk up as the day went along.

Even after being confined inside the stockade walls of the fort for less than a day, Dog and Horse seemed glad to be out. Dog in particular bounded all over the place with an energy that belied his years.

"How old is that critter, anyway?" Harrigan asked. "You've had him for as long as I've knowed you."

"Ain't neither of us spring chickens anymore," Preacher answered vaguely. "But I reckon we can still get bright-eyed and bushy-tailed on a mornin' like this."

It was beautiful, all right, with the sun coming up and spilling red and gold light over the valleys and the snow-capped peaks. The colors were soft at that time of day, like the world was nothing more than a giant canvas on which a heavenly painter spread His brush strokes.

But suddenly, crimson was a bright, hard ugliness as it sprayed out around the shaft of the arrow that struck Bob Mahaffey in the back of the neck and penetrated all the way through so the flint arrowhead stuck out the front.

CHAPTER 20

Mahaffey spasmed in the saddle, arching his back and making grotesque gagging sounds as he pawed at the arrow's shaft. The bloody arrowhead stuck out so far he could see it when he cast his eyes down. After a second, he toppled to the side and crashed loosely to the ground.

None of the other men had time to check on him, not that it would have done any good as fast as he was losing blood. They had troubles of their own.

More arrows whipped through the air. Rollin Brown let out a pained yell as one struck his upper left arm a glancing blow, ripping through the sleeve of his buckskin shirt and leaving behind a bloody gash.

Preacher and Harrigan hadn't been hit, but the way that storm of arrows was flying around them, it would happen soon enough.

They had ridden too near a grove of pines at

the base of a hill, Preacher saw as he wheeled Horse around. The Indians had hidden in those trees and waited for the four white men to ride into range. Preacher jerked his rifle to his shoulder, eared back the hammer, and fired at the pines.

Then he did the unexpected and kicked the stallion into a gallop straight at the trees. Harrigan and Brown followed his lead and charged after him.

Preacher put the reins between his teeth, slid the empty rifle into the sling he'd rigged for it on his saddle, and pulled both pistols from his belt. Horse closed the distance to the pines in a hurry. Preacher could already see figures darting around in the shadows under the trees.

More arrows whickered through the air around him, but he knew from experience it was harder to hit a target coming straight on. He thundered toward the enemies.

The advantage of knowing the woods were full of his enemies meant he could shoot just about anywhere and stood a good chance of hitting one of them.

Guiding Horse with his knees and the reins clenched between his strong teeth, he raised both pistols and fired. Smoke spewed from the muzzles as the weapons boomed. The heavy lead balls ripped through the shadows under the pines. Preacher heard somebody scream.

He jammed the empty guns behind his belt and

grabbed the butts of the two pistols sticking up from his saddlebags. His second volley tore into the trees. Harrigan and Brown fired their pistols as well.

"Come on!" Preacher shouted as he veered Horse to the side. They had dealt an unexpected blow to their attackers, hopefully throwing the Indians into a momentary state of confusion, preventing them from giving chase quickly.

Their only real chance of survival was to make it back to Fort Gifford before the warriors caught them.

Horse could have easily outdistanced the other two mounts if Preacher had let him run full speed, but he held the stallion back a little. Harrigan and Brown rode up alongside him. Preacher glanced over and saw that while both men looked worried, neither was panicking. He knew it wasn't Harrigan's first Indian fight, and figured it was probably true of Brown, as well.

"Are we heading for the fort?" Harrigan shouted over the pounding hoofbeats of their horses.

"Yeah!" Preacher yelled.

"What about Bob?" Brown called out.

"No chance for him!" Preacher replied. "He's bled dry by now!"

Brown's mouth twisted in a grimace under the blond beard. He and Mahaffey were friends, and no man worthy of the name liked to abandon a friend.

The grim reality was that Mahaffey was either dead or would be in a matter of minutes, or even seconds, and there wasn't a blasted thing they could do for him. Turning back would only amount to throwing their own lives away for no good reason.

Brown nodded reluctantly and leaned forward in the saddle, indicating he understood. He would stick with Preacher and Harrigan.

Preacher twisted in the saddle to look over his shoulder. Warriors mounted on wiry Indian ponies were boiling out of the trees to give chase. From so far away, he couldn't make out the markings on their faces, but he had a strong hunch those pursuers were part of Red Knife's war party.

By charging the ambushers and dealing out some damage of their own, Preacher and his companions had taken a slight lead. He figured they were about five miles from Fort Gifford. The chase wouldn't be a long one, no matter how it turned out.

"They might've heard us shootin', back at the fort!" Brown called.

"They knew we went out to hunt!" Harrigan yelled back. "They'll just think that's what they heard!"

"Not shootin' fast like we done!"

Preacher didn't take part in the conversation. He was saving his breath for riding.

And it was a breathtaking ride as they fled toward the fort. The horses sailed over small creeks and gullies, thundered along straight stretches, and careened recklessly around fallen trees and boulders.

Preacher looked over his shoulder from time to time. The warriors stuck stubbornly behind them. As he expected, most weren't gaining on them and some had even fallen back quite a bit.

But a handful of men mounted on particularly swift ponies were drawing closer. At that rate, they were going to ride those horses into the ground, but obviously they didn't care about that. In a short chase, a man with enough hate in his heart might sacrifice his mount to catch an enemy.

Preacher, Harrigan, and Brown galloped through a gap between a couple of small ridges. It was wide enough for the three of them, but not for the whole war party. The three warriors out in front went through the gap first, really the only ones who stood a reasonable chance of catching up to Preacher and the others.

They came up onto the flat beside the river. The walls of the fort were visible about a mile away. Harrigan saw them and let out a whoop. "We're gonna make it! They'll see us comin' and have the gates open!"

Preacher looked back again. The three Indians

closest were hanging on doggedly, with the rest of the war party straggling behind. But those three warriors were still dangerous. One in particular was mounted on a really speedy pony. The animal practically flew over the ground, its legs a flashing blur.

Brown's horse was beginning to labor. The animal was running a valiant race for life, but bone and sinew and muscle had their limits.

"Come on, Rollin!" Harrigan cried as he saw Brown's mount falter a little. "It's only a little ways now!"

"I'll make it!" Brown said. "You fellas go on and don't worry about me! I'll make it!"

The warrior in the lead was only about twenty yards behind him. As Preacher glanced back, he saw the way the man's face was painted and that was all the confirmation he needed to tell him that these were Blackfeet. Red Knife's bunch, had to be.

His knees clamped tight to his pony's sides, the warrior drew an arrow from the quiver on his back and nocked it to his bow, which he held in front of him at an angle so he could fire over his mount's head. He let fly. The arrow went wide. Preacher saw it go past from the corner of his eye.

The Blackfoot wasn't through. He pulled out another arrow and fired it after the fleeing men. Preacher knew it had found its target when he heard the thud of flint against flesh and Brown let out a loud grunt.

The mountain man twisted his head around and saw Brown sagging forward over his horse's neck. The feathered shaft of an arrow stuck up from the man's back. Preacher could tell that the head had penetrated deeply into Brown's body.

Harrigan saw what had happened, too. He cried, "Rollin!" and slowed his horse so he could reach over and grab his friend's arm. He steadied Brown and kept him in the saddle.

That son of a gun on the fast pony was drawing another arrow from his quiver. With Brown and Harrigan slowing even more, he stood a good chance of doing even more damage to them.

Once again, Preacher did the unexpected. He hauled back on the reins and pulled Horse to a sudden, skidding stop. Plucking the tomahawk from behind his belt, he drew his arm back and sent it flashing forward. He released the 'hawk perfectly.

It spun through the air with the force of Preacher's great strength. Adding the forward momentum of the fast-moving target, the tomahawk struck with tremendous force in the center of the Blackfoot warrior's forehead. The keenly-honed flint head cleaved through bone and brain, practically cutting the man's head in half. He toppled off his pony, the bow and arrow falling unfired from his hands.

Howls of outrage came from the other Blackfeet, but outrage couldn't make their tired ponies run any faster. Preacher wheeled Horse around again and galloped to catch up to Harrigan and Brown, who had raced past him when he stopped to throw the tomahawk. The three men rode side by side, with Brown in the middle still being supported by Harrigan.

When they were within a quarter mile of the fort, the gates began to swing open slowly, ponderously. Preacher saw men lining the parapet. Rifle barrels bristled all along the wall. The men inside Fort Gifford knew they were coming, all right.

So did Wiley Courtland and the rest of his party. As soon as the gates were open wide enough, Courtland and his men drove the herd toward the entrance, leaving the wagons behind. Preacher figured there was a good chance Langley was having a conniption fit, but once the horses started streaming through the opening, there was no stopping them. Nor could any white man deny shelter to another in such a situation.

Harrigan looked back and yelled, "We're gonna make it!"

Preacher thought it was tempting fate to make such a bold declaration, so he kept his mouth shut and concentrated on his riding.

"They're givin' up!" Harrigan exclaimed, sounding surprised.

Preacher looked over his shoulder. The rest of

the Blackfeet were falling back. They had slowed down, realizing they weren't going to catch up to the three men in time. The rest of the war party was slowly coming up behind them.

Preacher didn't heave a sigh of relief just yet. He and his companions might be safe for the time being, but they didn't know what else Red Knife had in mind.

As if in victory, the men on the wall whooped, shouted, and waved hats and coonskin caps over their heads as Preacher, Harrigan, and Brown covered the last two hundred yards to the fort. They slowed to a trot now that the Blackfeet weren't hot on their heels anymore.

Men were waiting to close the gates just as soon as they rode into the fort. They grunted and heaved, and the gates began to swing shut behind Preacher and his companions.

They reined in, and eager hands reached up to take the wounded Rollin Brown. Men lifted him from the saddle and carried him toward one of the buildings. Brown's head lolled loosely on his neck, and Preacher wasn't sure he was alive anymore.

Courtland's men had the horse herd under control. The crowd parted to let Langley through. The booshwa asked, "Where's Mahaffey?"

"He didn't make it," Harrigan replied with a

shake of his head. "The red devils got him with their first arrow."

Langley drew in a deep breath, his face grim. "What about Brown?"

"Don't know. Some of the fellas took him off to take care of him." Harrigan shook his head again. "It looked pretty bad, though."

"Damn it," Langley muttered. "I'm sorry I sent you out after more meat."

"Don't be," Harrigan told him. "We knew the risks. A man can't ever count on bein' safe out here."

Courtland pushed his way to the front, along with Otis Freeman. He gripped Preacher's arm. "Are you all right?"

"Yeah," Preacher said. "Harrigan and I were lucky. Come through it without a scratch."

"Well, thank God for that, anyway." Courtland looked over at Langley and added, "And thank you for letting us and our horses in. To tell the truth, I wasn't sure you would."

"I wouldn't leave any man out there to face those savages, even you." Langley started to turn away. "I should go let Judith know everything's all right—"

"Mr. Langley!" one of the man called from the parapet. "Mr. Langley, you better come look at this!" The fear in the man's voice made everyone on the ground glance up.

Langley strode over to the nearest ladder leading to the parapet and climbed up. More men streamed up the other ladders, including Preacher, Harrigan, Courtland, and Freeman. They gathered at the wall to look out across the rolling plains along the river. Preacher saw the Blackfoot war party about a quarter mile away.

But that wasn't what had prompted the man's frightened summons. More Indians were riding over a swell of ground behind the war party. They kept coming and coming, swarming over the little hill like ants.

"My God, how many of them are there?" Langley asked in a hushed voice.

Courtland sounded equally awed as he said, "There must be hundreds of them."

Preacher thought that was a pretty good guess. He put the number of Blackfeet at three hundred or so, and even though the tide had slowed down, more warriors continued to trickle over the rise and join the others.

"Looks like Red Knife rounded up a few friends before he came to call on us."

CHAPTER 21

A stunned silence hung over the parapet as the men stared at the huge Blackfoot war party. Finally one of them said in an awed voice, "I didn't know there were that many redskins on the whole dang frontier."

Preacher didn't say anything. He knew it was unusual for so many warriors to assemble in one place, but it wasn't unheard of. Each band tended to keep to itself, which made it difficult for a war chief to put together a large force. Red Knife must have called on several bands of Blackfeet and asked for their help in attacking the white interlopers.

"They were just playin' when they jumped us, weren't they?" Harrigan asked. "If they'd all hit us at once, we wouldn't have had a chance. They wanted some of us to get away and come runnin' back here."

"Yeah, more than likely," Preacher agreed. "Red Knife's puttin' on a little show right now. He knew if we hotfooted it back to the fort with a few warriors chasin' us, it would draw everybody out and he'd have a good audience when he let us see the real size of his war party."

"Why is he just sitting out there?" Beads of sweat appeared on Langley's face, despite that the day wasn't overly warm. "He has us outnumbered probably five to one. Why doesn't he go ahead and attack?"

"Don't rush things," Preacher advised. "He'll get around to it in his own sweet time." One of the warriors was sitting slightly ahead of the others, staring toward the fort, and he had a hunch it was Red Knife himself. "He's havin' too much fun right now. He thinks we're sittin' in here gettin' more scared with every minute that goes by."

Harrigan said, "He ain't far wrong about that."

"Someone should take a shot at him." Langley looked around at the men gathered on the parapet. "That would knock the wind out of his sails. Can somebody hit him from here? Preacher?"

The same thing had occurred to Preacher, and he had already gauged the shot in his mind. A ball from his rifle would carry that far, but it would take a minor miracle to hit what he was aiming at. "Lemme get my rifle, and I'll give it a try. You fellas keep an eye on him and sing out if he does anything."

There wasn't much chance of anyone on the parapet looking away from the war party. They were all staring raptly at the Blackfeet.

If luck was with Preacher and he actually killed Red Knife, it might make a difference. Even with a war party that size, getting inside the thick log walls of the fort would be difficult. The Blackfeet would lose a lot of men in the effort. Without Red Knife to drive them on to make the sacrifices, the other leaders of the war party would likely decide to turn and ride away.

It was a long shot, just like the one he was about to attempt, Preacher thought as he went down the ladder to fetch his rifle from the fringed sling hanging on Horse's saddle.

Judith Langley was standing on the front porch of the trading post as he crossed the compound to where the stallion stood, reins dangling. She shaded her eyes and looked at the crowd on the parapet.

She had to be wondering what was going on, thought Preacher. Somebody ought to tell her.

But not him. That wasn't his job.

He grabbed the two pistols from his saddlebags, loaded them and the two behind his belt, put all four behind his belt, and returned to the parapet with the long-barreled flintlock rifle. Men moved aside to let him get right up next to the wall. He peered over it. Red Knife hadn't moved, still sitting arrogantly on his pony ahead of the rest of the war party.

Preacher loaded the rifle with efficient, methodical movements as men called encouragement to him.

Quint Harrigan stood next to him. "You'll have to draw a bead on him pretty quick-like. If he sees that somebody's aimin' at him, he's liable to light a shuck."

"Somehow I doubt that," Preacher muttered. He knew when warriors conjured up their "medicine" before going into battle, it often gave them a feeling of invincibility, as if no knife or bullet or arrow could do them harm as long as they were protected by that magic. He had seen enough odd things during his years on the frontier not to completely discount the possibility.

Red Knife's stance struck him as that of a man who didn't believe anything could hurt him. And after gathering such a large war party he wouldn't want to display even the slightest sign of cowardice in front of them. His defiance of the white men had to be absolute.

Preacher rammed a charge and ball down the rifle's barrel, primed it for firing, and settled the butt plate against his shoulder. He crouched slightly so the barrel rested in the notch between two of the sharpened logs forming the stockade wall, and held it there, making the weapon a little steadier.

"Move back," Langley said in a voice made hoarse by emotion. "Give him some room."

"Got plenty of room," Preacher murmured as he nestled his cheek against the smooth wooden stock and peered over the barrel, figuring distance, elevation, and windage. "If you want to do somethin', you might try sayin' a prayer or two."

He drew in a deep breath and held it as he lined the sights on the distant figure. Then chuckled as Red Knife suddenly lifted the rifle he held. The war chief brought the gun to his shoulder and aimed it at the fort.

Preacher grinned. "Reckon he seen me. All right, Red Knife, if that's the way you want it. Let's you and me trade shots."

It took him only a moment to draw a bead on his target again. He squeezed the rifle's trigger, smoothly taking up the slack until the weapon boomed and kicked heavily against his shoulder.

Powder smoke spurted from the muzzle of Red Knife's rifle at the same instant, as if the trigger fingers of the two men were somehow inextricably linked.

Even with the heavy charges of powder behind the shots, it took a couple of seconds for the balls to travel the distance between the enemies. Preacher didn't move as he waited to see what was going to happen. The other men on the parapet seemed to be holding their breath in anticipation.

Dirt suddenly kicked up about fifty yards in front of the wall as the ball fired from Red Knife's rifle plowed into the ground.

Less than half a heartbeat later, the war chief's pony abruptly lunged to the side and toppled, throwing Red Knife into a rolling sprawl.

"Just a hair low," Preacher said. "Got the horse, not the man. Damn shame."

Because he knew he wouldn't get another chance.

Enraged howls went up from hundreds of throats. Red Knife scrambled to his feet, waving his rifle over his head and shouting. Like a tidal wave of horseflesh and humanity, the war party surged forward.

Preacher saw Red Knife swing up onto a riderless pony one of the warriors brought to him, but after that he couldn't pick out the war chief anymore. There were just too blasted many Blackfeet.

And each and every one wanted blood.

"Spread out along the wall!" Preacher bellowed as he reloaded his rifle. "Hold your fire until they get closer!"

"I'm in charge here!" Langley declared.

"Then you better start givin' orders," Preacher snapped. "Them Blackfeet ain't gonna wait around for you to figure things out."

Langley drew in a deep breath and shouted, "Spread out! Hold your fire like Preacher said!"

Courtland laughed, making Langley flush with anger. Preacher was a mite irritated with both. They had bigger things than their personal quarrel to worry about, namely several hundred angry Blackfoot warriors.

The feeling of fear was palpable in the air, yet the men took their places along the wall with no signs of panic. Most of the trappers at the fort had been through their share of battles against the Indians. Their calmness seemed to spread to the employees of the American Fur Company, some of whom were veteran frontiersmen as well.

Langley asked, "How long should we wait?"

"I'll give you the nod, and you can sing out." Preacher had no problem with Langley issuing the order to fire. "We got two things on our side. More guns, and these walls. Tell every second man to step back."

Langley called, "Every second man, step back!" He'd grasped what Preacher had in mind and went on without being told. "The men in front fire first! Then step back and reload while the others take their place!"

"You're catchin' on." Preacher grinned. His rifle ready, he pointed it at the charging Blackfeet. "Steady now, steady . . ."

Smoke and fire erupted from the muzzles of the war party's guns, but the Blackfeet didn't have all that many rifles and they weren't going to hit anything shooting from the backs of running horses. Preacher ignored those shots.

A moment later, warriors let arrows fly. The shafts arched through the air, nearly all of them failing to reach the fort. The few that made it that far stuck in the logs near the base of the wall.

"Now," Preacher called.

"Fire!" Langley roared.

The volley from the top of the wall crashed like thunder. Heavy lead balls tore through the front ranks of the Blackfeet, sweeping at least a dozen warriors from their ponies. Several mounts fell, causing the ponies right behind them to stumble and fall as well. The charge buckled in a welter of flailing legs and hooves.

Some awkwardness and confusion swept along the line of defenders on the parapet, but for the most part things went smoothly as the men with empty rifles stepped back and the ones who'd been holding themselves in reserve moved forward. With barely a pause, a second volley ripped out and smashed into the war party. The charge came to a confused halt.

The first group of men reloaded as fast as they could and without much delay as they moved into place again.

"Keep firing!" Langley shouted. "Make it hot for them, boys!"

The shots became a little ragged as reloading speeds weren't consistent. Some men just couldn't reload as swiftly as the others. But overall, the fort's defenders kept up a steady, devastating fire, cutting through the Blackfeet with withering effectiveness.

The warriors began to turn and flee rather than face the lethal lead storm.

"Tell the fellas to hold their fire," Preacher called to Langley.

The booshwa relayed the command. A few more scattered shots rang out, then an echoing silence descended over the outpost. Clouds of powder smoke drifted over the fort, stinging the eyes and noses of the defenders for a few moments before it began to break up.

The Blackfeet had left their dead—men and horses alike—sprawled on the ground. They would return for the bodies of their fallen comrades later, probably after dark. Until then, the corpses would have to lie in the sun, swelling and putrefying.

Preacher saw wounded warriors moving slightly. He heard their groans of pain. He knew no Blackfoot warrior wanted to dishonor himself in front of an enemy by crying out, but sometimes the agony was too much to hold back every sound.

Preacher's rifle was loaded. He lifted it to his shoulder, aimed at one of the wounded Blackfeet, and squeezed the trigger. The warrior jerked once as the shot hit him in the head, then he lay still.

"Good Lord, man!" Langley exclaimed. "That was cold-blooded murder."

"The hell it was," Preacher said as he reloaded again. "Puttin' that fella out of his misery was pure mercy. He was hit in the right side of the chest. That .50 caliber ball tore his lung to shreds, if it didn't do anything worse. Might've taken him ten or fifteen minutes to drown in his own blood, and those ten or fifteen minutes would've been the worst of his whole life."

The mountain man drew a bead on another badly wounded warrior. Just before he fired, he said, "I hope somebody will do me the same favor, if I'm ever in a fix like that."

Langley looked stricken, but he nodded in understanding. For several long minutes, shots continued to ring out from Preacher's rifle as he honored his fallen enemies the only way he could.

CHAPTER 22

The Blackfeet pulled back completely out of sight, going over the hill where they had made their dramatic appearance earlier.

Preacher didn't believe for a second they had given up, though, and said as much during a brief council of war with Langley and several other defenders, including Courtland, Freeman, and Harrigan. They were gathered near one of the blockhouses flanking the gates.

Langley clearly wasn't happy about having Courtland there, but he didn't say anything. Evidently, he was willing to put aside his animosity for the moment, since they were facing bigger troubles.

On the parapet along all four walls of the fort, men stood watch tensely, alert for any signs of a renewed attack by the Blackfoot war party.

"So you think the Indians will attack again?" Langley asked.

"I reckon you can count on that," Preacher replied. "Even if Red Knife was killed in the fightin'—and I got a feelin' in my bones we ain't that lucky—the other war chiefs who've thrown in with him will be mighty peeved at us now. They know they got us outnumbered by a lot. But they won't come straight at us out in the open again. An attack like that gives us all the advantage."

"You think they'll try to sneak up to the fort at night?" Courtland asked.

"They might," Preacher agreed. "The men who are on sentry duty will have to keep their eyes open wide. If a few of those varmints get inside the walls somehow and open the gates, the rest of 'em will pour in before we could stop them." He looked at Langley. "You'll need to post guards on that ditch that brings in water from the river."

"We might be able to block it off completely," Langley suggested.

Preacher shook his head. "We don't want to do that yet. The Blackfeet might decide to settle down and lay siege to the place. In that case, we'll need the water. You've got plenty of provisions and ammunition inside the walls?"

Langley nodded. "We can hold out for several weeks if we have to, where those things are concerned. But we shouldn't have to."

"How do you figure that?" Courtland asked, sounding doubtful.

"A supply boat from Fort Union will be here

within the next week to ten days. There'll be at least fifty men on it."

"That's not enough to turn the odds in our favor," Courtland pointed out. "We'll still be outnumbered by three to one."

"Yes, but something else on the boat *will* make a difference."

Preacher was getting a little irritated with Langley's secretiveness. "Why don't you tell us what that is?"

Langley smiled. "Cannons. Four of them, capable of firing six-inch balls. The boat can sit in the middle of the river and bombard those savages until they're all blasted to smithereens."

Preacher smiled at that news, too. He knew the Blackfeet wouldn't be able to stand up to such a barrage.

"The cannons are supposed to go in the blockhouses at each corner of the fort," Langley went on, "but they'll save us before they're even unloaded."

Harrigan said, "Then all we have to do is hang on and keep the Injuns out of the fort until the boat gets here."

"That's right," Langley said with a nod.

Despite being optimistic, Preacher had a hunch that chore might not turn out to be quite as simple as the booshwa made it sound.

* * *

In the calm, Preacher suggested to Langley that he might want to explain to Judith what was going on.

Langley glanced at Courtland then back at Preacher. "That's a good idea. She's probably frightened out of her wits, what with all the shooting. A woman needs her husband with her at a time like this." He went down the nearest ladder, leaving the other men on the parapet.

"Say, Preacher," Harrigan said. "I just got to thinkin'. . . . Where's that big ol' dog of yours? He didn't come back with us."

"He couldn't keep up with the horses, as fast as they were runnin' to stay ahead of those Blackfeet," Preacher said. "He's smart enough to have peeled off and gotten out of harm's way. Reckon he's not far off. He'll hang around and fend for himself until I get a chance to find him."

"I hope he's all right."

"It'd take a whole pack of wolves to give Dog any trouble. Even then, I ain't sure but what he'd have 'em outnumbered."

Harrigan chuckled, then grew serious again. "I'm gonna go see how Rollin's doin'. I ain't heard anything about him since we got back, and there hasn't been time to check on him until now."

Preacher nodded. "Let me know what you find out. I think I'm gonna stay here and keep an eye on Red Knife's bunch for a while."

Harrigan climbed down the ladder and hurried off toward the building where the wounded Rollin Brown had been taken earlier.

He came back about ten minutes later, and the hangdog expression on his red-bearded face told Preacher all he needed to know.

"Rollin didn't make it. He was still alive when we got here, but he only lasted a few minutes longer. Wasn't nothin' anybody could do for him."

"That's a damned shame," Preacher said. "He seemed like a good sort."

"He was. So was Bob Mahaffey. That's two good men dead because of those bloody-handed savages."

And they almost certainly wouldn't be the last, Preacher thought grimly.

From the air of tension gripping the fort, it seemed everyone expected the Blackfeet to attack again right away. But as the minutes and then the hours dragged past, it appeared that wasn't the case.

The lack of activity didn't make anyone relax, though. If anything, as the day went on nerves grew more taut and hearts slugged harder in the chests of the men watching from the walls.

Around midday, Langley sought out Preacher on the parapet. "My wife wants you to come down and have something to eat."

"I'm all right. The fellas have been passin' around canteens, so nobody's gettin' too thirsty. Don't have much of an appetite for food right now."

"You've got to eat to keep your strength up," Langley argued. "There's bound to be another attack sooner or later, and you'll have to help fight it off." He paused. "Besides, Judith insisted."

"Well, I can't very well argue with that, then," Preacher said with a smile.

"I'll take your place here on the wall," Langley offered.

Preacher nodded his agreement. He went down the ladder and crossed the compound to the trading post. Stepping inside, it took a second for his eyes to adjust to the dimness after the bright sunlight outside.

Judith stood behind the counter at the rear of the room.

"Hello, Preacher," she said, smiling at him. "I was hoping Ethan could convince you to come. We may be under attack by a horde of savages, but that's no reason to go hungry."

"I reckon that's a good way to look at it."

She motioned for him to follow her into the living quarters. A plate with an antelope steak and a thick hunk of bread sat on the table. "The fare isn't very fancy, I'm afraid."

"It'll do me just fine," Preacher assured her.

"And I have coffee on the stove."

"Even better."

While he ate, Judith sat down at the other end of the table. The scrutiny with which she regarded him made Preacher a little wary. He could tell something was on the lady's mind.

She asked abruptly, "What are the chances we'll survive this?"

So she wanted reassurance, he thought. He supposed he could do that. "We'll be fine. This fort's well built. The walls are plenty sturdy, and we've got plenty of powder and shot. We can hold out until that boat gets here from Fort Union with more men and those cannons your husband was talkin' about."

"Yes, Ethan told me the same thing. He seemed quite confident." Judith paused. "But I could see the fear in his eyes, Preacher. He thinks there's at least a chance the Indians will overrun us."

Preacher shrugged. "Anything's possible, I reckon."

"In that case, I have a favor to ask of you. I want you to promise to protect me."

That took Preacher by surprise. "That's more along the lines of somethin' your husband ought to be doin'. Or even . . ." He didn't finish the sentence.

Judith obviously knew what he meant. "I'm afraid neither Ethan nor Wiley would actually do what I have in mind. You see, when I say that I want you to protect me, I mean that I want you to protect me from being captured by the savages."

"Oh," Preacher said, understanding now.

"I'd take care of it myself, but I'm afraid that at the last minute I . . . I might falter in my resolve. And I don't want that to happen, Preacher. I really don't. So if you see there's no hope, perhaps you could come to me and . . . and . . ."

Feeling uncomfortable now, Preacher said, "It's best not to think about such things."

"I *have* to think about it now. Later, there may not be time."

She was right about that. And he could sympathize with her desire not to be taken prisoner by the Blackfeet. If he were to be captured, he would be facing a long, excruciating death by torture. But at the end of things, death *would* be waiting. That might not be true for Judith. She might endure years of misery and degradation at the hands of her captors.

Finally he said, "You never know how a fight's gonna go until you're in the middle of it. I can't make no promises except that if I can, I'll do what you want, ma'am."

She smiled again. "Thank you. That's a weight off my mind."

"But you better keep a pistol close at hand, just in case."

"And save it for myself?"

"That's up to you."

"I think I can do it. I just . . . wanted to be sure."

Preacher nodded and resumed eating. Neither of them said anything else.

When he returned to the parapet a little later, he didn't say anything to Langley about what he and Judith had talked about. He didn't see any point in it.

The day continued to crawl by. The spring sun was warm, and the growing stench from the bodies of warriors and horses got pretty bad. Preacher ignored it; he had smelled worse in his time.

Courtland asked, "Should we send out scouts, just to make sure the war party hasn't left? We'd feel rather foolish if we stayed holed up in here for a week or two until the boat gets here and it turned out the Indians were all gone."

"I'd rather feel foolish than be dead," Preacher said dryly. "Anyway, sendin' out scouts wouldn't accomplish anything except to get 'em killed. Red Knife's bunch is still out there."

"But how can you be sure?"

Preacher nodded toward the bodies. "They won't leave those poor varmints behind. They got to be tended to and given a proper send-off to the spirit world."

"I suppose you're right. I just hate this waiting."

"Red Knife's countin' on that."

Finally, the sun slipped below the horizon. As soon as it did, Preacher knew the danger increased.

Every instinct he possessed told him the Blackfeet would try something before morning.

Darkness settled in and thickened quickly. Preacher suggested Langley have a fire built in the center of the compound, creating light to see by when it came time to fight again. Soon, flames were leaping high and casting their flickering glare around the inside of the fort.

Preacher, Langley, Courtland, Freeman, and Harrigan stood together on the parapet, crouching slightly so their heads wouldn't be silhouetted against the glow from the fire behind them. The Blackfeet might not be very good shots, but there was no point in giving them easy targets.

"I'll bet they try to sneak up to the wall and climb over it before we can stop them," Langley said quietly. "They're stealthy bastards. We have to be ready for them."

"They might try that," Preacher agreed. "Or they might try somethin' even worse."

"Like what?" Langley asked.

Preacher didn't have to reply, because the next instant they could all see the answer for themselves.

Trailing streaks of fire, blazing arrows arched high in the sky and plunged down toward the fort.

Chapter 23

"Look out!" Langley yelled. "Everyone take cover!"

Gathered around the fire in the center of the compound, quite a few men scattered as the flaming arrows rained down. One man screamed as a shaft struck him in the back and knocked him off his feet. The burning head embedded itself in his body, and his coat began to smolder as he lay face down, jerking in death throes.

Some of the arrows fell among Courtland's horse herd. The flames made the animals panic, but with nowhere to stampede, all they could do was charge back and forth for a short distance.

One man got too close to the milling chaos, and a horse's shoulder bumped him heavily, sending him sprawling on the ground. He screamed as the horses trampled him. It was an ugly sound that cut off abruptly.

One of the arrows landed next to Preacher. He

stomped it out quickly and yelled, "Put out any fires that start! Don't let the buildings burn!"

The bonfire was in the middle of a large open area of hard-packed dirt. It wasn't going to spread. The flaming arrows, though, were falling all over the fort. Quite a few landed on the roofs of the buildings. Men grabbed buckets and raced to the ditch supplying water to the fort. They filled the buckets and ran back to throw water on the spreading flames.

The trading post was the most important structure in the compound. It held the largest supplies of food and ammunition. If it burned down, there was no way the defenders could hold out until the boat got here.

"Men on the wall!" Preacher bellowed. "Open fire on the redskins shootin' those arrows!" He thrust his rifle over the log and triggered a round toward the streaks of flame.

Other men followed his lead. A scattered volley rang out. If they hadn't scored any hits, at least they'd made the varmints duck. Fewer of the burning arrows flew into the air.

Then the Blackfeet changed their tactics. Instead of firing flaming arrows, they launched regular arrows, again sending them high so they arched down into the fort. The shafts impaled several men as they tried to keep the fires from spreading.

Death falling from the sky was too much for the nerves of some men. Like the horses, they began to panic and mill around.

Up on the parapet, Preacher bit back a curse and kept shooting as fast as he could reload his rifle. He wasn't firing completely blind. He had an idea where the Blackfeet were. He had a hunch what they would be doing next, too.

That hunch was confirmed when scores of howling warriors poured out of the darkness on all four sides of the fort and charged the walls. Some of them carried trunks of trees that had been felled and stripped of their branches, although several inches of those branches had been left to serve as hand- and footholds. If the Blackfeet succeeded in propping those tree trunks against the walls of the fort, they could scramble up them as easily as most men could climb a ladder.

Preacher shouted, "Stop 'em!" and lowered his aim. His rifle boomed, and one of the warriors leading the charge faltered and dropped his end of the tree trunk he was carrying. The trunk plowed into the ground, ripping from the hands of the other two warriors carrying it. The first man stumbled again and fell.

But even as he hit the ground, another warrior joined the other two. They picked up the trunk, and resumed running toward the fort. All along the line of attack, warriors fell as shots rang out, but more men took their place instantly.

The defenders on the parapet and in the block-houses kept shooting, in the hope they would kill enough Blackfeet to break the back of the charge.

Preacher wondered if that was possible. The warriors were willing to sacrifice their lives to wipe out their hated enemies, and their superior numbers allowed them to die and die and die until they would finally breach the fort's defenses.

Quint Harrigan appeared at Preacher's side. The red-bearded mountain man was panting from exertion. "I been goin' around the walls, makin' sure everybody knows what to do. We're holdin' 'em off, Preacher!"

"For now," Preacher replied grimly as he rammed a fresh charge down the barrel of his rifle.

Harrigan leveled his weapon and fired. He gave a grunt of satisfaction.

"Got another of the red devils." He dropped to a knee and reloaded.

Preacher squeezed off another shot and saw one of the warriors double over as the rifle ball punched into his guts. "Any of the fires from those arrows gettin' out of control?"

"Not yet," Harrigan reported. "Leastways I don't think so. But I been a mite busy." He raised up, took aim, and fired again. "Got that one in the head!"

"Best aim for the body," Preacher advised. "It's a bigger target."

Harrigan laughed. "To tell the truth, I was. Shot went a little high. But I was lucky, I reckon."

"We can all use a little luck right about now," Preacher muttered under his breath.

The Blackfeet were getting close. Preacher shot his rifle once more, then leaned it against the wall and pulled two of his pistols from behind his belt. He leaned forward, thrust them over the wall, and yelled, "Come and get it, you sons o' bitches!"

Some of the warriors shouted back at him, but the thunderous roar as smoke and flame erupted from Preacher's guns drowned out their defiant cries. The double-shot pistols and the heavy charges of powder sent four balls smashing into the forefront of the Blackfoot charge.

The damage was devastating. A couple of balls tore all the way through their targets and struck other warriors behind them. The assault broke as wounded men piled up on each other.

Some of the Blackfeet began to withdraw. Others milled around in confusion, which made them easy targets for the defenders on the wall.

Preacher tucked the empty pistols away. He left the other two in reserve and snatched up his rifle to reload it. In a matter of seconds he had the long-barreled flintlock ready to fire again. He drew a bead and dropped another warrior.

Men were shouting all over the fort, but suddenly some of those shouts took on an added note of alarm.

Preacher's head jerked around as he looked for the source. He spotted a knot of struggling figures on the fort's eastern wall, around the corner from where he was. In the flickering light of flames, he caught a glimpse of painted warriors among the defenders clad in buckskin and homespun.

"Quint!" he shouted to Harrigan. "Come on! They're inside the wall over yonder!"

Preacher didn't have time to reload his rifle, but he carried it with him as he hurried toward the spot where Blackfeet had penetrated the fort's defenses. The blockhouse at the corner was in his way, but a plank ran along the outside of it, forming a narrow, ledge-like pathway. He barely slowed down as he negotiated the plank with the agility of a mountain goat.

As he reached the parapet on the other side, a Blackfoot warrior climbed over the stockade wall and let out a harsh yell. He swung a tomahawk at the mountain man.

Preacher stepped inside the swing and smashed the rifle butt into the middle of the warrior's face. Cartilage tore and bone shattered under the force of the blow. The Indian went backward over the wall and plummeted to the ground below.

Reversing the rifle and gripping the barrel so he could use it as a club, Preacher waded into the melee. Quint Harrigan was right behind him.

More bones crunched and blood splattered as Preacher flailed away at the warriors. Several times he received minor cuts from knives or tomahawks wielded by his enemies, but he ignored the pain. Caught up in the heat of battle as he was, he didn't really feel it.

One of the warriors tackled him from behind and knocked him down on the parapet. The impact jolted the rifle from Preacher's hands. He plucked his knife from the sheath at his waist and drove the blade up and back.

There was a slight resistance as the razor-sharp weapon sliced into the Blackfoot's belly. Preacher ripped to the side with it and felt the hot gush of blood and the slick slide of guts spilling from the gaping wound he had opened up.

He threw off the dying warrior and rolled over. As he surged to his feet he changed his grip on the knife so he held it in more traditional fashion. His left arm went around the neck of a Blackfoot about to brain a fallen defender with a war club. Preacher jerked the warrior back and planted the knife deep in his body from behind. The blade rasped on ribs and then sank into the Blackfoot's heart. The warrior spasmed in death for a second before Preacher yanked the knife free and cast the corpse aside.

With his left hand, he picked up a fallen tomahawk. Using it and the knife, he struck again and again, right and left, doing terrible damage to the warriors who had scaled the wall and made it into the fort. The mountain man's arms were soon smeared with blood to the elbows, and crimson gore was splattered across his chest and face.

A sweeping blow with the tomahawk crushed a warrior's skull and knocked him off the parapet, falling to the ground inside the fort. Preacher looked around for another enemy to kill, but didn't see any. The Blackfeet had fled. It took a few seconds for the realization to penetrate the red haze hanging over his brain.

Quint Harrigan gripped his arm. "Preacher! Preacher, the redskins are gone! They lit out! They're pullin' back all around the fort!"

Preacher blinked away the fog of bloodlust and gave a little shake of his head. Bodies were scattered on the parapet all around the walls, white men and Indian alike. Death was no respecter of skin color. More littered the ground inside the fort where men had fallen off the parapet as they died.

Men stood at the walls, firing rifles at the warriors as they fled into the night. Indians seldom doubled back after retreating. Once an attack was over, it was over . . . until the next time.

Preacher drew in a deep breath. "Are you all right, Quint?"

"Banged up a mite," Harrigan replied. "How about you? You got blood all over you."

"Most of it ain't mine," Preacher said. "I'll be fine. Let's go see what those varmints cost us this time."

They began working their way around the walls, checking on the dead and injured. The Blackfoot casualties were five or six times as many as those of the defenders. A section of wall about twenty feet long was the only place the warriors had gotten into the fort. They had poured a lot of men into that gap, but most of them had died.

Elsewhere around the walls, a man had died here and there or been wounded by an arrow. That was true on the ground inside the fort, too. When Preacher did a quick count, he found only six of the defenders had been killed, with three times that many suffering wounds, most of them relatively minor.

Preacher and Harrigan were back on the ground when Ethan Langley came up to them. "We drove them off!" the booshwa said excitedly.

"Don't go to celebratin' just yet," Preacher warned him. "They'll be back."

A solemn look came over Langley's face. "Are you sure about that?"

"Sure as I can be," Preacher answered without hesitation. "They've still got us in a bad spot. They ain't just about to give up and go away." He looked around. "Have you seen Courtland and Freeman?"

"Not recently. And if anything happened to them, I don't care."

"You'd better care," Preacher said. "If we're gonna hold out until that boat gets here, we're likely gonna need every man . . . and every gun."

CHAPTER 24

Preacher found the missing men. Courtland had made it through the battle unharmed. Freeman had a bloody gash on his forehead, but insisted he was all right.

"What's one more scar matter to a man who's already as ugly as sin?" he asked with a grin.

Now that the shooting had dwindled away to nothing, the horses were finally settling down again. Courtland eyed them with anger and frustration. "Some of those animals are hurt, and that's going to have an effect on their value."

"They would've been a lot worse off if the whole place had burned to the ground," Preacher pointed out. "And that could've happened mighty easy, too."

The roofs of the fur warehouse, a couple of storage buildings, and one barrack were charred where flaming arrows had started small fires. Only the quick action by men risking their lives to fill buckets and throw water on the flames had saved the buildings.

"There's got to be somethin' we can do to keep those redskins from tryin' that again," Freeman said.

Preacher shook his head. "We can't see what they're doin' in the dark, so we can't stop them from shootin' those flamin' arrows. But we can be better prepared when they do. I'll talk to Langley about havin' plenty of buckets already filled before night falls again. We should go ahead and wet down the roofs real good to keep fires from startin' so easy."

Courtland snorted. "Good luck getting him to listen to any idea of common sense."

Preacher bit back the angry response that sprang to his lips. Clearly, Courtland and Langley were going to continue to nurse their hatred for each other, no matter what the circumstances.

They would be smart not to turn their backs on the other one during a fight, he mused. He wouldn't put it past either man to take advantage of the opportunity to get rid of his rival, once and for all.

Not that there was any real rivalry, Preacher reminded himself. Judith was married to Langley, and he hadn't seen any indication she would consider leaving her husband for Courtland, even though she had spoken up for her old beau a couple of times while the two men were arguing. That didn't mean anything serious. Judith was just trying to be fair.

The worst part about it, Preacher told himself, was that he was devoting precious time and energy to even thinking about that blasted mess, instead of concentrating all his attention on the threat from Red Knife and the Blackfoot war party.

He left Courtland and Freeman taking a closer look at the horse herd and walked toward the trading post. Harrigan caught up to him along the way and asked, "You reckon we'd better toss the bodies of those savages out of the fort? It's liable to make the rest of the varmints even madder if they can't tend to 'em in the Blackfoot fashion."

Preacher nodded. "I don't reckon they could get much madder at us than they already are, but it's the decent thing to do, and I don't see any reason not to be decent. Can you tend to gettin' that done, Quint?"

"Sure," Harrigan agreed. "What are you gonna do?"

"I want to make sure Miz Langley's all right and talk to Langley about gettin' ready for the next time Red Knife and his friends come callin'."

Harrigan nodded and hurried away.

Preacher had seen Langley disappear into the

trading post earlier, so he headed in that direction. Approaching the building, he noticed a small group of men standing on its porch. He heard loud, angry voices as he came closer.

"What's goin' on here?" he demanded as he went up the steps.

One of the men turned to him with a snarl. "I'll tell you what's go—" The man stopped short and took a step back. "Preacher! Sorry, I didn't realize it was you."

The fella was scared of him, thought Preacher. Well, it was true that he had a pretty fearsome reputation, although he rarely took advantage of it. "Just tell me what this is all about."

"Langley's got the door barred," another man said. "After all that fightin', we need powder and shot, and he won't let us in there to get it!"

Preacher frowned. "Let me through."

The crowd parted, and he stepped up to the door and pounded on it a couple of times with his fist. The booshwa didn't respond, so he shouted, "Langley! It's Preacher!"

A moment later he heard the scrape of wood on wood as someone inside lifted the bar on the door. Knowing there might be trouble if the men on the porch tried to bull their way inside, he turned to them and said firmly, "You boys stay back until I get this all sorted out."

One of the men began, "But we need—"

"Stay out here," Preacher cut in. "I know what you need. I'll find out what's goin' on and when you can get it."

Nobody argued with him. They all knew his reputation as a deadly fighter. But there was a lot of unhappy muttering behind him as the door opened a crack.

"Preacher," Langley said as he peered out cautiously through the narrow gap. "What do you want?"

"There are fellas out here who'll need more powder and shot before those Blackfeet make another run at us."

"I know that, and I plan to let them take whatever they need. But I have to make an accounting first."

Preacher's eyes narrowed. "An accounting?" he repeated.

"That's right. The company will want to know exactly what happened to those goods, especially since I won't have any pelts to show for some of them."

Preacher let out a disgusted snort. "You're tellin' me you're worried about those squinty-eyed varmints back East with their ledger books? You've got hundreds of angry Blackfeet outside the walls of this fort, and you're countin' pennies?"

"I've got a job to do," Langley insisted. "I was sent out here, and all the goods in this trading post were sent with me, so I could sell and trade for them and amass shipments of beaver pelts. Being attacked by the Indians doesn't change that."

Preacher didn't see how it could help but change things, but he didn't think he would get very far arguing with Langley. The man was stubborn as a mule. He had already demonstrated that with the grudge he held against Wiley Courtland.

"All right," Preacher said, "but whatever you've got to do, you'd best be quick about it. I don't think Red Knife and his bunch will be back tonight, but we can't count on that. You'd feel like a damn fool if you were in there countin' rifle shot while a hundred of those varmints were scramblin' over the walls with knives in their hands and murder in their hearts."

"It won't take long," Langley assured him. "And then everyone can take what they need."

Preacher started to turn away, but then he paused and asked, "How's Mrs. Langley?"

"Terribly frightened, of course. But she's a brave woman. She's holding up well."

Preacher wondered briefly if Judith had said anything to her husband about the promise she had extracted from him. He had a hunch that she hadn't. "Give her my best," he said gruffly.

Turning back to the other men, he held his hands up to get them to quiet down as they started talking loudly and angrily again. He heard the trading post door close behind him and the bar drop into place. "Settle down and take it easy. You'll get your ammunition."

"Yeah, when the booshwa finishes countin' every ball and every bit of powder," one man said bitterly. "We heard what he said. We're riskin' our lives for this outpost. Some of us have already been killed. He ought to throw the door open and tell us to take whatever we need."

Several men called out agreement with the man who had complained and Preacher recognized the sound. It was the noise of a mob in the making.

"Listen to me, damn it," he said sharply. "We all fought side by side against them Blackfeet. That includes Langley and the other fellas who work for the company. You start breakin' up into different bunches now and you may not be able to count on the man next to you when that war party shows up again. And you're gonna want to be able to count on him, because he may wind up savin' your life."

"Preacher's right," one of the men said. "This ain't the time to be worryin' about such things."

"It ain't the time to be worryin' about having every cent of the company's money accounted for, neither," the first man insisted stubbornly. "If this fort falls, the company loses everything!"

That argument made sense. Preacher said as much, then went on, "Langley knows that, too.

Give him a few minutes to finish what he's doin'. I reckon you'll get all the powder and shot you need after that."

The spokesman for the angry men looked at him with narrowed eyes. "We'll give him those few minutes like you want, Preacher. But he better not take too long."

Preacher stood in front of the door with his arms crossed, for the moment an immovable sentry. He kept his face impassive, but inside he was angry and frustrated that circumstances seemed to be maneuvering him into positions he didn't particularly want to take. He had intervened in the rivalry between Langley and Courtland, and now he was defending Langley's actions on behalf of the company when he found them just as petty and irritating as the other men did.

Luckily, he didn't have to wait long. The bar scraped out of its brackets again, and the door swung open behind him. Langley stepped out onto the porch and looked around. Most of the men were scowling at him.

"Help yourselves to powder and shot," he told them. "And any other supplies you need, too."

"You gonna charge us for 'em later?" asked the trapper who had spoken up earlier.

"No, I'm not. And if my employers back in St. Louis don't like that, they can damned well find somebody else to run this fort." Langley smiled faintly. "Assuming, of course, they don't have to do that anyway because my hair is hanging up in some Blackfoot lodge."

Preacher said, "In that case, there probably won't be no fort left for anybody to run."

Langley stood aside and waved the men into the trading post. He waited until they had trooped inside and then said quietly to Preacher, "You know, I'll probably lose my job over this anyway. But those men are fighting for all of us. I have to give them whatever help I can."

"That's the best way to look at it, all right," Preacher agreed.

"Still, I'd better go inside and, ah, keep an eye on the situation."

"Might not be a bad idea." Preacher knew some of those trappers, but not all of them. There might be some who would try to take advantage of the circumstances, even in the perilous surroundings.

Langley went into the trading post, leaving Preacher standing on the porch. He watched the activity around the compound as Courtland's men tried to quiet the horses, other men made sure all the fires were out except the main one in the center of the compound, and still others carried the bodies of the slain Blackfoot warriors onto the parapet and dropped them over the wall.

No matter how you looked at it, Preacher thought, war was an ugly business.

Red Knife had declared war on Fort Gifford, and only utter annihilation on one side or the other would end it.

CHAPTER 25

Preacher had been right when he said the Blackfeet probably would not attack again that night. Not a single arrow flew after the warriors retreated.

Sometime during the hours of darkness, though, the bodies of the slain warriors disappeared from outside the walls. The Blackfeet had stolen up and reclaimed them, just as Harrigan had predicted.

There was the matter of what to do about the defenders who had been killed. As the sky began to turn gray in the east with the approach of dawn, Preacher tied a rope around one of the sharpened logs forming the stockade wall and let the other end drop outside the fort.

Langley stood nearby watching him and frowned in puzzlement. "What are you doing, Preacher?"

"Goin' out to have a look around," the mountain

man replied. "We need to bury those poor fellas who didn't make it through the fight, but it ain't a good idea to open the gates and send out a burial detail until we're sure Red Knife and his varmints ain't lurkin' somewhere close by."

"I suppose that makes sense," Langley said with a nod. "But you're going alone? Shouldn't you take someone with you? That fellow Harrigan, maybe."

Preacher shook his head. "I can move faster by myself, and if I need to move, chances are it'll be fast."

"We could open one of the gates enough to let you out—"

"The rope's fine," Preacher insisted. "Leave them gates just like they are. And when I'm gone, pull up this rope, too. I'll holler when I'm ready for somebody to let it back down."

"All right," Langley said. "You know what you're doing."

"Damn right I do."

Preacher had rigged a sling on his rifle so he could carry it over his shoulder. The long-barreled flintlock was loaded, and so were the four pistols he carried behind his belt. It was a small arsenal, but if he ran into Red Knife, more than likely he would need every shot.

Preacher climbed carefully over the wall and gripped the rope. While Langley and several other men watched, he braced his feet against the logs and walked down the wall. It took only a moment for him to reach the ground.

He looked up and motioned with his thumb for the men to pull the rope back up. One of them did so, coiling it as he brought it in.

Preacher took his rifle from his shoulder and padded off into the gray shadows of dawn. After being stuck in the fort it felt good to be out there, moving around and breathing in the fresh, cool air of early morning. All of his senses were fully alert as he trotted west along the Missouri River.

He hadn't gone very far when his instincts warned him about a patch of darkness he recognized as a clump of brush. It was a good place for a couple of Red Knife's warriors to keep an eye on the fort, he thought. He slowed and brought his rifle to bear on the brush.

When movement exploded from it, he almost fired. But he held off on the trigger as he recognized the large, shaggy shape bounding toward him.

"Dog!" Preacher said softly.

The big cur raced over to him and reared up to put his front paws on the mountain man's shoulders. Preacher embraced him. "Good to see you again, you old varmint!"

Dog wagged his tail and licked Preacher's bearded cheek like a happy, innocent puppy, rather than the wolf-like, hundred-pound-plus hunting and killing machine he was.

"I knew you were bound to be around here

somewhere and we'd run into each other sooner or later," Preacher said. "You ain't hurt any, are you?"

Dog certainly seemed to be all right. He dropped to all fours again and ran around and around Preacher with boundless enthusiasm.

"Come on. We're scoutin' for Blackfeet."

Dog turned and loped toward the clump of brush from which he had emerged a few moments earlier.

"Come on," Preacher said again.

Dog stopped, looked back over his shoulder at the mountain man, and whined.

"What is it, you ol' scudder? You got a rabbit or somethin' in there?"

Dog whined again, and the sound took on a more urgent tone.

Preacher stiffened and his hands tightened on the rifle as he realized what Dog was trying to tell him. Something was in that brush, all right, and it represented a threat.

"Let's see what you got," Preacher said grimly as he started forward.

He used the barrel of the rifle to part the brush. The sun still wasn't up yet, but the eastern sky was rosy and golden, providing enough light for Preacher to see the buckskin-clad figures sprawled on the ground behind the brush.

Three Blackfoot warriors lay there, dark pools of coppery-smelling blood around the heads of two of them. Dog had ripped out their throats, probably before they were fully aware of what was happening. From the looks of it, Preacher's speculation had been right. Red Knife had left the men there to watch the fort.

The big cur had savaged the third man as well, but he was still alive, Preacher realized suddenly. He heard the man's ragged, shallow breathing.

Quickly but carefully, Preacher reached down and pulled a knife from its sheath on the warrior. He stuck it behind his belt and kicked the tomahawk laying beside the man into the brush where it was well out of reach.

The Blackfoot's injuries were severe. Big gashes covered his face and hands, and his right wrist was swollen and twisted unnaturally, showing that Dog had broken it with a wrench of his powerful jaws. The man had bled quite a bit, and Preacher wouldn't have given good odds for his survival.

But he was still alive, and Preacher wanted to talk to him. He set his rifle aside and knelt next to the warrior. Removing the wooden stopper of the water skin he'd brought with him, he held the skin to the unconscious man's lips and tilted it so some water ran into the warrior's mouth.

That brought him around, choking and gagging slightly.

Preacher set the water skin aside and drew the Blackfoot's own knife, laying the keen blade against the man's throat and pressing down just enough that the warrior knew what it was.

As the man's eyelids fluttered open, Preacher said in the Blackfoot tongue, "Be still, or I'll cut your throat."

Despite his injuries, defiance immediately began to burn in the man's eyes as he realized what was going on. His lips twisted in a snarl. "Go ahead, you white eater of carrion. End my life so I may join my brothers in the spirit world."

"You'll end up with them soon enough. Red Knife left you here to die."

"Red Knife will cut off your head and stick it on a pole!"

That angry threat told Preacher that Red Knife was still alive. He wasn't surprised.

"Why does Red Knife hate the white men so much?" Preacher asked. The war chief's hatred might be just on general principles, but something about the whole affair struck Preacher as personal.

"Because white men killed his sons!" the wounded warrior exclaimed. "They were only boys, and a group of trappers found them. They killed both boys and scalped them."

Preacher drew in a deep breath. That would be enough to do it, all right, he thought. Grief over the deaths of his sons had allowed the worm of madness to crawl into Red Knife's brain, as the Crow had put it.

One thing anybody on the frontier learned very quickly about the hostilities between red men and white was that wrongs and atrocities took place on both sides. Preacher had plenty of friends among the Indians, and often he was angered at the way they were treated.

At the same time, too many of them killed just for the sake of killing and considered spilling the blood of their enemies to be a sport. A deep streak of cruelty ran through many warriors, put there, perhaps, by the hard life they lived and leading them to unconscionable acts. Since long before any white man had ever set foot on the continent, the tribes had preyed on each other. Wanton slaughter was nothing new to the mountains and plains and forests.

So while Preacher might sympathize with Red Knife to a certain extent, it was a far cry from excusing the war chief's actions.

Hate gave the wounded man's voice more strength. "Red Knife has sent runners to all the Blackfoot villages from here to the Shining Mountains. He will bring a mighty army of warriors to destroy the white man's fort and avenge his sons. He will wipe the white men from the face of the earth, which rightfully belongs to the true people!"

"That ain't ever gonna happen, old son," Preacher said. "There ain't that many Blackfeet in the whole world."

"Red Knife will . . . will burn the fort to the ground!" The man's voice began to falter as the strength that had animated him a moment earlier faded. "The white men . . . will all die . . . and the other white men . . . will be too afraid to . . . come into our lands . . ."

Preacher didn't see any point in arguing with a man who was going to be dead in a minute or two. "Go to the spirit world, my friend, and may the hunting there always be good."

"I am not—" The warrior's head sagged back and his eyes glazed over. His spirit had started its journey to whatever destination awaited it.

Preacher left the bodies where they had fallen. When the three warriors didn't come back, Red Knife would send men to search for them. Preacher wasn't quite sure what they would make of it when they found the bodies. The dead men looked like they had been attacked by a pack of wolves.

It was a pretty fair description of what had happened to them, Preacher mused as he resumed his scouting with Dog at his side.

He went a mile upriver, circled back, skirted the fort, and explored the country east of the outpost. By the time he got back to Fort Gifford, the sun was well up and he was confident there were no Blackfeet close by.

As Preacher approached the fort he saw rifle barrels sticking out over the walls and was glad the defenders weren't letting down their guard. A man appeared with the rope, holding it up as if asking if Preacher wanted him to throw it down. The mountain man recognized Quint Harrigan's bristling red beard.

Preacher shook his head and pointed at the gates. "Open 'em up!" he called. "It's safe for the time bein'."

The heavy gates swung back. Ethan Langley strode outside the fort as soon as the opening was large enough.

Harrigan was right behind him, grinning. "I see you found that dog o' yours."

"What else did you find?" Langley asked in a brisk tone of voice. He hadn't had any sleep for more than twenty-four hours, like the rest of them, but he was holding himself together pretty well for someone who wasn't a veteran frontiersman.

"The Blackfeet have pulled back a ways," Preacher reported. "I don't know exactly where they are, but they're far enough off that we ought to have time to lay our dead to rest without them botherin' us."

Several men had emerged from the fort behind Langley and Harrigan, among them Wiley Courtland and Otis Freeman. One of the fur trappers in the group suggested, "Maybe we ought to make a run for it while we got the chance."

"Where are you gonna go?" Preacher asked. "Red Knife's put out the call far and wide for more warriors. No white man's gonna be safe anywhere in these parts until that varmint's dead."

"So what are you sayin', that we should just wait here for those savages to kill us?"

"We should hold out until the supply boat gets here with more men and those cannon," Langley said. "When they do, we'll wipe Red Knife and his men off the face of the earth."

A wry smile tugged at the corners of Preacher's mouth. The booshwa had no way of knowing it, but he had just echoed the threat made by that dying Blackfoot warrior.

As far as Preacher could see, the odds were just about even on which side would get wiped from the face of the earth first.

CHAPTER 26

The six men who had died in the battle were buried on top of a small hill about a quarter mile from the fort. Preacher and several other men went along with the burial detail to act as guards. From the top of the hill they could see a pretty good distance all around. The Blackfeet might still be able to sneak up on them, but at least it was less likely with men keeping watch.

Langley brought his Bible from the trading post and read over the graves while the other men took off their hats and caps and stood around solemnly, knowing it was mostly a matter of luck they weren't among the ones in the ground.

The short service over, everybody headed back to the fort, not losing any time getting behind the sturdy gates and the thick stockade walls. Most of the men heaved sighs of relief when the gates were closed and barred.

With no real work to be done other than keeping watch for the Blackfeet, Preacher said to Langley, "Pick out some men to stand guard. Everybody else needs to get some rest while they can."

"I'm not sure anyone can relax enough to sleep under these circumstances," Langley argued. "Those savages could come back at any time."

"They could," Preacher agreed, "but they can't get near the fort in broad daylight without bein' seen. And when a man who's tired enough gets a chance to sleep, you'd be surprised how quick he forgets about everything else."

Langley shrugged. and said, "I suppose. It's worth a try, anyway."

"Count the men off in fours, and have different shifts on guard duty," Preacher suggested. "Change 'em out every three hours. That way everybody gets to rest." He added, "I'll be part of the first watch."

"That's not necessary. You were already up all night, then you went out and did all that scouting. You should get some sleep now."

When the mountain man opened his mouth to object, Langley smiled and raised a hand to stop him. "It was your idea to take turns standing guard, Preacher."

"All right, all right," Preacher grumbled. "Reckon I *am* a mite tired. I'm not as young as I used to be, you know."

"You have more strength and vitality than any five men here put together. But go and rest, anyway. I'll arrange the guard details. There's a small extra room in my living quarters with a bunk in it. Why don't you go there and lie down?"

"Figured I'd just find a corner somewhere and curl up." If it was good enough for Dog, it was good enough for Preacher.

"There's no need for you to do that," Langley insisted. "Go sleep on a real bed."

That would feel sort of odd to a man accustomed to such a rugged life as he was, thought Preacher, but he supposed he could give it a try. He nodded his thanks and started toward the trading post.

Judith stood on the porch, resting her hands on the railing. "Can I do something for you, Preacher?"

"Your husband's settin' up guard shifts. "We only need about a dozen men at a time keepin' an eye out for the Blackfeet. So the rest of us are gonna get some shut-eye. Mr. Langley said I could use the spare room in your livin' quarters."

"Of course. I'll show you where it is." She smiled. "I hope you don't expect too much. It's really not very fancy."

"I wouldn't know what to do if it was. My idea of fancy is any piece of ground without too many rocks in it."

The trading post was empty as she led him into it. The men had already gotten everything they needed, at least for the moment.

Judith said, "It was very frightening last night,

wasn't it? I mean, when the Indians attacked and all those fiery arrows came raining down on the fort."

"I knew what you meant. And yeah, any man who wasn't scared had to be just too blasted dumb to know what was goin' on."

"Even you were afraid?"

Preacher let out a snort. "I know I got this reputation as the big lobo wolf of these parts, but that don't mean I never get scared. Reckon I get just as scared as anybody else when things are goin' bad."

Judith shook her head. "I really doubt that."

"It's the truth," Preacher insisted. "Maybe the difference is that when things are goin' bad, I feel like I got to put 'em right again, and that means doin' something. Takin' action. And once you start doin' that in the middle of a fight, you're too busy to remember that you're scared. All you're tryin' to do is get from one chore to the next. From one minute to the next, I guess you could say."

"That sounds like a good way to look at things. When the battle was going on, I . . . I didn't do anything but sit in here and hug myself and pray that I would survive." She stopped and turned to look intently at him. "I should have been out there helping. Then I would have been too busy to be frightened, like you said."

Preacher shook his head. "Not in a fight like that. That was no place for you. Do you know how to load a gun?"

"Not really. I've seen Ethan do it, of course."

"Get him to teach you," Preacher suggested. "That way, if there's ever a need for it, you can reload for the men while they're fightin'."

"All right. That sounds like a good idea."

"You might even get him to show you how to shoot a rifle, too, after this is all over. It's a mighty good skill to have out here."

"You sound confident we're all going to live through this siege."

"Well, that's another thing," Preacher said. "If you go into a ruckus thinkin' you're gonna lose, chances are you will. As long as my heart's beatin' and my blood is flowin', I don't intend to give up, no matter what the odds against me."

"I think you deserve that reputation you have. Come on."

Judith took him through the living quarters to a door leading into a narrow space not much more than an enclosed lean-to on the back of the building. But as Langley had said, the room had a bunk in it, and when Preacher saw the straw mattress, he realized just how tired he really was.

"I'll let you get some rest," Judith said. "But before I go, there's one thing . . ."

"Yes, ma'am?" Preacher prompted.

"You didn't forget about the promise you made to me, did you?"

"No, ma'am," he told her with a solemn shake of his head. "I sure didn't."

He didn't mention the fact that he could have been killed in that wild melee on the parapet, in which case he would have been unable to keep the promise.

Judith seemed to be aware of it, anyway, because she reached into the pocket of her dress and took out a small pistol, which she held up to show him. "Just in case. I had Ethan load it for me. I told him I wanted to be able to fight if the Indians broke in here."

"He believed that?"

"He acted like he did, anyway."

Preacher nodded. Sometimes acting like you believed something was the only way to get through the bad times.

He wasn't certain how long he had been asleep when something roused him. Not long enough, that was for sure. As soon as he'd stretched out on the bunk, he had fallen into a deep, dreamless slumber.

Now voices somewhere nearby had disturbed his sleep. They weren't loud, but they held a definite undertone of anger as they went back and forth.

"—shouldn't be here," he heard Judith Langley say.

"I had to see you."

The other voice was somewhat muffled, but Preacher didn't have any trouble recognizing it. It belonged to Wiley Courtland.

"There's no telling what's going to happen," Courtland went on. "We may not live through this."

"Preacher says you should never go into a fight expecting to lose."

"I don't give a damn what Preacher says," Courtland snapped.

The mountain man snorted as he sat up on the bunk. Courtland obviously didn't give a damn about a lot of things. As Judith had told him, he shouldn't be in the booshwa's living quarters, at least not without Langley present, too. It just wasn't proper.

Courtland continued, "I had to tell you how I feel about you, Judith."

"I know that already, Wiley. You've made it perfectly clear, despite the fact that you should have accepted my decision graciously."

"I'm sorry. I can't be gracious when it comes to losing the woman I love."

"Are you sure you love me? Or is it that you just don't want to lose to Ethan?"

"I'll show you how much I really love you," Courtland said harshly.

Preacher didn't like the sound of that. He swung his legs off the bunk and stood up. The last thing in the world he wanted to do was get mixed up deeper in that blasted romantic triangle, but he wasn't going to stand by and do nothing while Courtland made advances to another man's wife.

Judith said sharply, "Wiley, don't."

"You don't mean that," Courtland argued.

"I most certainly do. I love my husband."

For the moment, Preacher stayed where he was. If Judith had cried out, or if he'd heard the sounds of a struggle, he would have stepped in to put a stop to it.

But evidently Judith's rebuke of Courtland had made him hesitate. Preacher wasn't going to interfere if he didn't have to. Judith would probably be embarrassed if she knew he had overheard most of the conversation.

"Your husband doesn't love you," Courtland persisted. "If he did, he wouldn't have dragged you out here to this godforsaken wilderness where you're bound to be killed."

"Ethan swore he'd protect me, and I believe him. The job was too good to turn down. He's going to be an important man in the fur company someday."

Courtland laughed. It was an ugly sound that grated on Preacher's ears.

"You know better than that." Courtland smirked. "He'll never be more than a flunky stuck in some out-of-the-way trading post. If you stay with him, you'll grow old before your time from all the hard work and danger. And that's *if* you survive the Indians and the wild animals and the terrible weather."

"And what could you offer me?" Judith asked. "You're a trader now, too, only in horses instead of furs."

"That horse herd was just an excuse to come out here and find you."

Preacher heard Judith's quick intake of breath.

"Then it's true?" she asked. "You knew I was here all along, like Ethan said?"

"Of course I knew! I asked around until I found out about Langley taking the job with the fur company, and it wasn't difficult to find out where he'd been sent. Don't mistake what I'm saying. I plan to make a nice profit on the horses. But the real reason I came is so I can take you back to St. Louis with me. You'll be safe there, and I can give you a comfortable life."

"I . . . I have a life." Judith's voice trembled with emotion. "My life is here, with Ethan."

"You're wrong. I'm taking you back. We can leave now, today, while the savages are gone. I don't care about the horses anymore. I'll tell Otis to get whatever he can for them and send me my share of the profits. The only important thing is that you'll be with me, where you belong."

Preacher heard feet moving on the puncheon

floor and figured Judith was backing away from Courtland.

"You're insane," she said. "I'm not going any-where with you, Wiley. For one thing, Preacher says it's not safe to leave the fort, even though the Indians have withdrawn for the moment."

"The Indians are gone!" Courtland insisted. "And if we move fast enough, we'll be far away from here before they ever come back. They won't bother us."

"I don't care! I'm married. I won't leave my husband!"

"You will! If I have to drag you—"

Judith cried out then, as Preacher had expected her to earlier. Like it or not, his interference couldn't be postponed any longer. He opened the door and stepped into the main room of the living quarters.

Courtland and Judith stood beside the table. His hands were clamped tightly on her upper arms, and she was shaking her head as she tried to pull free from his grip. Her face was pale with fear.

Preacher crossed his arms. "That's about enough."

CHAPTER 27

Courtland's head jerked around toward the mountain man, grimacing. "Preacher. I didn't know you were here."

"I reckon you didn't," Preacher said in a flat, hard voice.

"Look, my friend, this is none of your business. It's between the lady and me."

"When I see somebody treatin' a woman rough, I make it my business. Let go of her."

"I'm not hurting her—"

Preacher took a step closer. "I said let go."

Courtland took his hands away from Judith's arms and moved back.

As soon as she was free, her hand dipped swiftly into her pocket and came up with the little pistol she had shown Preacher earlier. She pulled back the hammer as she lifted the gun and pointed it at Courtland's face. His eyes widened as he found himself staring down the weapon's barrel no more than six inches away. "Judith, don't!" he exclaimed. "For God's sake—"

"I don't blame you for wantin' to shoot him, ma'am," Preacher broke in, "but it might be a good idea to hold off on it. We're liable to need every man we got when Red Knife shows up again." He could see how tense her finger was on the trigger.

Courtland was mighty close to death, and he seemed to know it, too. His face had gone almost as pale as his hair.

Judith drew in a deep breath and lowered the pistol. Carefully, she let the hammer back down. "Get out of here, Wiley. I don't ever want to see you again."

"You don't mean that." A note of desperation came into Courtland's voice as he spoke.

"I mean every word of it," Judith insisted. "I was willing to accept you as a friend. I wanted to be fair to you. But you've forfeited all that by coming here today and behaving like you did. I see now that we can't be friends after all."

"Of course we can—"

"No." The finality in Judith's tone meant there wouldn't be any more argument.

Courtland realized that and his features hardened into a taut, angry mask. "All right," he snapped. "If you're sure that's the way you want it."

"It is," Judith said.

"I hope you don't have cause to regret that decision someday. Someday soon."

Preacher said, "I think the lady told you to get out."

"I'm going." Courtland gave Judith one more hard look, then turned and stalked out of the living quarters.

Preacher heard his footsteps thudding heavily on the floor in the trading post, then the front door opened. A second later, it slammed behind Courtland.

Judith went pale and started to tremble. She had been holding her emotions in check while Courtland was there. "I . . . I never expected him to do something like that. I knew it bothered him that I chose Ethan over him, but I really did hope that . . . that we could be friends . . ."

"Some fellas just can't seem to see things that way," Preacher said as he came closer to her. "I reckon Courtland's one of 'em." He gestured toward the pistol. "Might be a good idea to put that away."

She lifted it again and stared at it as if she had never seen a gun before and couldn't understand how it had gotten into her hand. After a second she slipped it back into her pocket. "I really was going to shoot him, you know."

"I know. And he knew it, too. He wound up more scared of you than he was of me."

"I don't know about that." Judith gave Preacher

a wan smile. "If he knew how badly I was shaking inside . . ."

"You kept it under control. That's mighty important."

"Maybe. But I . . . I . . ." With a shudder, she stepped toward him.

Preacher reacted instinctively and put his arms around her. There was nothing sensual or romantic about it. He was just comforting a fellow human being, as awkward as that made him feel. He became even more uncomfortable when Judith started to cry. He felt the sobs shaking her body, although she cried in silence.

Given the circumstances, he supposed it was an understandable reaction when Ethan Langley appeared in the doorway, saw them standing like that, and exclaimed, "What the hell is going on here?"

Preacher looked up and saw the angry expression on the booshwa's face. "Miz Langley's mighty upset. Reckon you should be over here instead of me."

"Damn right I should be," Langley snapped as he strode forward. "Take your hands off my wife!"

Preacher stepped back from Judith.

"Ethan, it's not—"

He didn't let her finish. "For God's sake, Preacher, it's bad enough I have to worry about Courtland! Now you're making advances to my wife, too?"

"Ethan, listen to me!" She moved closer to him, putting a hand on his arm as she got between him and Preacher. "It's not what you're thinking."

Preacher was glad Judith had intervened, because judging by the look on the booshwa's face and the way his fists were clenched at his sides, he was ready to throw a punch. Preacher didn't want to hurt the fella, especially over a misunderstanding, but it wasn't his nature to be attacked and not fight back.

"Can't you see I was crying?" Judith went on.

Her tear-streaked cheeks made that pretty obvious, Preacher thought. "I was upset, and Preacher was just trying to comfort me, that's all. It's like he . . . he was my uncle . . . or my grandfather."

Preacher wasn't sure if that made him feel much better or not.

Langley still glared at him, but the man's fists unclenched. He looked at his wife. "What were you upset about?"

A hollow laugh came from Judith. "I listened to that battle for what seemed like hours last night, Ethan. I . . . I didn't know but what any minute a horde of screaming Indians would burst into the trading post and kill me . . . or worse. I didn't know if you were dead or alive. Don't you think all of that is enough to make a person upset?"

"Of course it is," Langley said with a worried frown. "I didn't mean to make things worse, Judith. I'm sorry."

He went to her and took her in his arms. She pressed her tear-dampened face against the front of his shirt.

Langley looked over his wife's shoulder at the mountain man and said gruffly, "Sorry, Preacher. I didn't understand what was going on."

Preacher gave him a curt nod. It was as much forgiveness as he felt like allowing.

Judith hadn't told her husband the real reason she was upset because she didn't want Langley going after Courtland again. Despite her anger, she knew open warfare between the two men wouldn't do anybody any good.

Preacher gave her credit for that. Besides, the things she had said to Langley were no doubt true. She *had* feared for her life, and his, during the battle with the Blackfeet.

"How long did I sleep?" Preacher asked.

"A couple hours," Judith replied. "I'm sorry I disturbed you."

Preacher shook his head. "That's fine. Nothin' to worry about."

"Go back and get some more rest," Langley suggested. "Your turn on guard duty won't come up for a good while yet."

After the confrontation with Courtland, Preacher wasn't sleepy anymore, but before he could decide what to do, Quint Harrigan appeared in the doorway between the trading post's main room and the booshwa's living quarters.

"Hate to bother you folks," Harrigan said, "but I reckon you'd better come take a look at this, Preacher. You, too, Mr. Langley."

"What is it?" Langley asked.

"We got company again." Harrigan didn't have to explain what he meant by that.

Preacher understood.

The Blackfeet were back.

It was a mite quicker than he'd expected. He'd found Red Knife's scouts who'd been selected to keep an eye on Fort Gifford. Pulling the war party back, well away from the outpost was all part of Red Knife's plan. He had hoped the white men would think it was safe to flee the fort, and then he could pounce on them while they were out in the open.

Courtland had almost fallen for that trick. He had wanted to leave the fort and take Judith with him, thinking they could make a run for it. But if they had, they would have been running right into the jaws of death.

Langley turned back to Judith. "Will you be all right?"

"Of course," she replied, summoning up a smile and using the back of her hand to wipe away the damp tracks of her earlier tears. "You go with Mr. Harrigan."

Langley nodded and glanced at Preacher. "Are you coming?"

"You couldn't keep me away."

The three men left the trading post. An electric atmosphere gripped the compound as they strode across it. The men on guard duty stood tensely on the parapet, and they were joined by a number of men who were supposed to be resting. No one was talking, and the expectant silence added to the eerie feeling in the air.

Langley went up one of the ladders first, followed by Preacher and Harrigan. When they were on the parapet, several of the men at the wall stood aside to let them step up and get a good look.

Preacher wasn't surprised by what he saw. Five hundred yards away, the Blackfoot war party waited, some mounted on ponies but most on foot.

The warriors weren't just the survivors of the previous attacks. The war party had grown to bigger numbers, just as the dying scout had said that it would.

As Preacher turned, he saw the ranks of Blackfeet weren't just on one side of the fort. They were lined up all around it.

"My God," Langley said in a choked voice. "We're surrounded. They have us completely cut off. We're trapped."

"We already were," Preacher said grimly. "But now, every man jack can see that for himself, so there won't be any more talk about makin' a run for it. Anybody who tries to slip through those lines will be dead mighty quick."

"But what are we going to do?"

"Same thing we were plannin' on before. We'll hold out until that supply boat gets here and brings those cannons with it."

"Can we actually do that?" Langley didn't sound convinced.

Preacher tilted his head toward the Blackfeet. "We're about to find out, because here they come again!"

CHAPTER 28

The Blackfeet launched several hundred arrows into the air at once. While the shafts arched high in their flight, Langley bellowed at the men in the compound, "Take cover! Take cover!"

They scrambled for whatever shelter they could find as the arrows began to fall. The men on the parapet knelt down as low as they could so the wall protected them. The arrows couldn't reach the small space where the parapet butted up against the logs.

As long as the riflemen on the wall were forced to take cover, they couldn't fire at the charging warriors. Preacher knew they were going to have to risk standing up again.

He moved first, rising high enough to thrust his rifle barrel over the wall. The storm of arrows had slackened some, because half the war party was running toward the fort while the other half continued firing the flint-tipped shafts.

Some of the warriors carried blazing torches to set the walls on fire. Flaming arrows hadn't done the trick, but maybe the blazing brands would.

"Get the ones with the torches!" Preacher shouted to his fellow defenders. "Don't let 'em get to the fort!"

He aimed the rifle, ignoring the arrow whipping past his head less than a foot from his ear. The rifle boomed and kicked against his shoulder. He saw the man he had targeted suddenly stumble and clap a hand to his chest where the rifle ball had gone into his body.

The warrior hung on to the torch with his other hand, and kept running. But only for a couple of steps. He faltered and pitched forward onto his face as death caught up to him. The torch flew from his hand, rolled in the dirt in front of him, and went out.

Unfortunately, there were dozens more just like him, equally intent on setting the fort on fire. They charged all four walls at once. Preacher heard fast, frantic rifle shots all around him but didn't know if they would be enough to stop the deadly charge.

Somebody should have sung out a warning and alerted everybody in the fort to the threat before those Blackfeet got that close. Maybe the guards thought they were just seeing small scouting parties and didn't realize the danger they were in until it was too late.

No matter how it had happened, it was too late to worry about that now, Preacher told himself. All that mattered was stopping the varmints.

And if they couldn't, at least they had to stop any fires along the wall from spreading. As he reloaded, Preacher shouted, "Langley! Get men with buckets of water up here!"

Langley jerked his head in a nod to show he understood and headed for the closest ladder. As he grasped it, an arrow arched down and stuck in the top rung. The shaft quivered from the impact.

He kicked it loose, swung onto the ladder, and started down.

Quint Harrigan had taken a position at the wall close to Preacher. He drilled one of the attackers, then grinned at Preacher and called, "Stubborn varmints, aren't they?"

He staggered suddenly, his eyes widening in pain and shock. An arrow was stuck through his neck, appearing so suddenly it was almost like magic.

Preacher shouted, "Quint!" and took a step toward his friend, but it was too late to do anything for Harrigan. The life was already fading from his eyes as he wheeled around aimlessly and plunged off the parapet.

Sorrow and grim anger welled up inside Preacher as he saw Harrigan fall. He turned back to the wall. His rifle was loaded and ready to go. He drew a bead and fired, but he didn't take any satisfaction from the way a Blackfoot warrior's head exploded as the ball bored through his brain.

Quint Harrigan was just as dead either way.

Another warrior snatched up a fallen torch and the attack continued.

Men carrying buckets of water scrambled up the ladders onto the parapet. Preacher pointed to where the base of the wall was on fire about twenty feet to his right. "Dump your buckets there! Some of you stay back in reserve!"

It was utter chaos along the parapet as men fired at the attackers while others tried to extinguish the flames breaking out here and there. All the while, arrows continued to fall. Men screamed in pain and shouted curses and whispered prayers. Clouds of powder smoke rolled through the air and stung eyes and noses. The Indians were so close Preacher set his rifle aside and started using his pistols. At least one Blackfoot fell with every shot he fired.

Through eyes watering from the smoke, Preacher saw the attackers falling back. Their efforts to torch the place had failed, and the deadly accurate shots from him and the other defenders were driving them off.

He leaned out to look back and forth along the wall. There were some charred places, but the wall was intact, without too much damage done. He faced the men and ordered, "Make sure all the fires are out!"

Several men had formed fire lines, and continued passing buckets from the ditch to the ladders and up to the parapet.

Preacher looked around. Several bodies slumped here and there with arrows protruding from them. The attack had cost the defenders more men, and Quint Harrigan was among them. The red-bearded trapper's body lay on the ground, blood from his mangled throat forming a dark puddle around his head.

Harrigan was far from the first friend Preacher had lost, and doubtless he would be far from the last, too. But the man's death still hurt. He had been a valiant fighter, and could always be counted on for a quick grin and a joke.

Preacher didn't dwell on those thoughts as he made sure his rifle and all four pistols were reloaded. The best way to honor Harrigan's death was to be ready when the men who had killed him attacked again.

Preacher figured the war party numbered at least four hundred. The fort's defenders had inflicted a lot of casualties on the Blackfeet, but they were still overwhelmingly outnumbered.

The walls of Fort Gifford were the only things standing between the white men and death.

Red Knife was smart enough to know that, which was why he had concentrated his efforts on the walls. As long as the Blackfeet were willing to die, he could continue his attack again and again until the defenders were whittled down to the point that they couldn't hold the walls.

When that happened, it would be all over.

It was a race between certain death and the arrival of the supply boat from downriver.

In any siege, there were lulls in the action, and that was just the case. The Blackfeet withdrew, but not out of sight. They wanted the fort's defenders to know they were still there.

Preacher was well aware Red Knife wanted the men in the fort to sit in there and contemplate their imminent death.

People who thought of Indians as ignorant savages were really the ignorant ones, Preacher mused as dusk finally settled over the landscape after a long day of waiting. Red Knife was a good example of the sort of intelligence and cunning Preacher had come up against many times in his adventurous career.

In the end, the outcome was likely to depend on brute force, and the war chief had it all on his side, at least for a while. Four cannon and plenty of powder and shot could change that in a hurry . . . and Red Knife didn't know the boat was on its way upriver. If he wanted to take his time, it was just fine with Preacher.

Otis Freeman came up beside the mountain man and leaned on the wall to peer out into the gathering shadows. Fires were visible along the Blackfoot lines. They would be cooking their supper soon.

"I haven't had a chance to tell you I'm sorry about your friend Harrigan," Freeman said. "I talked to him some. Seemed like a good fella."

"He was," Preacher agreed. "I didn't know him all that well, but you could count on him in a fight and he was always ready to smile, even in the middle of trouble. I'll miss him."

"Too bad we can't bury him and the others."

Six men had lost their lives in the battle that morning. The survivors couldn't venture outside the walls to lay them to rest, not with the war party waiting only a few hundred yards away, so the bodies had been wrapped in blankets and put in the trading post's root cellar. It was a temporary solution and one surely destined not to work out well, but it was the best they could do.

"We'll make sure they're tended to proper once this is all over," Preacher said.

"They'll have a nice funeral pyre when the whole place is burned down around us."

Preacher shook his head. "You folks give up too

easy. As long as a man's still alive and can fight, he's got a chance, even if it ain't much of one. I'll take a slim chance over none, any day."

Freeman chuckled. "Yeah, you're right about that, I suppose. Still, I sort of wish I'd never signed on to help Wiley bring those horses out here. It seemed like a good idea at the time."

"The two of you are old friends?" Preacher asked.

"No, not really. We've known each other for a few years. I drove some, now and then, for his freight line. This was a chance to do somethin' more than just workin' for wages. I figured we could maybe make a real business out of it. You know, bring a couple herds out every year. Wouldn't be too long until our horses were all over the frontier."

"It wasn't a bad idea. Maybe it'll work out yet."

"We'll see. We've got to live through the next few days first."

Freeman was right about that, thought Preacher . . . and living through the next few days wasn't going to be easy.

CHAPTER 29

Time crawled. Somehow, minutes became hours and hours became days. Tension so thick hung in the air over the fort sometimes it seemed difficult to breathe. It was hard to believe men could be bored while waiting to die, but that was exactly what happened to the defenders of Fort Gifford.

Unfortunately, over the next several days, any time the boredom was broken meant bloody fighting and more death.

The Blackfeet attacked at least once a day, showering arrows into the fort until it seemed impossible they would have any left. Indeed, as the number of shafts decreased with each attack, Preacher began to think maybe they really were running out. They couldn't recover the ones that fell inside the walls, and they didn't have an endless supply.

Several times, the warriors tried to set the fort

on fire. Preacher and the other riflemen on the parapet drove them off with deadly accurate shooting.

In each battle, though, several defenders died or were wounded so badly they were out of the fight. Judith Langley was kept busy not only cooking but also tending the injured men as best she could. It was probably good for her, Preacher thought. Having so much to do wouldn't allow for time to be scared. For her sake, he hoped that was true at least part of the time.

The men had a gaunt, hollow-eyed look about them. No one was sleeping much. Only about forty men were left alive in the fort, and guards had to be posted around the clock. There was no telling when the Blackfeet might attack again.

Preacher was standing on the trading post's porch drinking a cup of coffee when Ethan Langley came up to him. The booshwa's face was haggard and drawn. He looked like he had lost twenty pounds in the past week.

"Another few days and the boat will be here," Langley commented. "I'm starting to think we might make it after all, Preacher."

Preacher was feeling unusually pessimistic. "You don't even know for sure the boat's comin'."

"It was supposed to be here sometime between the seventeenth and the twenty-fourth. Today is the fifteenth."

"That's if it didn't get delayed somehow, or the trip wasn't canceled completely."

"The company would have sent word."

"Which wouldn't have gotten here yet, either."

"You're the one who told everybody not to give up hope," Langley pointed out.

Preacher smiled humorlessly and shrugged. He took a sip of his coffee. "You're right about that. Reckon the strain's startin' to get to me."

"I don't believe that. You're Preacher."

"Yeah, well, that don't make me no damned miracle worker!" Wearily, Preacher rubbed a hand over his face and then muttered, "Sorry. Too little sleep and too much killin'. It starts to wear on a body after a while."

Langley nodded. "Yes, indeed it does. I'm amazed we're all holding up as well as we are."

"What about Miz Langley? Every time I see her she's got a smile on her face, but she must be about wore out."

Langley looked concerned. "Yes, she's been my rock. But even a rock will wear down eventually." He grunted. "At least Courtland has kept his distance. I have to be thankful for that. With everything else that's going on, Judith doesn't need him annoying her, too."

Preacher didn't say anything. From the sound of it, Judith still hadn't mentioned the confrontation with Courtland. It was the smart thing to do.

Courtland had been in the thick of every battle,

and Preacher didn't think the man had gotten so much as a scratch. That was the way it seemed to work sometimes. Lady Luck watched over one man while turning her back on another, and there was no real rhyme or reason to her choices.

Not all of the men Courtland had brought with him had been so fortunate. Boylan was dead, skewered by an arrow during one of the ruckuses, and Prince was laid up with a bad wound in his leg. Freeman, Elkins, and Dalton were still able to fight, although they had picked up a few nicks and bruises.

"If we do get through this," Preacher said, "we'll have Miz Langley to thank for some of it. She's been an inspiration to everybody."

"I agree, although she's too modest to see it that way."

Preacher drank the last of his coffee and handed the empty cup to Langley. "If you're goin' in, you can take this for me. I'm headed back up on the wall. That coffee ought to keep me goin' for a while."

Langley glanced up at the sky. "The sun will be going down in another hour or so. Do you think they'll attack again tonight?"

"I reckon you can count on it."

Darkness had fallen. The Blackfeet had demonstrated they were willing to attack at any hour of the day or night, so the defenders couldn't let down their guard. Preacher was on the parapet near the gates with every sense on alert when Otis Freeman approached him.

"Preacher, have you seen Wiley?"

"You mean here, lately?" Preacher frowned in thought and shook his head. "No, I can't say as I have. Not since some time this afternoon."

Freeman rubbed his jaw. The gash on his forehead was healing, but it would leave an ugly, puckered scar. As he had mentioned earlier, it wouldn't really make much difference. "It's been a couple hours since I saw him. I looked around the fort, and I can't find him."

"He's got to be here somewhere," Preacher said.

"Maybe. Maybe not."

"You're thinkin' he might've gone over the wall and took off for the tall and uncut?"

"I'd hate to think that he'd abandon us, but if he's not here . . ."

Preacher nodded toward the darkness outside the fort. "No way he made it through all them Blackfeet without them catchin' him. If he went out there, he's likely dead by now." The mountain man paused. "Either that, or they're savin' him."

"Why would they do that?"

"To put on a show for us. They might tie him to a post and build a fire at his feet and burn him that way. Or they could build a fire and hang him upside down over it, so his brain cooks until his head explodes. Or just torture him for five or six hours so we hear him screamin' the whole time." Preacher shrugged. "There's not much tellin' what they might decide to do, but you can count on it bein' pretty bad."

"Good Lord," Freeman muttered. "I hope he's still here and I just couldn't find him. I wouldn't wish something like that on my worst enemy."

"Neither would I," Preacher agreed. "If they've got him and they try somethin' like that, I'll do my best to put a bullet in his head. That'd put him out of his misery and cheat those varmints out of their sport."

"Maybe it won't come to that. I'm gonna go look around some more."

"You do that. I hope you find him." Preacher had a hunch Freeman wouldn't be able to locate Courtland, though. There weren't that many places inside the fort for someone to be.

More time passed. When Preacher's shift on guard duty was over, he climbed down from the parapet. The past few days he had taken to sleeping on the ground next to the fur warehouse instead of in the extra room in the booshwa's living quarters. With a ladder only a few steps away, he could get back on the parapet in a hurry any time trouble broke out.

At the moment, despite the nearly non-stop exhaustion that gripped all the defenders, he was more hungry than sleepy, so he headed for the trading post where Judith Langley kept a fire burning in the stove and a pot of stew simmering on it nearly all the time. Preacher thought he might get a bowl of it before he turned in.

When he came into the trading post he didn't see Judith, or anyone else, for that matter. It was possible she was over at the barracks where the wounded men had been taken, changing their dressings or using a cool rag to wipe the foreheads of the men who had fevers.

As Preacher moved toward the back of the room he heard someone talking. The door into the living quarters was slightly ajar, and the voices came from in there. One of them was female.

Preacher didn't think anything of it as he leaned his rifle against the wall near the stove. He figured Judith and Langley were back there talking. Then he remembered seeing Langley outside as he headed across the compound. So it wasn't the booshwa in the living quarters with Judith.

That still didn't have to mean anything, but when her voice suddenly got louder, filled with anger and alarm, Preacher knew something was wrong. He wasn't a bit surprised when he stepped closer and recognized Courtland's urgent tones.

The fella just didn't know when to give up, Preacher thought disgustedly. He hadn't learned last time, so maybe the lesson ought to be a mite more stern.

"—*have* to come with me, Judith," Courtland was saying as Preacher came up to the door. "You don't have any choice. It's your only chance. Otherwise you'll die tonight."

"You're mad!" Judith told him. "Wiley, for God's sake, what have you done?"

Preacher shoved the door open. "Yeah, Courtland, I want to know that, too. What are you up to, you—"

He didn't get a chance to finish the question. At that moment, someone outside the trading post shrieked in pain, shots began to roar, and a man yelled in sheer terror, "They're here! *The Indians are inside the walls!*"

CHAPTER 30

In the split second Courtland whirled around to face him and all hell broke loose outside, Preacher knew the horse trader had something to do with what was happening. Without knowing how it was possible or what Courtland hoped to gain, every instinct in the mountain man's body told him it was true.

Preacher grabbed one of the pistols tucked behind his belt.

At that same instant, Courtland's hand shot out and snatched up the oil lamp burning on the table beside him. With a shouted curse, he threw it at the mountain man.

Preacher flung up his left arm to shield his face. The lamp broke, sending blazing oil cascading down his arm. The sleeve of his buckskin shirt protected his flesh, but he still felt the fiery heat.

Courtland barreled into him, dragging a screaming Judith behind him. The collision knocked Preacher off his feet. He made a grab for Courtland's leg but missed. And he couldn't shoot with Judith between him and Courtland.

The two vanished through the door leading into the main room of the trading post.

Preacher scrambled to his feet and slapped out the flames still burning on his oil-soaked sleeve. Not all of the oil had landed on him, and he spent precious time stomping out patches of fire on the puncheons where oil had spilled on the floor.

Once he was confident the building wasn't going to burn down, he jerked a second pistol from behind his belt and rushed to the door.

Stepping onto the porch was like stepping into a nightmare.

He might have saved the trading post from burning—for the moment—but the barracks of the wounded men was ablaze, and the blood-chilling screams Preacher heard over the roar of gunshots and the crackling of flames told him some of the badly injured hadn't been able to get out.

The Blackfeet seemed everywhere, shrieking war cries and laying waste to the defenders with tomahawks, knives, and clubs. Arrows hummed through the air, but most of the slaughter was being carried out close up.

The gates stood wide open, so there was no doubt how the warriors had gotten into the fort.

Despite being overrun and outnumbered, the men were putting up a fight. Preacher saw desperate struggles going on everywhere he looked. Before plunging into the melee, he saw Otis Freeman on top of the parapet using a broken rifle to flail away at the Blackfeet surrounding him. Blood streamed from a dozen wounds, but Freeman stood tall, swinging the rifle, breaking bones, and crushing skulls.

But suddenly Freeman lurched forward and toppled off the parapet. As he fell, Preacher saw the tomahawk lodged in the back of Freeman's head. The weapon had shattered his skull and buried itself in his brain, killing him.

Preacher didn't see Courtland or Judith, but he figured they had to be around, unless they had made their way through the chaos and escaped through the gates.

Considering at least a couple of hundred bloodthirsty Blackfoot warriors were still outside the fort, Preacher didn't think it was much of an escape.

Those thoughts flashed through his brain in a matter of seconds. Then he leaped down from the porch and threw himself into the battle.

A warrior lunged at him, tomahawk lifted for a killing blow. Preacher raised the pistol in his right hand and fired it into the Blackfoot's face at a range of two feet. The warrior's head blew apart in a pink spray of blood, bone, and brain matter. Preacher stepped aside to let the body collapse beside him.

He pivoted and fired the left hand pistol, gunning down a warrior about to plunge a knife into the back of a defender already struggling with two opponents.

Preacher's shot delayed the man's death only a second. A knife raked across his throat and opened up a gaping wound from which blood poured. The man went down, gagging and dying.

As half a dozen warriors charged him, Preacher stuck the empty pistols behind his belt and grabbed the other two guns tucked away there. His thumbs pulled the hammers back as he lifted the pistols. The weapons roared and spouted smoke and flame. Three Blackfeet went down like they had been scythed.

Preacher didn't wait for the remaining three to attack him. He charged ahead and smashed the empty pistol in his right hand into the nearest man's face. Bone crunched under the blow's terrible force and the warrior flew off his feet.

Preacher ducked under a swinging tomahawk and swept the pistol in his left hand up and around. The barrel shattered the Indian's jaw and sent him spinning senseless to the ground.

The final warrior thrust his knife at Preacher. Twisting away, the mountain man couldn't avoid it fully. He felt the blade's fiery bite as it went into his side, but the wound was a shallow one. Before the warrior could launch a backhanded stroke with the knife, Preacher drove his heel into the man's right kneecap, snapping it. The Blackfoot yelped in pain as his leg folded up under him and dumped him on the ground. Preacher brought his foot down on the man's neck, crushing his windpipe.

The men Preacher had killed or put out of action in that brief whirlwind of bloody violence didn't even make a dent in the attacking forces. The Blackfeet continued to swarm over the compound, wantonly killing every white man they found. It was murder, pure and simple, and Preacher knew there was no way he could stop it.

All he could do was take as many of the attackers to hell with him as he could.

Except he didn't have to go to hell, he realized as he stowed the empty guns behind his belt, snatched a couple of fallen tomahawks from the ground, and waded into the slaughter.

Hell had come to Fort Gifford.

Preacher didn't feel the wounds, didn't taste the blood in his mouth, didn't even hear the shouts and screams anymore. He felt the hot rush of blood in his veins and heard the trip-hammer slugging of his heart. He was wrapped up in a cocoon of madness where nothing existed except death . . . the deaths of Blackfeet he struck down with the tomahawks, right and left, right and left, and his own inevitable end. At that moment, in that place, the entire universe was a massacre . . . Preacher's massacre. He embraced it because there was nothing left to do.

Suddenly tackled from behind, he was knocked off his feet and driven to the ground. He twisted around to strike out when he heard a familiar voice.

"Preacher, no! It's me, Ethan Langley!"

Preacher almost brained Langley with one of the tomahawks anyway. Finally realizing who the man was, the madness holding Preacher in its grip broke.

The booshwa clutched at his arm. "Have you seen Judith?"

After giving his head a little shake to clear it, Preacher said, "She was with Courtland."

"Courtland! What—"

"I think he let the Blackfeet in here." Preacher wasn't sure how—or why—Courtland had accomplished such an act of treachery, but his gut told him that was what had happened.

The two men were sprawled on the ground near the trading post. It was a momentary island in the sea of bloody chaos. Bodies, red and white alike, littered the ground around them.

The stockade walls were on fire and so were most of the buildings inside the compound. It was only a fluke the raiders had turned their attention elsewhere for the moment. The respite surely wouldn't last long.

"You were . . . you were shouting and hitting at the air with those tomahawks," Langley said. "You had already killed all the savages within reach."

"Reckon I went a mite loco," Preacher admitted, "but I'm all right now. In fact, I'm thinkin' we're gonna make our stand here, Langley. You still got kegs of gunpowder in the tradin' post, don't you?"

"A dozen or so. But I have to find Judith—"

"There's nothin' you can do for her now." Preacher's voice was harsh and unrelenting. "Go grab some of those kegs while you got the chance."

"What are you going to—"

"Just get the powder!" Preacher ordered. He pulled himself to his feet.

Langley did the same and staggered into the trading post, reappearing a minute later with two wooden kegs tucked under his arms.

Preacher took one of them and smashed the top open with a tomahawk. He slung the powder all over the ground in front of the trading post. As he took the second keg from Langley, he said, "Go get more."

Langley obeyed. Preacher supposed the man's brain was too numb to do anything except follow orders. He threw the contents of the second keg near that of the first, using the last of it to lay a short trail to the base of the porch steps.

Suddenly he spotted a familiar figure striding arrogantly across the compound. A grin appeared on Preacher's face as he shouted, "Red Knife!"

The Blackfoot war chief heard him and turned. His face twisted in hatred. He shouted guttural commands, and a dozen warriors raced toward the trading post.

Preacher pulled one of the empty pistols from behind his belt and knelt as if he were praying. Actually, he cocked the gun and rested the hand holding it on the ground, waiting until the charging warriors, bristling with knives and tomahawks, were almost on top of him.

He pulled the trigger.

The hammer fell and the flint struck. A spark leaped from it, landing in the powder trail and igniting it. Sparks shot along the ground, leaping and dancing, and when they reached the powder Preacher had scattered on the ground, it went off as well with a great flash. The warriors charging through it suddenly found themselves engulfed in fire.

Preacher leaped back onto the steps as Langley emerged from the trading post carrying two more powder kegs. Preacher grabbed one and heaved it into the flames. It exploded in a huge incendiary burst and spread blazing death to more Blackfeet.

Langley followed suit and threw the other keg into the fire. It blew up, too. Flames shot high in the air. The stench of burning flesh clogged Preacher's nostrils. He was in Hades, all right, and he figured he'd soon be shaking hands with the Devil.

A devil named Red Knife.

It was not to be. A tomahawk came streaking through the flames and smashed into Preacher's head. He felt himself falling, toppling down, down, into red-shot darkness. He cursed, disappointed that he had missed his chance to kill Red Knife before dying himself.

Then the darkness claimed him, and all was oblivion.

CHAPTER 31

Death hurt like hell, and it was noisy, too. Instead of hearing harps playing and angels singing, Preacher heard flames crackling and men screaming. That wasn't right, he thought. Death was supposed to be peaceful. That was why whenever somebody died folks said, "Rest in peace."

There was a perfectly reasonable explanation for that, considering the sort of life he'd led, he told himself. He really was in hell. The real thing, not a battle in some wilderness outpost. He could expect a lot of pain and racket, and it would go on for all eternity.

It was sort of puzzling, though, how Satan's imps were yelling to each other in Blackfoot.

That oddity finally prompted him to open his eyes and realize he wasn't dead after all.

The next thing to it, maybe. His head pounded with agony and his mouth was full of blood. The coppery taste of it made him gag. A great weight pressed down on him. When he tried to move, whatever it was yielded slightly, but the weight itself didn't go away. He was trapped.

He couldn't see anything, crowded as he was by all the stuff around him. Through a sudden red glow, Preacher caught a glimpse of a lifeless eye only a couple of inches from his face. A dead man's face was pressed right up against his.

In fact, he was completely surrounded by dead men.

It took all of Preacher's iron will to keep from shouting in horror as he figured out he was lying in a pile of corpses, awash in the blood leaking from them. His stomach lurched. He fought to control it. He couldn't allow himself to be sick, any more than he had allowed himself to cry out.

If he did anything at all to alert the Blackfeet that he was still alive, in a matter of moments he would be as dead as all the other luckless fighters in the gruesome pile.

The faint, reddish glow revealing Preacher's grim surroundings faded, and he realized someone must have walked past carrying a torch. A member of Red Knife's war party, no doubt. No white man would be walking around unmolested. He still heard screams now and then and knew the warriors were finishing off the few surviving defenders.

The Blackfeet believed he was already dead, or

they would have taken quick steps to ensure it was true.

It was that head wound from the tomahawk, he thought. A gash in the scalp always bled like a son of a gun. He must have *looked* so convincingly dead they'd picked him up and tossed him in a pile with the other corpses.

Preacher's thoughts were fuzzy and meandering. The tomahawk might not have killed him, but it had given him such a wallop it was hard to think straight. His brain wandered back a few moments to what happened before he lost consciousness.

Actually, one white man might be able to walk around inside the fort without the Blackfeet killing him.

The traitor, Wiley Courtland.

Preacher had no proof Courtland had let the warriors into the fort. But if he hadn't, why had he gone to Judith and told her she had to go with him, that she had to get out of the fort right away or else she would die tonight?

The answer was that Courtland had known what was about to happen. Even in Preacher's muddled state, he knew that made the most sense.

Courtland's earlier disappearance from the fort had to be considered, too. Had he gotten out and gone to make his deal with Red Knife, then slipped back in to get Judith? That seemed feasible, although there were plenty of blank spots that needed to be filled in.

Time for that later, Preacher told himself. He forced his thoughts toward a much more basic problem.

How in the world was he going to get out of there?

Sooner or later the Blackfeet would get around to burning the pile of bodies in which he lay. He had to escape before that happened, which meant he had to get out from under the stifling weight. If he could reach the open, he could make a run for it. The odds would be against him, but it was still dark. At least he would have a chance of giving them the slip.

A chance, however slim, was all he wanted.

Preacher began by moving his arm, slowly and carefully. It was doubtful the Blackfeet were watching the bodies very closely, since they believed everybody in the pile was dead, but they might notice if those corpses started shifting. Preacher moved an inch at a time, knowing slow progress ought to be invisible in the flickering light from the flames of burning buildings.

The stench of blood and the human wastes released at the moment of death sickened him, as did the clammy feel of lifeless flesh all around him. He forced down the primitive impulse to scream. Slow and steady, he told himself. Slow and steady. Shift here. Shift a little more. Plant a foot against a blood-slick corpse and push.

Preacher had never undertaken a grimmer

task than crawling through corpses stacked like cordwood. Since he couldn't see much of anything, he hoped he was working his way toward the end of the pile and not burrowing deeper into the charnel mound.

When the crimson glow of firelight reappeared and grew stronger, he knew he was getting closer to the edge. Keep going, he told himself. When he got to a point where he could see, then he could pause and figure out his next move.

A man's voice shouted not too far away. It took a second for Preacher to realize the bitter curses were in English.

The voice belonged to Ethan Langley.

Preacher was just as shocked to find out that Langley was still alive as he was by his own continued existence. The screaming had stopped, so he'd figured the Blackfeet had succeeded in wiping out the rest of the fort's defenders.

Langley was not only still alive, he was furious.

Preacher had a hunch only one man could be the target of that much anger from the booshwa.

Sure enough, Courtland's voice came to Preacher's ears. "Let him go. I'm not afraid of him."

"Ethan, no!"

That was Judith, Preacher thought. Courtland would have seen that she stayed alive. If the horse trader had made a deal with Red Knife, as Preacher suspected, the war chief might have honored Courtland's wishes.

But Courtland was taking an awful chance. Even if Red Knife had given his word, he might consider it meaningless since Courtland was white. Red Knife could turn on them and slaughter both.

Cautiously, Preacher pulled himself in the direction of the light and the voices. He eased aside a dead man's leg and found himself with a narrow gap through which he could see into the compound. His eyes narrowed against the nightmarish glare of flames consuming the trading post and the fur warehouse next to it. The blazes were enormous, casting waves of heat across the ground inside the ruined fort.

About forty feet away, Ethan Langley stood between two Blackfoot warriors, who released him at a guttural order from their war chief. Red Knife faced Langley and Courtland. A dozen feet separated the former rivals. Judith stood next to Courtland. His hand clamped around her arm kept her from running to her husband.

Langley looked like he was in pretty bad shape. Blood from several wounds stained his shirt, and his face was smeared with gore. But he was on his feet, even though he didn't seem too steady, and he glared defiantly at Courtland and Red Knife.

"A chance to kill you, that's all I ask, Courtland," Langley rasped in a voice hoarse from smoke. "Give me a knife, or even just my bare hands. I don't care. Just a chance."

Courtland laughed. "And why would I do that? I have what I want. Judith is mine now."

"No!" she cried. "I'm not, and I never will be!"

Courtland ignored her and went on. "Do you know why I asked Red Knife to have his men spare your life, Langley?" He didn't wait for an answer. "I want to kill you myself. You've had it coming for years, and finally I'm going to rid myself of you, once and for all."

"A fair fight, an unfair fight, I don't care," Langley pressed. "If I get my hands on you, I'll kill you."

Courtland shook his head. "I'm not that big a fool." He shoved Judith toward Red Knife. "If you'll hold the lady for me, Chief . . ."

Proving he'd had enough of the delay, Red Knife spoke in English. "End this, Courtland. It does my people no good."

"Don't worry, I'm going to finish it myself right now," Courtland assured him.

Red Knife took hold of Judith's arms from behind as she screamed at Courtland, "I hate you! I'll never love you, Wiley, never! I'll never forgive you for what you've done!"

"Then I can't make things any worse between us, can I?" Courtland asked coolly. "Still, you'll cooperate with me, Judith. If you want to live, you'll have no choice."

"I don't want to live!" she cried. "Not after this!"

"Judith, no!" Langley exclaimed. "You have to survive somehow—"

"No!"

"Time to end this." Courtland drew a pistol from his belt and cocked it.

While they were carrying on Preacher had been easing himself forward, still moving slowly and carefully. He had abandoned any thoughts of getting away. Like Ethan Langley, he wanted to kill Courtland. He had fought side by side with the man, had almost considered him a friend, but he felt only a deep loathing for him. Courtland had cast aside everything in order to get what he wanted. He was lower than a snake in Preacher's eyes.

Preacher tried to pull his right leg up, but suddenly it wouldn't budge. His ankle was trapped in the angle between a couple of dead limbs. It was like the corpses had latched on to him and didn't want to let him go. He imagined they were trying to pull him back deeper into the pile, and a fresh wave of horror surged through him.

But he was more horrified by what he witnessed next, unable to do anything except lie there and watch events unfold.

Courtland cocked the pistol and raised it to aim at Langley. The warriors flanking the booshwa moved aside, well out of the line of fire.

Courtland smiled. "Burn in hell, Langley."

Judith screamed and twisted enough to ram her knee into Red Knife's groin. As the war chief grunted in pain, his grip on her slipped and she pulled free. She dashed toward her husband.

Just as Courtland pressed the pistol's trigger.

The ball struck Judith in the back, passed all the way through her body, and burst out the front of her dress in a spray of blood. She staggered as her eyes widened in shock. She gasped, "Ethan!" as Langley howled, "Nooooo!"

Then Judith pitched forward onto her face and lay motionless as the red stain on the back of her dress continued to spread.

CHAPTER 32

The tragic scene froze everyone into place, but only for a split second that seemed much, much longer.

Then Langley, no longer being held by the warriors, lunged at Courtland, his arms outstretched and his fingers hooked into claws as he screamed out his hate.

At the same time Preacher gave his leg a violent wrench, and it popped loose from the macabre grip of the corpses. Covered in blood from head to foot, he hauled himself out of the pile and stumbled to his feet.

"Courtland!" he croaked in a harsh, hollow voice.

Courtland's head jerked toward Preacher, who looked like he had just climbed up out of a grave to come back and avenge the dead. The distraction gave Langley the chance to reach Courtland

and crash into him, locking his hands around the man's neck as they both went down.

For a second it looked like Langley might get his wish and Courtland would die at his hands.

But the Blackfoot war chief stepped in and plunged a knife into Langley's back.

Langley screamed. His body arched in agony. Courtland heaved him aside and scrambled away. Langley looked around and crawled toward his wife with the handle of the knife still protruding from his back. He stretched out a hand toward her . . .

And slumped down dead before he could touch her. His hand rested on the ground, reaching for her.

Red Knife rapped a command and several warriors charged toward Preacher. Even if he was afraid the bloody figure was a spirit, the war chief was pragmatic enough to see whether or not knives and tomahawks would strike it down.

Preacher's brain worked as swiftly as it ever had and he quickly realized that the several warriors between him and Courtland eliminated his chance to kill the horse trader. He also realized that simplified things. He had to live.

He had to kill Courtland before he died, which meant he couldn't die at the hands of the warriors moving toward him.

The closest warrior swung a tomahawk at his head. Preacher went low, moving under the blow and wrapping his arms around the man's thighs. With a yell, he lifted the warrior off his feet and sent him spilling over his back. When the man dropped the tomahawk, Preacher's hand flashed out to snatch it from the ground. He pivoted, brought the tomahawk up, and used it to rip open the belly of another warrior.

Preacher used his shoulder to knock the disemboweled man aside. The tomahawk crunched into the forehead of a third warrior. Red Knife shouted orders, summoning more and more of his men.

Preacher already had what he wanted, though: a narrow lane through the men trying to kill him. Arrows whipped past his head, but he was moving so fast none of the archers could draw a bead on him. In fact, several of the hastily fired shafts missed him and struck other warriors.

The Missouri River was a hundred yards away. Preacher ran toward it, arms and legs pumping and flying. Shapes appeared in front of him and tried to stop him, but he smashed them down without slowing. The same madness that had come over him earlier had him in its grip again. Then his only goal had been to kill. Now his aim was to escape . . . so he could kill again.

The thought that he was already dead flashed through his mind. Maybe his body was so filled with arrows it looked like a pincushion, and he just didn't know it. He figured the fatal message would catch up to his crazed brain any second.

But until it did, he kept running and fighting.

Suddenly, the river was in front of him, its surface silvery in the moonlight instead of muddy. He threw the tomahawk aside and left his feet in a long, clean dive that carried him far out from the shallow bluff forming the bank.

He struck the cold water and went under. Icy shock careened through his body, numbing it from every pain as effectively as his temporary madness had. The frigid sensation braced him and cleared his mind. He stroked with his arms and kicked his feet, still under the surface.

It was too dark to see much of anything, but he sensed disturbances in the water around him and knew the Blackfeet were firing arrows at the spot he had disappeared. He swam away from it, but the arrows followed. They were firing blindly, but weren't missing by much. Preacher held his breath, kept swimming, and trusted to luck.

Gradually fewer and fewer arrows fell around him. When it felt like his lungs were going to explode, he paused and drifted to the surface. He turned onto his back so only his mouth and nose emerged into the air. Forcing himself not to gulp down a breath the way he desperately wanted to because that might draw attention, he drew in air shallowly, slowly, drifting along with the river's current, until the wild hammering in his head slowed somewhat.

If it had been daylight, he wouldn't have stood

a chance. But in the darkness he went unseen, and when he dove back down to swim underneath the surface again, he did it gently, with no splash.

Preacher gave thought to Red Knife's next move. He might send men along both sides of the river to search for the mountain man. In that case, Preacher would just have to elude them. On the other hand, the war chief might not want to go to that much trouble. He had destroyed the fort and he had killed dozens of the hated white men. It might be enough to satisfy him for a while.

Either way, Preacher was willing to pit his skills against those of the enemy. He was patient, and he was stubborn. He was going to get away. He could feel it in his bones, although he couldn't feel much of anything else in the icy water.

But even if he escaped, it wasn't over.

Far from it.

By morning, Preacher was miles downriver. Chilled through and through, unable to go any farther, he crawled out onto the bank and let the rising sun warm him. When he finally stopped shivering and was able to raise his head and look around, what he saw didn't surprise him.

He appeared to be alone in the vast wilderness surrounding him.

Red Knife had decided Preacher was dead or he didn't care one way or the other. All that really mattered was that no Blackfeet were waiting to kill him.

But it didn't mean they might not come along later.

He staggered to his feet and looked around for a place to hole up. He found it in a narrow crevice in the side of a bluff about five hundred yards away from the river. It was barely big enough for him, but he was able to sit with his back against the rough dirt wall and rest. He meant to keep watch, but his eyes closed and he slept.

When he woke up, the sun was low in the sky. It was late in the day, and he was ravenously hungry. With his sore muscles protesting, he climbed out of the crevice and looked around for something to eat. He found some tiny, bitter berries in a clump of brush and gobbled them up. They were better than nothing.

In the last of the fading sunlight, he stripped off his bloodstained clothes and took stock of his physical condition. His rangy, powerful body was marked all over with gashes and bruises. The knife wound in his side had crusted over, and he hoped it wouldn't fester. He didn't have any whiskey to pour on it or any herbs with which to make a poultice.

So, he was starving, beaten up, and he had lost quite a bit of blood. His muscles trembled from weakness. He wouldn't stand a chance against a Blackfoot boy, let alone a full-grown warrior.

That didn't stop a grin from stretching across his bearded face as he climbed back into the ragged buckskins.

He was alive. And Wiley Courtland . . .

That varmint didn't know it yet, but he was dead.

By the time another day and a half had passed, some of Preacher's strength had returned. It wasn't the first time he had been on his own and unarmed in the wilderness. He had rigged a snare and managed to catch a rabbit. His flint and steel had still been tucked away in a pocket, so he'd been able to build a small fire and roast his catch, but he would have eaten the critter raw if he'd had to. At night he'd returned to the hidey hole in the narrow crevice.

After finishing off his second catch, Preacher doused the fire with sand and started back upriver toward the fort, reaching what was left of it a little before dusk. Piles of ashes and rubble marked the location of the buildings, and charred lines on the ground showed where the walls had been. Dead horses lay rotting, but a huge pile of bones testified grimly as to how the bodies of the defenders had been burned, just as Preacher expected.

Somewhere in that pile were the remains of Ethan and Judith Langley. At the very least, Preacher hoped they were together.

He was sitting on the riverbank with his back to the scene of carnage and destruction when he heard a familiar whicker. His head came up sharply as he called, "Horse?"

The stallion emerged from the brush on the far side of the river, and Preacher's heart leaped more when he saw the big shaggy shape beside Horse. Both of his trail partners had survived the massacre. Dog and Horse knew how to take care of themselves. He wasn't surprised, but he was awfully glad to see them.

They plunged into the river and swam across to him, shaking themselves off as they emerged from the water. Preacher hugged them. Horse bumped his shoulder happily, and Dog licked the mountain man's bearded face. The reunion made Preacher feel better than he had any time since before the fort fell.

He slept that night with Dog curled against his side.

In the morning, in the rubble of one of the buildings, he found a bone-handled knife that had survived the blaze fairly well. With it, he carved a spear, and for breakfast he and the big cur had roasted fish.

Something was nagging at him. The night before, he had spotted an orange glow in the sky to the west. It was faint, but he saw it well enough to know a big fire was burning there.

Armed with the knife and the makeshift spear, he wanted to see what had caused the glow.

He was as close to a purely primitive state as he had been in a long time. Almost everything about civilization had been stripped from him. As he trotted along on Horse with Dog at his side, he might as well have been one of the ancient denizens of this land, one of its original settlers.

He had ancient cunning as well, and when his instincts warned him to be careful, he paid attention to them. Dropping to hands and knees, he crawled up a hill until he could peer over its grassy crest.

An Indian encampment was below, several hundred yards away. It was no tribal village, though, rather the camp of a war party pausing to let its wounded members heal some before resuming their journey home. Preacher's eyes narrowed as he spotted the tall, proud, arrogant figure of Red Knife striding around the camp.

How about that, he thought to himself. The universe had a way of balancing itself out, at least every now and then.

Preacher watched the Blackfoot camp for a long time, but didn't see Wiley Courtland among the warriors. Had Red Knife betrayed and killed him? Or had Courtland left, his horses gone and Judith lost to him forever?

There was one way to find out: ask Red Knife. That would mean slipping into the camp, capturing the war chief, and getting back out again without being discovered. After the ordeal he had been through, Preacher wasn't up to that, and there was no telling how long the Blackfeet would stay there before pulling out. With a sigh, he withdrew from his vantage point and started back to the fort to figure out his next move.

When he got there, the supply boat was tied up at the riverbank, and the men it had brought were standing around staring in horror and confusion at what was left of Fort Gifford.

CHAPTER 33

Captain Robert Creighton tipped the bottle and let amber liquid pour into the tin cup of coffee in front of Preacher. "That ought to give you some strength. My God, what an ordeal you've been through!"

"It was pretty bad," Preacher replied with typical understatement. He sipped the whiskey-laced coffee and felt its welcome warmth spread through him.

The two men were sitting at a small table in the captain's cabin. Creighton, a tall, lanky, balding man, shook his head in amazement. "I'm not sure there's another man alive who could have lived through it."

Captain wasn't a military title in this case. Creighton worked for the American Fur Company, just like Ethan Langley had. He was in charge of the supply boat *Stag* that had come up the Missouri, past Fort Union, all the way to Fort Gifford.

The boat was crowded. Between the crew and the fur trappers who had bought passage on it—trust the company to find ways to make money by any means they could—thirty men had come upriver on the *Stag*. Crates of provisions, ammunition, beaver traps, axes, and other supplies were stacked on the deck.

Most important to Preacher, the four cannon Langley had told him about were lashed to the deck, two on each side of the boat to balance their weight.

Preacher had a blanket draped around his shoulders to ward off any lingering chill. He had eaten a good meal of biscuits and salt pork, and was drinking his third cup of coffee. He felt almost human again.

"I had a good reason for stayin' alive," he said in response to the captain's comment. "If Wiley Courtland's still alive, I aim to find him and see to it he pays for what he done."

"You have no proof this man Courtland was in league with the savages," Creighton pointed out. "In fact, given everything that happened while he was bringing that herd of horses to Fort Gifford, it would seem more likely they were mortal enemies."

"Reckon they were, then," Preacher said. "Red Knife hadn't had much luck gettin' past the fort's walls, though. He might've been willin' to strike a bargain with Courtland and let him live, in return for his help gettin' inside the fort."

"I suppose. How do you propose to find out?"

"I'm gonna ask Red Knife . . . before I kill him."

"You plan a clandestine mission into that Indian camp?" Creighton asked with a frown.

Preacher drained the last of the coffee. "No, I plan to blow hell out of that Indian camp. Or I should say, *you're* gonna blow hell out of it."

Creighton's frown deepened. "You mean to launch an attack on the Blackfeet with those cannon? I'm not sure I can allow that. They belong to the American Fur Company."

"So did Fort Gifford," Preacher snapped, "and Red Knife burned it to the ground. I've got a hunch the company would want you to settle that score. And I want a distraction so I can get into the camp and get my hands on Red Knife. Can you do that for me, Captain?"

Creighton sat there without saying anything for a long moment. It was clear he considered Preacher's request a dilemma. He was the sort of man who liked to have specific orders before he did anything. Bold action didn't come naturally to him.

He had seen that pile of bones, though, and seen the rest of the devastation left behind by the war party. Finally he nodded. "I'll help you. I don't know exactly what it is you want me to do, though."

Preacher grinned. "I'll explain the whole thing to you."

* * *

Dawn had not yet arrived the next morning when Preacher knelt at the top of the rise overlooking the Blackfoot camp. The eastern sky was gray, though, and provided enough light for him to see the warriors beginning to stir. He had worried they'd be gone.

But that wasn't the case. They had waited a day too long.

He glanced to his left. The Missouri River ran there, about a quarter mile away. Captain Creighton would be maneuvering the *Stag* into position.

The plan called for him to shut down the boat's engine while it was still far enough away that the Indians couldn't hear it. From there, men would wade ashore with heavy ropes and haul the vessel upriver against the current. It would be hard work, but it could be done. They were more than willing to make the effort after hearing about the massacre carried out at Fort Gifford.

Preacher looked the other way at the ten men who had come with him. He hadn't had any trouble getting volunteers. They were all fur trappers, and knew they wouldn't be safe as long as Red Knife was around. With Preacher leading them, they would hit the camp from one side while Creighton bombarded it from the other with those cannon.

The mountain man knew there was a chance Red Knife would be killed in the barrage. If that happened, he might not ever find out what had happened to Wiley Courtland. But the souls of the men who had died inside the fort cried out for vengeance, and Preacher was going to give it to them. Red Knife's war party would never again carry out such wanton slaughter.

Dog sat beside Preacher, waiting. A low whine came from the big cur.

"I know you're anxious to get down there, old fella," Preacher said quietly. "So am I. It won't be much longer now."

He had borrowed a rifle from a man on the boat and taken a couple of pistols from a crate bound for Fort Gifford. He still had the bone-handled knife he had found in the rubble. It felt good to be armed again.

The sky had started to take on a rosy tint. It brightened as Preacher and his companions waited. He kept looking toward the river, waiting for some sign of the *Stag*. If anything had happened to delay the boat, or worse still, if it had run aground, the plan was ruined. Even though the war party appeared to have shrunk to half the size it had been when the fort was destroyed, it was still much too big for a small force to attack without the help of those cannon.

Suddenly, as red and gold continued to splash across the heavens, heralding the start of a new day, the prow of the *Stag* nosed into view around the bend just below the Blackfoot camp.

The men hauling the vessel were on the river's south bank. The Missouri was wide, but not so wide it would make any difference. The camp was well within range of those big guns. Creighton's crew had turned them so they all pointed toward the enemy. The captain, like Preacher, had served in the War of 1812 and knew how to handle the cannon.

"All right, boys," Preacher said softly. "Won't be much longer now . . ."

Several of the Blackfeet were awake and moving around, but they weren't paying attention to what was happening on the river. The *Stag* seemed to inch forward with maddening slowness, but finally it was in position. The men holding the ropes tied them to trees and scrambled back aboard. Preacher couldn't make out the details from so far away and in the light of dawn, but he knew the men designated as gunners were getting ready to touch off the charges.

The sun peeked over the horizon behind Preacher. Down below in the camp, a sleepy warrior ambled toward the river but stopped abruptly and let out a shout of alarm when he saw the boat. Captain Creighton couldn't have gotten a better signal.

A cannon boomed and sent smoke billowing into the air. The heavy ball was a gray streak flying through the air. It smashed into a sleeping warrior and turned his head to pulp before bounding on to kill several more men.

"Come on!" Preacher shouted as he surged to his feet and lunged down the slope toward the camp.

Creighton had the big guns firing one at a time, so by the time all four had thundered out their challenge, the first cannon had been reloaded and was ready to fire again. The steady barrage continued as Preacher ran down the hill with Dog bounding along beside him and the other men right behind him.

Chaos reigned in the Blackfoot camp. Men died without ever knowing what was going on. Death seemed to come from nowhere, striking them down right and left. It was like the heavens had opened up to rain lightning bolts, even though there wasn't a cloud in the sky on the beautiful early morning.

By the time the warriors finally realized where the attack was coming from, Preacher's companions were among them, opening fire and cutting them down.

Preacher headed directly to where he had seen Red Knife the previous evening. Along the way he emptied his rifle and pistols, and with each shot another Blackfoot fell. He didn't take the time to reload.

A familiar voice roared orders and tried to rally

the panicking warriors. Preacher followed that voice and spotted his quarry through the confusion.

"Red Knife!" he bellowed.

The war chief whirled toward him. Surprise etched on Red Knife's face as he recognized Preacher. But that reaction lasted only a second before he roared a defiant, hate-filled challenge, lifted the tomahawk in his hand, and charged toward the mountain man.

Preacher threw his empty pistols aside and jerked the bone-handled knife from his belt. Darting aside as the tomahawk swept down at his head, he met Red Knife's assault with an attack of his own. The blade flashed out and cut deeply across Red Knife's chest. The war chief grunted in pain, sweeping the tomahawk around in a back-handed strike Preacher barely avoided.

Back and forth they lunged at each other, evenly matched. Preacher's left arm went numb when the flat of the tomahawk's head struck his shoulder a glancing blow. Red Knife was bleeding from several wounds inflicted by Preacher.

Only a few days had passed since Preacher had been tossed into a pile of corpses and left for dead. Most men who had gone through what he had wouldn't even be able to get out of bed. But he was on his feet and fighting, letting his rage fuel his battered body and holding his own against the war chief. He forgot about everything else going on around him and concentrated only on his opponent.

The tomahawk smashed into his side where he'd been wounded in the earlier battle. Fiery pain shot through him, and for a second everything turned hazy around him. Red Knife sensed an advantage and bulled in, swinging the tomahawk at Preacher's head.

At the last second, Preacher jerked aside. The tomahawk barely grazed his long, gray-shot hair as he fell backward. Off balance, Red Knife stumbled too close to the mountain man. Preacher grabbed the front of the war chief's buckskin shirt with his free hand and planted a foot in Red Knife's belly. The Blackfoot flew through the air and crashed down with stunning force.

Preacher was on him in the blink of an eye, holding the blade against his throat. All it would take to send the razor-sharp edge slicing through flesh was a little more pressure.

He held off and rested a knee on the inside of Red Knife's right elbow, forcing the war chief to let go of the tomahawk. Then Preacher leaned closer over him. His lips drew back from his teeth in a snarl as he demanded, "Where's Courtland?"

"The white traitor?" Red Knife swallowed, which wasn't easy with a knife held so tightly against his throat. "Gone."

"You killed him?"

"Why? He kept his end of the bargain, but still

he lost all he wanted. The white woman was dead at his hand." An ugly chuckle came from Red Knife's mouth. "Nothing I could do to him was worse than that."

Red Knife had a point there, thought Preacher. "Which way did he go?"

"East. Will you go after him?"

"Damn right I will," Preacher muttered.

"Then he will die. More than ever, you are the Ghost Killer."

And with that, Red Knife lunged up from the ground. The blade cut deep into his neck and blood spurted, rising in a crimson fountain as Preacher pulled back in surprise.

Unable to live with the shame of his defeat, Red Knife had chosen his own way out. It didn't really matter. He had beaten Preacher to the throat cutting by only a moment, after all.

Preacher wiped off the bloody knife on the war chief's buckskins, retrieved his guns, then stood up and tucked them into his belt. The cannon had fallen silent, and it was easy to see why. The bombardment had devastated the camp, and Preacher and the men with him had finished the job. Blackfoot bodies lay everywhere. Some members of the war party might have survived and fled, but surely not many. Those who had would carry the tale of the thundering death that had come in the dawn.

One massacre for another, Preacher mused as he looked around. And sometime in the future, another war party would wipe out another fort to avenge what had happened there. On and on, a never-ending cycle of violence stretching all the way back to the dim, misty beginnings of mankind. Where it would end, Preacher had no idea.

All he knew was that particular part of the cycle wouldn't end until he found Wiley Courtland.

CHAPTER 34

Fort Union was larger and more substantial than Fort Gifford had been, with thick earthen walls that wouldn't burn and tall blockhouses to protect them. The booshwa didn't live in the back of a log trading post but rather in an actual two-story house with whitewashed walls and a red roof. The land on which the outpost sat, at the confluence of the Missouri and Yellowstone Rivers, was considered to be Assiniboine territory, and the tribe got along well with the white men who had built the fort. Various bands visited frequently, setting up their lodges outside the walls and making a holiday of it.

It was as far west as the American Fur Company had been able to penetrate safely, as the destruction of Fort Gifford proved.

None of that mattered to Preacher. To him, Fort Union was just the starting point in his search for Courtland.

He had come back downriver on the *Stag*. Captain Creighton had balked a little at taking Horse aboard, but in the end agreed. The boat returned with the same cargo it had left with. There was no place to leave it upriver, although some of the trappers bound for Fort Gifford had bought supplies before they scattered to seek their fortunes in fur.

With the boat tied up at the dock built out into the river, Creighton said to Preacher, "I have to go talk to the booshwa about what happened at Gifford so he can write a letter back to the company and let them know. I don't suppose you'd want to come with me?"

"You saw what was left. You can explain it all just as good as I can."

"I wasn't there," Creighton pointed out. "You were."

"The Blackfeet got in, killed everybody, and burned down the fort. Can't get much more simple than that."

Creighton sighed and nodded. "I suppose. But he may insist on talking to you anyway, since you're the only survivor."

"Maybe I'll be here, maybe I won't," Preacher said with a shrug. "And I ain't the only survivor. Dog and Horse lived through it, too, but I don't reckon they'll feel any more like talkin' than I do."

He left Creighton on the boat and walked through the open gates into the fort with Dog beside him and Horse trailing behind. A long building to the right ran the entire length of the wall. It served as trading post, tavern, and barracks for the men. Preacher intended to ask in there if anybody had seen Courtland. With hair so fair it was almost white, most folks would remember him.

Preacher tied Horse to a hitch rack in front of the tavern, told Dog to stay, and went inside.

He'd been hoping to pick up Courtland's trail there.

He hadn't expected to find the man himself.

Courtland was sitting alone in a rear corner of the big smoky room. A jug sat on the table in front of him, but he didn't appear to be drunk. He looked like a living dead man, gaunt and hollow-eyed.

He saw Preacher at the same time the mountain man spotted him.

Preacher tensed, expecting Courtland to reach for the pistol laying on the table beside the jug. Courtland didn't move, except to cock one white eyebrow in surprise.

Then he smiled.

Preacher almost lost control of his emotions then. It would have been simple enough to pull both pistols from behind his belt, walk up to Courtland, and blow the man to hell. But that wouldn't provide him with any answers to the questions still puzzling him.

More than a dozen men were in the tavern

drinking, playing cards, talking, and laughing. None seemed to notice the looks passing between Preacher and Courtland.

Stiff-legged, Preacher walked across the room toward the horse trader.

"Red Knife assured me you had to be dead," Courtland said quietly as the mountain man came to a stop in front of the table. "He said you were badly wounded, and his men were bound to hit you with their arrows when you tried to get away in the river. Somehow, though, I didn't believe him. I had a feeling I'd be seeing you again."

"In this life or the next," Preacher growled out. "If I *had* been dead, I would've been waitin' for you at the gates of hell."

"I don't doubt it for a moment. How *did* you survive?"

"Divine providence."

Courtland looked puzzled.

"The Good Lord must've kept me alive so's I can kill you," Preacher explained.

"That could be," Courtland said with a shrug. "Although this"—he looked around at the inside of the tavern—"this is already hell on earth, isn't it?"

Preacher used a foot to pull back one of the empty chairs at the table and sat down. "I reckon any place would seem like hell on earth to you, after what you did. You know how much blood you got on your hands, Courtland?"

"I only care about some of it," Courtland murmured.

"Judith's."

Courtland's wry smile was gone, and in its place was a look of pain. "I never meant for her to be hurt. I just wanted what was best for her. You can't see that, can you, Preacher?"

"You didn't have any right to decide what was best for her."

"But I loved her. Don't you see? Of course I had the right."

"So you were responsible for the deaths of dozens of men, all because a woman picked somebody else."

"'The face that launched a thousand ships, and burnt the topless towers of Ilium . . .'," Courtland mused. "Although you don't know what I'm talking about, do you?"

"Don't sell me short," Preacher snapped. "I may not have read Homer, but a friend of mine can quote him all day and half the night, if he's of a mind to. Name of Audie."

"A learned man, from the sound of it. Well, then, I suppose he might understand what a man will do for love."

"You didn't do anything for love. You did it for hate." Preacher paused. "I ain't sure *how* you did it, though."

"And that's puzzling you, I can tell. It really wasn't difficult. You gave me the idea."

"Me?" Preacher exclaimed.

"That's right. When you went over the wall on that rope. It was easy enough for me to do the same thing. I was supposed to be on guard duty that night. Instead I just left."

"Nine times out of ten the Blackfeet would've killed you out of hand."

"Maybe. But I was desperate, and I was going to die anyway when the fort fell. When I asked to see Red Knife several warriors took me to him, and I made my proposition. I'd leave the rope down when I snuck back into the fort. His men could climb up and hide in the blockhouse where I was posted, and wait until they were ready to strike."

"Wait a minute. There were always two men in those blockhouses."

"Of course there were. I took care of the man who was on duty with me."

"You killed him, you mean," Preacher said.

"Slit his throat. Couldn't have him see me coming and going, now could I?"

Preacher was breathing a little harder as he struggled to control himself. "You let those warriors in, and nobody noticed 'em until they were openin' the gates. Is that the way it worked?"

"Exactly. And Red Knife had a large force ready to rush the gates as soon as they were open . . ." Courtland shrugged again. "You know the rest."

"And in return?"

"Judith and I were to get safe passage out of there, to wherever I wanted to go."

Preacher's eyes narrowed. "Did you really think she wouldn't have told anybody what you'd done?"

"She would have had to rely on me for her safety. Besides, she would have come to love me. She always loved me. Somehow Langley just blinded her to that fact."

Several seconds of silence went by before Preacher said, "Mister, you're as crazy as a man can be. You never would've got away with it."

Courtland reached out lazily and picked up the jug of whiskey. "I guess we'll never know, will we?"

He exploded out of his chair and swung the jug as hard as he could at Preacher's head.

The mountain man was ready. He'd been ready for Courtland to try something ever since he sat down. He jerked backward, and the jug passed harmlessly in front of his face. The chair tipped over with a crash as he came to his feet.

Courtland snatched the pistol from the tabletop. The gun roared, and Preacher felt the hot sting of burning powder against his cheek. The ball flew past his ear and smashed into a keg behind the bar as men in the tavern shouted in alarm and scrambled for cover.

There wouldn't be any more shots. Courtland stood with the smoking pistol in his hand and slowly looked down at the bone handle of the knife sticking out from his chest. Even as the gun was going off, Preacher had brought the knife up from under the table and buried the full length of the blade in Courtland's body.

Courtland's eyes widened with the realization he had only seconds to live. He tried to say something, but couldn't get the words out. He licked his lips before rasping, "You . . . you've done me . . . yet another favor . . . my friend."

"I ain't your friend," Preacher said harshly. "And you can tell it to the Devil."

Courtland winced, sagged, and twisted, landing on his side as he toppled onto the table. Preacher reached down to pull the knife free, but then he stopped. The blade was right where it was supposed to be, in the traitor's heart.

He left it there as he turned and walked out of the tavern.

TURN THE PAGE FOR AN EXCITING PREVIEW

Welcome to the peaceful little town of Doubtful, Wyoming,
which has more than its fair share of kill-crazy gunslicks,
back-shooters, and flat-out dirty desperadoes.
It also has a sheriff named Cotton Pickens,
who tries his best to keep law and order
without getting his head blown off before breakfast.

DOUBTFUL'S GOT A NEW DEPUTY . . .
FOR THE MOMENT

Cotton Pickens got where he is by virtue of a quick
draw and slow wit. He knows the difference between
lawbreakers you have to lock up . . . and the kind
you might as well just let go. Deputy Rusty Irons,
though, ain't the sharpest tool in the shed.
Someone kidnapped his mail order brides.
They were probably doing him a favor,
but a deputy in love is blind.

As for the various carny barkers, medicine show
con artists, and revival-meeting fly-by-nighters who
pass through Doubtful, Cotton just tries to keep
the peace and keep the traveling hucksters
moving on. But in one terrible moment, it all
goes straight to hell as the town explodes in a
frenzy of killing and bloodshed. That's when a
lawman like Cotton earns his pay, saves his soul,
or loses his life by looking evil straight in the eye.
Of course, there's also the matter of keeping
his new deputy alive and in one piece.

SUPPORT YOUR LOCAL DEPUTY
A COTTON PICKENS WESTERN
by William W. Johnstone
with J. A. Johnstone

Coming in March 2013 wherever Pinnacle Books are sold.

CHAPTER 1

My deputy, Rusty Irons, was as itchy as a man ever gets. We were at the Laramie and Overland stage station waiting for the maroon enameled Concord stage to roll in. He couldn't come up with proper bouquets, not in the barely settled cow town of Doubtful, Wyoming, but he managed some daisies and sagebrush he'd collected out on the range.

Rusty was waiting for his mail order brides. That's right, Siamese twins from the Ukraine, joined at the hip. He'd ordered just one, but they sent him the pair. He'd gotten the hundred-fifty-dollar reward offered for Huckster Bob, wanted dead or alive. Rusty got him alive, collected his reward, and applied the money to getting himself a wife.

So there we were, waiting for the stage to roll in. It was an hour late, maybe more.

Well, my ma always said there's nothing worse than a sweating bridegroom, and Rusty filled the bill. He had sweat running down his sides. His armpits had turned into gushers.

"Well . . . you get to be best man," Rusty sputtered.

"If I don't arrest you for bigamy first," I countered.

"I looked it up; there's no law in Wyoming Territory against it."

"Well, I'll arrest you for something or other," I said. "You found a preacher who'll tie the knot?"

"No, but I'm going to argue that all he has to do is marry me to one of 'em."

"What'll you do with the other?"

"I can't auction her off, so she gets to be the spectator."

"They speak English?"

"Not a word. They're from Lvov, Ukraine."

"Well, that's a good start. You won't get into arguments," I pointed out. "My ma always said the best part of her marriage was when my pa was snoring."

Rusty, he just grinned. "You're the result."

I wasn't sure how to take that, but thought I'd let it pass without a fistfight. His armpits were leaking worse than ever and I didn't want his sweat all over my sheriff suit and pants.

"You figure they're joined facing the same way?" I asked.

"I wouldn't marry them if one was facing backwards. Here." He pulled out a tintype.

The image of two beautiful blondes leaped out at me. It looked like they were side by side, except they had on a single dark skirt.

Rusty pointed to one of the women. "This one here's Natasha, and the other is Anna."

"You know which one you'll hitch up with?"

"We'll toss a coin. Or maybe they've got it worked out."

"What if one wants you and the other doesn't? Or you want one and not the other?"

Rusty, he just grinned. "Life sure is interesting."

Word had gotten out, and a small crowd had collected at the wooden stage office on Main Street. Some of the women squinted at Rusty as if he was a criminal, which maybe he was. But mostly they were wondering what sort of twisted beast would want to marry Siamese twins. Fifty of the good citizens of Doubtful stood in clumps, whispering and pointing at Rusty as if he belonged in the bottom layer of hell.

Rusty, he just smiled. "I'm glad you got me that raise."

"You'll need it," I replied.

I'd gone to the Puma County supervisors and talked them into raising Rusty's wage by five dollars, because of his impending wedlock and his faithful service as my best and most useful deputy. That put him up just two dollars below my forty-seven-a-month sheriff salary, but I didn't mind.

I saw Delphinium Sanders, the banker's wife, glaring at both of us as hard as she could manage. And George Waller, the mayor, was studying us as if we belonged in a zoo—which maybe we did. I sure didn't know how things would play out, or who'd marry whom, but it made a late spring day real entertaining in the cow town of Doubtful.

Hanging Judge Earwig was there too, and thought maybe he'd do the marrying if no one else would. He was broadminded, and didn't mind if people thought ill of him. He might even marry both the twins to Rusty, seeing as how there wasn't any law against it. That'd come later, when the next legislature got moralistic. Or maybe Rusty could take his gals to Utah and find a Mormon cleric to fix him up, but I didn't put much stock in it. Utah had outlawed that sort of entertainment.

The stagecoach sure was late. Dry road, too. The dry spring meant no potholes or mud puddles. The waiting was hard on Rusty.

"Hey, Rusty, you got a two-holer, or are they gonna take turns?" some brat yelled.

I went after the freckled punk, got an ear, and twisted it. "Cut that out or I'll throw you down a hole and you'll stink for a week."

"Aw, Sheriff, this is the best thing to hit Doubtful in a long time."

"You're Willie Dickens, and your ma didn't raise you right. I let go of your ear, you promise to respect people?"

"Anything you say." Willie yanked loose, smirking.

I let him go. The whole thing was turning into an ordeal for my deputy sheriff, instead of a moment of joy. It wasn't hard to tell what all them good folks of Doubtful were thinking. The marriage would have a threesome in the bedroom.

And still no coach.

Then, about the time I was ready to head back to the sheriff's office and look over the mail, we spotted the coach rounding the hill south of Doubtful. It was coming along at a smart clip, maybe faster than usual because them drays looked pretty lathered.

"Well, Rusty, here it comes," I said.

Jonas Quill, the jehu, pulled back the lines slightly, and the sweated horses gladly quit on him while the coach rocked gently. He yelled down at me. "We got held up, man."

"Held up?"

"Four armed men, masked."

By then, the maroon door of the coach had swung open. Six passengers emerged; four rumpled males, mostly whiskey drummers, and two frightened women in bonnets, both gray-haired.

No Ukrainian Siamese identical female twins.

Rusty seemed to leak gas.

"Clear away from here," I yelled at the mob. We got trouble."

"Where are they?" Rusty asked.

"Don't know, but we got business. Sheriff business." I looked at the six who had just gotten off the stagecoach. "You passengers, stick close here. I'll want statements from all of you."

One woman looked annoyed and started off.

"You, too, Mrs. Throckmorton."

"I surrender to my fate," she said, and kept on going.

Rusty looked shell shocked, so it was up to me. "Quill, tell me. What happened and what got took?"

"Nothing got took. Just the twins."

"My mind isn't quite biting this cookie, Quill."

"Three masked men on saddle horses, another in a chariot."

"A what?"

"A two-wheel chariot hung on two trotters. Man driving it was masked, too."

"A chariot like them gladiators used?"

"A two-wheel stand-up cart, with a lot of gold gilt and enameled red on it. They stop my coach, one has a scattergun aimed at me. They open the door, point it at the twins, and say 'ladies get out,' but the twins, they don't speak a word of English, so the masked men prod the ladies out with their revolvers. That takes some doing—four legs, one skirt—but they get the Siamese twins out, get them into the chariot, and the man with the whip smacks the butts of those trotters and away they go, the three of them standing in that chariot."

"That's it?"

"The others want the twins' luggage, and they load it on a packhorse."

"And you didn't fight it?"

"They made us drop our weapons," one of the drummers said.

"What else did they take? The mail? Anything in the lockbox?"

"Nope," said Quill. "The foreign women and their bags is all."

"Did they give any reasons?"

"They said not to shoot 'cause we'd hit the women, and that was true. They headed due west, over some off-road route."

"Good, we'll have some tracks to follow," I said.

"Them were my brides," Rusty complained.

"Real purty, they were. But sure hobbled up." Quill frowned. "I can see the direction your steamy little brain's taking, Irons."

Things were getting a little out of hand.

"Rusty, you interview the male passengers, and I'll interview these women. Meanwhile, you people, clear out of here." I waved my arms to shoo them out.

But no one moved. Half the town, it seemed, had flooded in.

* * *

Rusty and I got what we could from the passengers. Nothing was taken except the Ukrainians. No one was forced to empty pockets. No valuables ended up in bandit pockets. The kidnappers were young, well masked, rode easily, wore wide-brimmed hats and jeans and dirty boots. They were polite with no apparent accents and offered no reasons. Treated courteously by the bandits, the Ukrainian twins went peaceably, not understanding a bit. They were even smiling.

"Were they hostages? Will they be returned for a reward?" Rusty asked the drummers.

"Nope, no sign of it," said one in a black bowler.

"Who'd want female Siamese twins?" Rusty asked.

"They were real lookers," another salesman ventured.

Rusty whipped out his tintype. "These the ones?"

They studied the black and white a while. "Not sure, but seems so," one said.

"Did these women seem in distress?"

"Nope, they thought it was all pretty merry."

The passengers had been detained long enough, so me and Rusty cut them loose, cut the jehu loose, and headed for Turk's Livery Barn. We had some hard riding in front of us.

CHAPTER 2

Rusty, he wanted a posse. He was plumb irate. Them was his brides got stolen, and he was rooting around, looking for ways to hang the wife-rustlers at the nearest cottonwood tree.

"Hey, cool 'er off," I said. "Go saddle up and take some fixings. I'll get Critter, and we'll get this deal shut down in no time."

"Who'll run the office?'

"I'll send Burtell." I was referring to a part-time deputy.

"I want a posse. That was Anna and Natasha who got took. I want plenty of armed men."

"This'll be the easiest kidnapping we ever solved. Where can they hide? We got some dudes in a red and gold chariot, kidnapping beautiful Siamese twins in one skirt, and they speak Ukraine, or whatever the tongue is. We got 'em cold, Rusty."

He didn't want to believe it, and I didn't blame him. He got robbed out of two real pretty gals, and a lot of real fine nights once he got hitched to one or the other . . . or both.

But my ma, she used to say twins were double the trouble. She'd settle for twin cocker spaniels, but not any pair that would put her out some. In truth, if we got them joined-up twins back, I wasn't sure Rusty could handle the deal.

He turned toward the office where he'd left his horse and I continued on to Turk's Livery Barn, fixing to saddle up Critter the Second. The first got his throat slit, and I looked hard before I found the Second, who was meaner than the first, so it worked out all right. I don't know what I'd do with a gentle horse. Horses are like women. If they don't buck when you're riding them, they're no good.

Critter was out in the yard, which wasn't good. He kicked down any stall he got put into, so Turk often put him outside. I got the bridle and went after him, and sure enough, he headed for a corner in the fence and waited for me, his rear hoofs itchy to land on me. I tried moving along one rail and he switched that way, so I tried the other rail, and he switched that way.

"Critter, dammit, we're going to look for some women. Or one woman. I don't have it straight. So shape up," I yelled.

He turned and eyed me, and settled down. I bridled, and brushed, and saddled him without trouble. Critter was a philosopher.

"Dog food," called Rusty as he led his horse toward the barn. "He needs to be turned into dog food."

"I won't argue with it," I called back.

"Shouldn't we have a buggy or a cart?" Rusty asked. He was thinking about how to transport the Ukrainian ladies. You can't expect Siamese twins to climb up on a horse, but maybe a pair of horses would work if they crowded close.

I ignored his question and stared at him. He was armed to the teeth, with a saddle gun and a pair of mean-looking Peacemakers hanging from his skinny hips. He was gonna get his women back, even if he burned some powder. "You got any idea why them gals got took?"

"It sure is interesting," I replied.

Turk spotted us. "You going after them stage robbers?"

Rusty nodded. "That's my women they took."

"Double the feed bags," Turk pointed out. "You sure got odd tastes."

That was my private opinion, but I wasn't voicing it. Rusty was the best deputy I had, and I didn't want to rile him up.

Word spread through town like melted butter, and they were all watching as we rode out. Mostly watching Rusty, not me. The women stood along Main Street with pursed lips, and I could read their every thought.

Soon we were trotting down the Laramie Road,

heading for the ambush spot, so I could see what was to be seen, and we could see what the chariot wheels did to the turf. It should be easy enough to follow that cart, and with a little luck I'd have the bandits in manacles and heading for my lockup in a day or two.

Rusty, he sure was silent.

"What are you thinking, Rusty?"

"Maybe I won't marry after all. They'll be plumb ruined. I was marrying double virgins, and now look at it. It's a mess."

"You sure got big appetites, Rusty. Double everything—double marriage, double honeymoon, double household, double mouths to feed."

"Yeah, that's me," he said, a little smirky. Somehow he was seeing that as proof he was double the rest of us. He looked over at me. "What if they both expect babies at the same time, eh?"

I didn't push it. Life sure was going to be interesting.

Critter loved to get out, and he was pretty near popping along. Rusty's nag had to trot now and then to catch up. We were riding through empty country, nothing but hills and sagebrush, and not worth anything except to a coyote. But that was Wyoming for you. Ninety percent worthless, ten percent pretty fine.

It took us about three hours to reach the ambush place, well chosen to hide the ambushers behind a curve in the road. The jehu had given me a pretty good idea of it. Signs were all around there, all right—some iron-tire tracks, some hoofprints, some handkerchiefs, and plenty of boot-heel dimples in the dun clay.

And sure enough, the iron-tire tracks led straight west, off the road and over open prairie. So we followed them.

"We'll nail 'em, Rusty. How can we lose? Look at them tracks, smooth and hard."

But the tracks gradually turned and finally came entirely around, heading for the Laramie Road, maybe a mile south of where the ambush happened. And there they disappeared. Those clean iron-tire tracks vanished. We messed around there a while, widening out, looking for the tracks, but it was as if that chariot had taken off from the earth and rolled on up into heaven.

Rusty was having the same sweats as me. That just couldn't be. Big red and gold chariots didn't just vanish—unless through the Pearly Gates. I wondered about that for a while. Were them Ukrainian ladies taken on up?

The road had plenty of traffic showing on it, and we scouted it one way and then the other, checking hoofprints, poking at ruts, and kicking horse turds, but the fact was, the kidnappers had ridden off into the sky, and were rolling across cumulus, or maybe thunderheads, to some place or other.

"You got any fancy theories, Cotton?" Rusty, he

sure looked gloomy. Like he had been deprived of a night with two of the prettiest gals ever born.

"We could ride on down to Laramie and see what's what," I said.

"Who'd want 'em?" Rusty asked.

"Some horny old rancher, I imagine."

"Well, there's no man on earth hornier then me." It was dawning on him that he'd lost his mail order bride—or brides, I never could get that straight—and he was sinking into a sort of darkness.

I thought it was best to leave him alone. "I'll get ahold of the sheriff, Milt Boggs, and tell him what's missing, and for him to let us know if we got a red chariot and two hipshot blondes floating around southern Wyoming."

"We catch them, what are you going to charge them with?" Rusty wanted to know.

"Now that's an interesting question," I said. "My ma used to say people confess if you give them the chance."

"Well, she inherited all the brains in your family," Rusty said, just to be mean.

Truth to tell, my mind was on what might happen when we got back to Doubtful without two hip-tied blondes and a red chariot and a mess of crooks trudging along in front of my shotgun. Townspeople'd be telling me to quit, or maybe trying to fire me again. Seems every time I didn't catch the crook or stop the killer, they wanted to fire me. I've spent more time in front of the county supervisors trying to save my sheriff job than I've spent running my office.

About dusk, we got back in town, and all we raised were a few smirks. Like no one thought kidnapping Siamese twins from the Ukraine was worth getting lathered up about. Especially when it was all Rusty's problem. He was the only one got shut out of some entertainment. So we rode in by our lonesome selves without a parade of bandits and bad men parading in front, and without those brides. People sort of smiled smartly, and planned to make some jokes, and maybe petition the supervisors to get rid of me, and that was that.

Me, I felt the same way. If Rusty hadn't mail-ordered the most exotic womanhood this side of Morocco, it never would've happened.

Turk showed up out of the gloom soon as we rode into his livery barn. "Told you so."

"Told us what?"

"That you'd botch another job again."

I was feeling a little put out with him, and if there were any other livery barns in town, I would have moved Critter then and there. My horse chewed on any wood he could get his big buck teeth around, and sometimes Turk sent me a bill for repairs, but I could hardly blame Turk for that.

Rusty unsaddled, turned out his nag, and disappeared. He was feeling real blue, and I didn't blame him.

"Hey," Turk said, "while you gents were out the Laramie Road, chasing Ukrainian women, a medicine show came up the Cheyenne Road and set up outside of town."

"Medicine show?"

"None other. Doctor Zoroaster Zimmer's Three Way Tonic for digestion, thick hair, and virility. Three dollars the six-ounce bottle, thirty-five dollars a dozen. And you get to watch a juggler, belly dancer, an accordion player, and a dog and pony act, and then lay out cash for the medicine."

"Zimmer? Seems to me he's on a wanted dodger in my office. Whenever he hits town, jewelry and gold coins start vanishing, and dogs howl in the night. I think his tonic's mostly opium, peppermint, and creek water, but I'll find out."

"Yeah, Sheriff, and guess what? I wandered over there to have a gander. He's driving a big red-enameled outfit with gold trim. But there's no chariots or Ukrainian blondes in sight."

CHAPTER 3

Doubtful, it had growed some, and was fixed in the middle of some of the best Wyoming ranch country around. So there were plenty of people in the Puma County seat, and also plenty more out herding cows and growing hogs and collecting eggs from chickens. There were even some horse breeders around town, most of them raising remounts for the cavalry.

The town was half civilized. I knew the rough times were over when some gal named Matilda opened up a hattery. I don't know the proper name of a hat shop, but it don't matter. Hattery is what she operated, and she did nothing but sell bonnets and straw hats full of fake fruit to the town's ladies. And gossip, too. All the local gals went in there to gossip about the rest of us. Sometimes I got a little itchy about sheriffing in a halfway civilized town and thought I should pack up and head for the tropics.

But my ma, she always said don't shoot a gift horse between the eyes, and that's how I looked at my job.

That eve, Rusty quit early on me and headed off to his cabin to nurse his disappointment. He had his heart set on marrying the Ukrainian beauties and never having to have a conversation with his women because he didn't understand a word they said. I thought it was a fool's dream, myself. What if they was saying mean things about him, in their own tongue, maybe even at night with the pair of them lying beside him?

The town was drawing everything from whiskey drummers to medicine shows these days, and I intended to get out to the east side to have a close look. Half the shows rolling through the country roads of the West were nothing but gyppo outfits, looking to con cash out of the local folks, while swiping everything that wasn't nailed down tight. And if they could get a few girls in trouble while robbing citizens and peddling worthless stuff, they did that, too, and smiled all the way to the next berg.

I'd wander over there. But first I'd patrol Doubtful, as I did every evening—wearing my badge, walking from place to place, rattling doors to see if they were locked, and studying saloons closely to see if there was trouble. Sometimes there was, and the barkeeps would be glad I wandered in at a moment when some drunken cowboy, armed to the teeth, was picking a fight.

So I did my rounds, seeing that all was quiet at Maxwell's Funeral Parlor, and no one was busting the doors at Hubert Sanders' Merchant Bank. I peered into Barney's Beanery, and saw that it was winding down for the eve, and peered into the dark confines of Leonard Silver's Emporium. I checked the office of Lawyer Stokes, and saw no one rifling his file cabinets. McGiver's Saloon was quiet, and so was the Last Chance, where I saw Sammy Upward yawning, his elbows on the bar, looking ready to close early.

I spotted a few posters promoting Dr. Zoroaster Zimmer's show. The man had a string of initials behind his name, but I never could figure out what all they meant, but the PhD meant he was a doctor of philandery or something like that. The KGB puzzled me, but someone told me it was British and had to do with garters and bathtubs. You never know what gets into foreigners. At any rate, Professor Zimmer had them all, and they followed his name like a line of railroad cars. I thought I'd like to meet the gent.

Denver Sally's place, back behind saloon row, looked quiet, the evening breezes rocking the red lantern beside her door. Most of her business came on weekends. The Gates of Heaven, next door, looked as mean as ever. Who knows all the ways a feller wants to get rid of his cash?

Doubtful was peaceful enough, that spring evening. So it was time to drift out beyond saloon row, east of town and take a gander at the medicine-man show. A mess of those shows were wandering through the whole country, setting up in dark corners of little towns, and running an act or two across a stage set up on a wagon. The medicine man would step out and peddle his stuff, and when he gauged he'd done all the selling he could, he'd pull up stakes and head for the next little town and do it all over again.

Sure enough, east of town on an alkali flat, a couple of torches were going.

I moseyed closer and saw two fancy red and gilt wagons—one with a lamplit stage—and a makeshift rope corral with some moth-eaten drays in it. Maybe twelve, fifteen suckers were watching a jet-haired woman in a grass skirt wiggle her butt and make her bosom heave. I'd never seen that, and it seemed entertaining, but I had sheriff business to do, namely, look for a red and gilt chariot, and two blond Ukrainian women joined at the hip.

It took a quick prowl around the rear of the place, and into the other wagon, to satisfy myself no one was hiding a chariot or Siamese twins, blond or any other color. Whoever kidnapped the ladies, it wasn't that miserable outfit.

I spotted a gent smoking a cigar back there, and thought he might have some answers. He saw the glint of my badge even before we spoke. He sucked on his gummy cheroot, and knocked off the ash. "You looking for something, Sheriff?"

"Just keeping an eye on things. How many people you got in this outfit?"

"Six and the professor."

"Any women?"

He stared at me as if I were an idiot. "That's Elvira Smoothpepper out there. And we got Elsie Sanchez, the Argentine firecracker."

"No Ukrainian blondes?"

"You got eyes, don'tcha?"

"Who else is in the show?"

"Sheriff, there ain't anyone with a wanted poster on him. There's me and another teamster. He's the accordionist, and there's a tap dancer named Fogarty, and the professor."

"What does the professor sell? What's his medicine?"

The gent smiled. "Try it sometime and come back and tell me."

"Any chariots around here?"

"Any what?"

"Oh, never mind."

"You all right, Sheriff? Want to lie down? That second wagon, it's got bunks. Had a little too much?"

"Who's the professor?"

"He's whatever he is at any moment. Right now, he's a medicine man, and he's working the rubes for a few bucks."

"Yeah, well, I'll go watch the show," I said.

"It beats pissing on a fence post."

Half of the crowd was cowboys, out from the saloons. I recognized a few, most of them that hung out at Mrs. Gladstone's Sampling Room. They were tied up with the Admiral Ranch, other side of the county. But there were some locals too, including the mayor, George Waller, who looked embarrassed when he saw me.

"I just came to view the competition." Waller was a merchant, and any outfit that sold anything was competition, as far as he was concerned. "Maybe you should arrest the whole lot."

"What for?"

"They're all crooks."

"Well, that's progress. You show me one act of crookery, and I'll pinch the person straight off."

Elvira Smoothpepper was making her belly roll and the grass skirt sway, and that was pretty entertaining. The accordionist got to wheezing away, and pretty soon the act creaked to a stop, and out came Professor Zoroaster Zimmer, in black silk top hat and tails, and a grimy white vest that looked a little worse for wear.

I'd never seen the like.

He spotted me at once, and welcomed me. "Ladies and gents, here's the sheriff of, ah, Puma County, Wyoming. Come to see our little show, and maybe endorse my product, namely, the Zimmer Miracle Tonic, guaranteed to cure piles, insomnia, gout, St. Vitus Dance, and all bowel troubles. Welcome, Mr. Sheriff.

"Now, esteemed friends, I want to tell you about a product that should need no introducing, since it sells itself. You need only ask your neighbor, who has the remedy on his shelf, ready to use, and you'll see how effective it is. Mr. Sheriff, please come up."

"Me?"

"Of course, you. Step right up, my friend."

"I haven't got anything ailing me, Doc."

"Oh, my friend, do you have restless nights? Toss and turn nights?"

"Naw, I sleep like a log."

"Do you ache after a long day on your horse?"

"Now, you're talking about Critter, the orneriest critter on four legs. Yes, I'll allow that I ache some after a long ride on that beast."

"Were you out on him today, Sheriff?"

"Pretty near the whole blasted day, Professor."

"Then you must feel weary, right down to the bone."

"Well, we were out looking for some blond Ukrainian women who are attached at the hip. They plain disappeared."

The crowd got mostly dead silent, and a couple of snickers came from some of them cowboys.

"I think you are very weary, sir, after a day of searching for blond Ukrainian women. Are you a bit worn?"

"I am done in."

"Well, perfect. I would truly like to have you sample Doctor Zimmer's Tonic and report the results to all these fine folks."

"My ma, she used to say, one drink is enough."

"Oh, this is not drink, sir. This is an elixir to balm the soul, elevate mood, celebrate life, and rejoice in your own splendid body. Now how old are you?"

"I forget; past thirty, anyway."

"Ah, the shady side of thirty. Let me tell you, my friend, that is when Doctor Zoroaster Zimmer's Tonic works wonders the fastest. It works wonders at any age, sir, but especially after thirty."

The maestro of this here event reached for a bottle of the stuff, which was sitting on a little shelf with a gold halo around it, so the bottle looked like a saint.

He sure was smiling. He grabbed that stuff, pulled the cork, and poured a little into a tumbler, handing it to me while all them cowboys and Mayor George Waller watched.

I remembered what my ma used to say—no guts, no glory—and I downed the stuff in one gulp.

Well, it took a moment to work through me, like the glow of a lot of fireflies, and then I plumb keeled over. The accordionist caught me going down.

THE FIRST MOUNTAIN MAN SERIES BY
WILLIAM W. JOHNSTONE

__**The First Mountain Man**
0-8217-5510-2   **$4.99**US/**$6.50**CAN

__**Blood on the Divide**
0-8217-5511-0   **$4.99**US/**$6.50**CAN

__**Absaroka Ambush**
0-8217-5538-2   **$4.99**US/**$6.50**CAN

__**Forty Guns West**
0-7860-1534-9   **$5.99**US/**$7.99**CAN

__**Cheyenne Challenge**
0-8217-5607-9   **$4.99**US/**$6.50**CAN

__**Preacher and the Mountain Caesar**
0-8217-6585-X   **$5.99**US/**$7.99**CAN

__**Blackfoot Messiah**
0-8217-6611-2   **$5.99**US/**$7.99**CAN

__**Preacher**
0-7860-1441-5   **$5.99**US/**$7.99**CAN

__**Preacher's Peace**
0-7860-1442-3   **$5.99**US/**$7.99**CAN

Available Wherever Books Are Sold!

Visit our website at **www.kensingtonbooks.com**